Long Walk Home

Don Helin

Publisher Page
an imprint of Headline Books, Inc.
Terra Alta, WV

Long Walk Home

by Don Helin

copyright ©2018 Don Helin

To order additional copies of this book or for book publishing information, or to contact the author:

Headline Books, Inc.
P.O. Box 52
Terra Alta, WV 26764
www.headlinebooks.com

Tel: 304-789-3001
Email: mybook@headlinebooks.com

Cover photos by BigStock: johnanderson, mimagephotography, & Glynnis Jones

Publisher Page is an imprint of Headline Books

ISBN 13: 9781946664198

Library of Congress Control Number: 2017957751

PRINTED IN THE UNITED STATES OF AMERICA

To Elaine for her love and support – Love always

Acknowledgements
Thanks to all the members of the Pennwriters
Fourth Wednesday Writers Group,
and a special thanks to my four readers—
Dennis Royer, Debbie Beamer,
Roger Smith, and Dennis Hocker.

To Cathy, Patti, Ashley, and all the staff at Headline Books
You are the best

1

Upper Manhattan, Monday, 9:00 a.m.

Zack Kelly reached up to knock on the door, then stopped. It stood ajar a few inches. "Mr. Olney," he called, "are you here? Mr. Olney?" He could smell a mixture of mildew and fried food.

His daughter, Laura, stood behind him. "It's so quiet, I feel like I should whisper."

Zack had taken a ten-day leave from his duties working for the president's national security advisor to enjoy a long overdue July vacation with Laura. She was a tall, slender young woman, with long brown hair pulled up in a ponytail, beautiful blue eyes, and a bright smile. A freshman at George Washington University this fall, she'd earned a spot on the soccer team. God, he loved her.

"This hallway is quiet." He knocked again. "That's funny, Olney said he'd be here."

Zack pushed against the door, rewarded by a loud squeaking sound as it opened another few inches. "Mr. Olney? It's Zack Kelly. I called you earlier." Still no answer.

He stepped into an inner hallway, Laura close behind him. A dining room stood to his left, the living room straight ahead. He smelled coffee. Smelled good.

The living room contained a three-person couch with a coffee table in front of it, what must have been a 42 inch television in the corner, and a number of lounge chairs scattered across a wall-to-wall beige carpet. A large picture window provided a panoramic view of the Hudson River.

"Look at that view...there," Laura screamed and pointed. "Dad!"

A gray-haired man lay on the floor of the living room, a gash across his forehead. Blood pooled around his head, soaking the rug.

Zack rushed over to him and knelt. "Mr. Olney?" He checked Olney's neck for a pulse. Steady but faint. "Mr. Olney, can you hear me? Laura, call 911."

Laura grabbed the cell out of her pocket. "What's the address?"

Zack called it out as he hurried down the hallway to the bathroom and grabbed towels. He returned and knelt again. Bruises covered Olney's face, the gash across his forehead oozed blood.

Laura pocketed her cell. "They're on the way."

Zack opened Olney's shirt. More purple bruises. Poor bastard had been beaten with something heavy. He pressed the towel over the head wound, the towel turning red. "Tell them . . ."

"All right, don't move." A heavy-set, red-faced man stood in the doorway, a gun in his hand pointed at Zack. "Stay exactly where you are."

***

Eagle watched the five men and two women sitting at the kitchen table in the aged, but quiet motel. The room smelled of pizza and beer. The early morning sunlight filtered through the purple curtains, reflecting off the glass framing the various prints on the wall.

Maps of Manhattan and the Hudson River lay scattered across the table. He shuddered to think what they were about to do, but he couldn't show fear. "All right, we arrive in separate cars at 8:15. Then we walk into the terminal and wait for the next call to board."

The red-haired man, code-named Horse, shook his head. "We can't all get there at the same time. It'll look too damn suspicious."

Horse pissed Eagle off when he argued. Always arguing. "What the hell are you talking about? People arrive there all the time in bunches. Not many guards. It won't look suspicious at all."

Horse glared at Eagle. "Yeah, but they're not all wearing ball hats pulled down over their foreheads, dark glasses and black boots."

"He's right," Dog, a slender woman with short brunette hair, answered. "We can't walk in there like fucking puppets and say, 'god damn, hello'. They'll spot us in a heartbeat."

Eagle swiveled toward Horse. "All right, smart-ass. What do you suggest?"

"We should start arriving around seven o'clock, have breakfast, sit around, but we must all arrive separately and go through security separately, maybe at twenty minute intervals."

Coyote stood and began to pace around the room. "I agree."

Eagle knew he'd lost. He hated to lose, but this was too important. "It's settled. Too much is riding on this for us to fight. We arrive in 20 minute increments." He turned to the woman who had taken the name, Kitten. "Tomorrow you go to the station and check everything out."

Kitten leaned forward. "I'll do that."

Eagle liked her. She was not only smart, but with her long blond hair and athletic figure, cool looking. "Be careful."

"I'll be fine. I did a tour of duty in the secretary's office on the seventh floor of the State Department building. We called it, 'Mahogany Row.' Constantly under the watchful eye of the Diplomatic Security Service. All that fucking sensitive compartmentalized information. I survived working there and lived to tell about it. I'll survive this."

Eagle smiled. "I know you will."

The eight stood in a circle and clasped hands as they had done so many times before. It would start in three short days. They would be forgotten warriors no longer.

2

Zack looked up at the chunky intruder, measuring the distance to him and that damn gun. Too far. Couldn't risk it, particularly not with Laura here. "Look buddy, take it easy with the gun."

"Stand up," the man said. "No sudden moves. And I'm not your fucking buddy."

Zack stood and moved in front of Laura. "Just be careful with the gun." He pointed. "This guy was laying on the floor, bleeding, when we got here. I think it's Chester Olney. We've called an ambulance. Should be here in a couple of minutes."

"You're not in a position to tell me a damn thing. Now, show me some fucking ID before I get really pissed off."

Zack reached into his back pocket and pulled out his wallet. He took out his military ID and handed it over. "My name is Kelly. This is my daughter."

Laura stayed partially hidden behind her dad.

Studying the ID, he glanced at Zack. "Zack Kelly, army colonel, six foot, 195 pounds, looks about right. I'll hang on to this for a while."

He glanced up. "What do you do?"

"I work for the president's national security advisor, Admiral Steele."

"Steele? I've heard his name. He's helped the NYPD out a few times."

Zack nodded, trying to figure how to proceed. "Why are you here?"

The man's voice sounded raspy, probably a life-long smoker. "I'll ask the questions, wise guy. You feds think you're a big deal. Well here in New York, you're not."

Oh, shit, Zack thought, that didn't go very well. He glanced around, looking for something to throw at the guy or disrupt his line of vision. Nothing. Better play the contrite soul. "Look, I made arrangements to meet with Mr. Olney. He was my dad's partner."

"You're Roger Kelly's kid? I heard you was coming."

Heard I was coming to New York? Who else knows I'm here? "I never believed the rumors my dad might have been a dirty cop. Now can you put away the gun? We need to bring the EMTs in here as soon as they arrive. Which should be pretty quick."

Holstering his pistol, he handed back Zack's ID, then turned to the slender, dark-haired woman standing by the door. "Huna, go downstairs and guide the ambulance guys up here."

"Will do." She turned and headed out the door.

Zack slipped further in front of Laura. "Now, who are you?"

The man pulled out a badge. "Detective Inspector Martin Dempsey, NYPD. You just saw Sergeant Huna leave."

Cops. Zack breathed a sigh of relief. "I'm here because I wanted to hear Mr. Olney's story about what happened the night someone shot and killed my dad."

Dempsey slipped the badge back into his pocket. "A pisser your old man got hisself killed. How old were you when it happened?"

The story still frustrated Zack, but he wasn't going to say much until he knew more about Martin Dempsey. "Just a kid. Now maybe you can tell me why you're here."

"We got a call about noise in this apartment. I was in the area and knew Chester so I told dispatch I'd take the call. Figured you was the guy who assaulted my friend."

"Me? My daughter and I just got here. He's taken one hell of a beating. We tried to help."

Dempsey nodded. "I don't believe in taking chances. Now what are you doing here after all these years? Stirring things up?"

"My dad died a hero in a drug raid, then a bunch of bastards claimed he was a dirty cop. Those rumors almost killed my mom. We had to move to Minneapolis because of the gossip. Now I'm back to see who's responsible for all the shit and get it straightened out."

Footsteps sounded in the hallway. A male EMT hurried into the room, pulling a stretcher on wheels behind him, followed by a female EMT.

The male EMT knelt next to Olney and checked for vital signs. "What's his name?"

Dempsey walked over to the man. "Chester Olney."

The EMT wiped away blood from Olney's face and bandaged his forehead. "Mr. Olney, can you hear me?"

Olney moved his arm and moaned.

"Do you know where you are?"

"My . . . . my apartment."

"We're going to take you to the hospital. Get the docs to check you over."

A moan, then a quiet, "Okay."

The two moved Olney onto the stretcher and together pulled him out of the room.

"Can we hitch a ride to the hospital with you?" Zack asked. "I'd like to see how he's doing."

Dempsey didn't answer, but Sergeant Huna said, "Sure, you can ride with me. The inspector is staying to look for evidence and meet the forensic folks when they arrive."

Zack wrapped his arm around Laura and followed Huna out the door. They rode the elevator to the first floor. A number of people crowded around the front door at the end of the tiny hallway. "Were you the ones who called the police?" Zack asked.

An older man shook his head. "I didn't hear anything."

A gray-haired woman leaning on a cane next to him also shook her head. "Me, neither."

Zack puzzled about that. If no one had called the police, how did Dempsey know to come over here? Something strange going on.

***

Zack and Laura sat next to Sergeant Huna in the waiting room of Mount Sinai Saint Luke Hospital, Zack drinking a cup of needed coffee. On the way in, Huna told Zack that Saint Luke was one of Manhattan's few Level 1 trauma centers. Fortunately for Olney, the hospital was on 114th Street, only a few blocks from his apartment.

Laura leaned close and whispered, "Do you think we should call Grandma Ethel? She'd probably want to know what happened to Mr. Olney. Didn't she know him?"

Zack thought for a moment, then nodded. "I'm going to step out into the hallway. If the doc comes in, let me know." He eased his way past all of the troubled people waiting for word about loved ones and out the door.

Pushing in his mother's number, he waited until he heard her familiar voice. "Hi, son. How's the trip going? Are you and Laura having a good time?"

"Well, not really. We stopped to see if we could talk to Chester Olney about dad."

"How is he? My goodness, I haven't heard from him in years."

"Not so good. When we arrived at his apartment, we found him on the floor, beaten up."

"What?"

"Fraid so. Laura and I are at the hospital now waiting to hear how he's doing. There's no family here as yet."

"Oh, my," his mother replied, "he's such a nice man. I heard his wife died a few years ago, and I don't believe they had any children. Maybe I should fly out and see if I can help him. I always liked Chester. He was such a good friend to me after your father died."

"Why don't you wait until we can find out more."

"No, I'll fly out. If he's in such bad shape, he'll need help doing things for a few days. Maybe I can even sneak in a couple of dinners with you and Laura while I'm there. I don't see either of you as much as I'd like.

Zack knew his mother. Once she made up her mind, no changing it. "When you make reservations, fly into Newark Airport. We can drive over and pick you up."

"Okay, Newark it is. I'll call and let you know when I'm scheduled to arrive."

"See you soon." Zack returned to the waiting room and sat next to Sergeant Huna.

An attractive woman, probably around thirty, she sat working on her laptop. "Can I help you, Colonel?"

"My daughter and I arrived at Olney's to talk with him, then the next thing I know, I'm staring down the barrel of a revolver. What's the deal with Dempsey?"

She chuckled. "He tends to be a little quick on the draw, but Dempsey's a good cop. He's been around a long time." She lowered her voice. "Maybe a bit too long, but I do believe he means well. You say your dad was a cop here in New York?"

Zack nodded. "He died in the line of duty when I just a kid."

"That's terrible. I'm so sorry."

"The worst part is that a few weeks after his death, rumors started that he was a dirty cop."

She thought for a moment. "Was his name Roger Kelly?"

"That's right. How did you know?"

"The story still goes around the force. As a matter of fact, I heard it first at the police academy during my training."

Zack's eyes got wide. "What? Your training?"

"That's right. It appears the operation wasn't well planned. I heard they had to move quickly and as a result, lost two officers. And then," she looked away for a moment, "well, I don't want to add rumor to fact."

"Go ahead. I've heard it all," Zack said. "The story was my dad had been on the take from some mafia asshole."

Huna looked away. "Oh, here comes the doctor."

A slender red-haired man in blue scrubs appeared at the doors to the surgical ward and looked around the room. Huna raised her hand. "Are you Chester Olney's doctor?"

"Yes, I am. Are you family?"

Huna shook her head and pulled out her badge. "Police. We found Mr. Olney in his apartment. He'd been assaulted. How is he doing? I'd like to talk with him as soon as possible."

"He took quite a beating," the doctor replied. "It could have been much worse, but for his age, he's in good shape. You should be able to talk to him in a few minutes. Do you know any of his family? We're having problems notifying a next of kin."

"Sorry," Huna said. "I'd be happy to check and see what I can find out."

"That would be great. I'll get back to you as soon as he can have visitors." He walked back through the set of double doors.

Zack leaned over to Huna. "Do you think I could talk with him after you finish?"

"I'll have to check with the doctor and see what he says. But I'd think that should be okay. Where are you and your daughter staying?"

"Over on Staten Island at the Navy Lodge."

A few minutes later, the doctor returned to the waiting room. "You can go in now, officer. He's awake, but in a lot of pain. It's probably best if you don't stay too long."

***

He walked the two blocks along Astor Place, checking behind him every fourth step as always, then turned right to 3rd Avenue. Stepping into the book store for a moment, he picked up a magazine, pretending to read it while looking out the front window. No one looked familiar.

He put the magazine back and stepped outside, continuing along 3rd Avenue. When he arrived at his apartment building, he walked up the cracked steps and stopped at the top. Looking around once more, he inserted his key in the lock and stepped inside.

The dark hallway was not very welcoming, but he didn't expect it to be. He just hoped it was safe. When he reached the landing between the first and second floor, he looked out the dirty window. Saw no one who looked familiar. Good.

At the top of the stairs, he walked down the corridor to the third door on the left and stopped. Pulled out his key and inserted it in the deadbolt and heard the satisfying click. Now the second key, He inserted it in the other dead bolt and heard the second click. Checking the tiny string between the door and the frame. Not broken. Good.

Reaching behind himself, he pulled the knife out of the sheath and stepped inside. Dark and quiet. Keeping the door open for a moment in case he had to make a run for it, he walked around the apartment, checking. Checking. How he stayed alive. Always checking.

Stepping back to the door, he closed it and locked the two dead bolts. Before turning on any lights he walked to the window. Keeping his back against the wall, he peeked out past the window frame. Saw no one who looked suspicious. He pulled the shade down and turned on the light.

He looked around the barren one-room apartment. Two chairs facing the TV, a single bed in the corner and a hotplate. Casey Matheson was home.

3

Mount Sinai, Saint Luke Hospital, noon

Sergeant Huna returned to the waiting room about twenty minutes later. She stopped in front of Zack. "Mr. Olney doesn't remember much about what happened. He says his doorbell rang and he thought it was you. When he opened the door, two men forced their way in and beat him up."

"Just like that," Zack said. "Doesn't make any sense. They didn't say anything? Did he know them?"

"Apparently not. I agree his story doesn't seem to make much sense."

Zack stood as did Laura. "When we got there, I found the street door locked. I was about to buzz Olney's apartment when a women opened the door to leave. I told her we had an appointment with Mr. Olney and she let us in. Now my question remains, how did those two guys get in?"

"I didn't ask, but he's pretty screwed up in the head right now. Oh, his assailants they did tell him to keep his fucking mouth shut."

"About what?"

Huna's answer was halted by the arrival of the doctor. He glanced at Zack. "The police say it's important for you to see Mr. Olney, but please, only stay for a few minutes."

Huna gave him her card. "If he remembers anything to help us, give me a call. Actually, I can wait a few minutes and give you a ride to wherever you're going."

"That would be great," Zack replied. "I'm not sure where we'll be headed. Probably depends on what Mr. Olney says."

"No problem. I always have paperwork to do." She smiled. "Thank heavens for computers."

"Thanks." Zack turned to Laura. "Come on, let's go in for a few minutes."

Olney's room was the third door on the left. Zack passed a nurse hurrying down the hall and a couple of orderlies pushing a stretcher.

When they entered, Olney's head was propped up on a pillow, his eyes closed. Opening his eyes, he turned toward them and asked, "Who are you?"

Zack was amazed at the number of bruises on his face. "Mr. Olney, my name is Zack Kelly. This is my daughter, Laura."

"Oh, Roger's boy. You look just like him. And what a lovely young lady."

Laura blushed. "Thank you."

Zack placed his hand on Laura's shoulder. "I've been told I look like my dad, but I really don't remember much about him. Laura and I are in New York for a visit. While I'm here, I wanted to talk to you about my dad. I'd like details on what happened the night he was killed."

Olney took a deep breath. He started to cough. Laura reached over and helped him drink some water through a straw.

"Thank you," Olney said. "Let me see if I remember right, your mother came from somewhere in the Midwest. She didn't care much for New York, and sure didn't like ball games. Quite an artist, I remember."

"Yes, she is. Well known for her art in the Twin City area."

"How is she? I always enjoyed her company. Is she still painting?"

"She is," Laura replied. "I only wish I'd inherited a little of her talent."

Zack put down his coffee cup. "Hospital coffee. Not so great. Can you tell me what happened that night? Also, tell me where I might review the incident case file."

Olney leaned back, then he started to cough again.

Laura reached over to the bedside table and held the glass for Olney to drink more water.

"Thanks," Olney said. "I'll never forget it. Damn muggy August night, almost like last night. The two of us had been assigned to the drug task force. We received a tip from an informant that a major drug purchase would go down at ten o'clock. Since it was already seven, we didn't have much time to develop our strategy and get organized."

"Did you have many of these operations?" Laura asked.

Olney nodded. "The mayor was on the war path about drugs. He demanded we bring down the Angelo Family who were the leading suppliers of drugs in the city."

Olney started to cough again. Laura gave him more water. "Would you like us to come back tomorrow?"

"No, let me see if I can get this out without coughing up my lungs."

Zack waited. "Take your time."

"I was wounded in the same operation. The difference was I got shot in the leg, but your dad in the head."

He looked toward the window for a moment. "It's almost like yesterday in my mind. There were fourteen of us, divided into three groups. Lieutenant Frank Tomlinson was in charge. Your dad and I were assigned to the group going in the front, another team spread out in the back, the third would block from the sides."

Olney motioned for more water. After Laura helped him drink, he continued. "I keep wondering if I could have done more."

Zack wondered the same thing. Goddamn Olney lived and his dad had died.

"Don't second guess yourself," Laura said. "I'm sure you did all you could."

"I still relive that night. Dream about it. Nightmares. We busted down the front door and the shots started spraying us. Your dad and I were pinned down, but we returned fire. We received covering fire from the side and Tomlinson gave us the order to move in. We wore body armor, but your dad fell right away. Hit in the head. I got shot moving over to try and help him.

It was a botched operation all the way." Tears formed in his eyes. "Your dad died in my arms."

Zack felt himself tearing up. Years of sadness over his dad's death had infected his mind.

Laura reached over and put her arm around Zack's shoulder.

"Why?" Zack's voice rose. "Why was it botched? Was there an after action report? I'd like a copy."

"Tomlinson managed to hush it up. I was released from the hospital in time for your dad's funeral. We had hundreds of cops turn out. Guys came all the way from the Midwest."

"I remember that," Zack said. "But why did the rumors start about my dad?"

"I've never been able to prove it," Olney said, "but I think Tomlinson planted those rumors to shift blame from himself. The story started that your dad had been tight with the Angelo family and they killed him so no one would find out."

Zack's voice rose again. "Why the hell would he do that?"

"Tomlinson was a political creature, on his way up. If he didn't pass the blame to someone else, it would settle on him. A real bastard."

The anger built, eating at Zack. "But didn't you defend him?"

"Of course I did, but rumors are like a flood. They roll around long enough and people begin to believe them as they sweep over everything."

Zack stood. "Where is this Tomlinson character? Is he retired? I want to talk with him."

Olney shook his head. "He won't be hard to find. He's the New York City Police Commissioner."

* * *

Zack called Tomlinson's administrative assistant and gave her his name, then set up an appointment for three o'clock. He briefed Huna on what Olney had told him and thanked her for the offer of a ride, but said he and Laura would have lunch, then catch the red line from the hospital. They had to transfer to get to Tomlinson's office, just a block south of Worth Street near Battery Park.

When they arrived at Police Plaza, Zack showed his military ID and Laura her driver's license to get past the police officer at the door. "We have an appointment with Commissioner Tomlinson," Zack said.

The officer checked with Tomlinson's secretary and waved them through the security gate. Once through the maze, they took the elevator up to the commissioner's office.

Zack entered Tomlinson's outer office to see a marvelous view of the East River spread out before him. Did Tomlinson frame his father? Set him up? Well, Zack sure as hell wasn't going to let it ferment any longer.

A petite redhead sat behind the reception desk. "May I help you?"

"Zack and Laura Kelly to meet with Commissioner Tomlinson."

She looked at a book, then dialed a number. "Colonel Kelly is here to see you." She pointed toward a closed door. "Right in there. He's waiting for you."

Zack pushed the door open, wondering if this was all part of Tomlinson putting him on edge. Tomlinson was short, maybe 5' 8" but stood straight. His blue eyes watched Zack through dark-framed aviator glassed. He ran his hand over short clipped gray hair.

"Zack Kelly. I'm Frank Tomlinson," He stuck out his hand and Zack accepted it. "Please call me Frank." Tomlinson had a habit of talking in short bursts. "And who is this lovely lady?"

"My daughter, Laura."

He shook hands with Laura, then motioned toward a grouping of chairs. "Please be seated. Can I get you something to drink? Coffee? Maybe some iced tea?"

"Coffee would be nice. Laura?"

"Iced tea, please."

As they sat, Tomlinson pushed a button on his intercom and asked for a pot of coffee and some iced tea. "Zack, I'm sorry about your father. An outstanding police officer and a fine man.

We worked together for almost two years. All the time, I had the highest respect for him."

"Can you tell me what happened the night someone shot and killed my father?"

Tomlinson leaned back in his chair. "Let me think for a minute. We had been alerted a major drug shipment would be arriving at a certain warehouse. We organized our team to go in and make arrests. When we went in, it was like they knew we were coming. And they had automatic weapons. Your father was one of the first officers to be hit."

"How was it organized?" Zack asked.

"What do you mean?"

"You may not be aware, but I've been with the army rangers long enough to know how much planning goes into an operation to ensure the lowest number of casualties."

"Thank you for your service. If I remember right, we divided into three teams."

"Was everyone in flak jackets?"

"Absolutely."

Zack wasn't sure how to proceed. "What went wrong?"

"We analyzed the operation from every angle during our after action review," Tomlinson said. "I think we planned it right. After extensive study, we concluded the dealers must have known we were coming and were ready for us."

"Are you saying someone tipped them off?"

"That's what we concluded."

Zack took a sip of coffee to give himself time to think. "Were there any casualties other than my father?"

"Yes, we had three wounded police officers."

"How about the dealers? How many of them were killed."

"Six wounded. None fatally."

"Did you determine who fired the shot that killed my father?"

Tomlinson looked down and shook his head. "In all the mayhem, we never found out exactly who fired the shot."

"Wouldn't ballistics give you the fatal bullet, then you could determine the weapon? Couldn't you get finger prints off the specific weapon?"

"I can't remember now why, but we didn't get it. However, all of them were arrested. Two were sentenced to twenty years in jail."

Zack steamed. "They killed a police officer. I thought the code of blue would go after the killer without letting up. That's what we'd do in the army."

"Let me think a minute how to put this."

"Commissioner, you don't need to protect me or Laura. I lived through the shame of the rumors about my father. How did you know for sure he was a dirty cop?"

"We had the testimony from three of the dealers. They were all members of the Angelo Family."

"Isn't it a serious enough charge, you would need proof from more than three Mafia drug dealers to determine if they were lying."

"All three told us he worked for the family. He had provided information about our operations over the past six months."

Zack had to be careful here. It wouldn't do any good to piss Tomlinson off. "You took the word from a couple of Mafia hoods. They killed a NYPD police officer, for heaven's sake."

Thomlinson's gaze swept the room, like he was composing himself. "You may be upset and I understand why you are, but you must realize we wouldn't have gone forward if we weren't sure." He stopped for a moment. "Only a handful of people know this, but we had an undercover officer inside the family operation. He confirmed what we feared. Roger Kelly had been taking payouts from the Angelo family. If it hadn't been for his testimony, it might have been different."

"Who was this man? I'd like to talk to him."

"I'm sorry, but he died six years ago. We never released his name because his family could still be in jeopardy."

"Commissioner, as you may know, I work for the president's national security advisor. In my official duties, I've reviewed a number of case files. Would it be possible to review the incident file? It would mean a lot to me."

"Sergeant Dempsey mentioned to me you work for Admiral Steele. The admiral has been a great deal of help to us on a number of cases."

Zack smiled. "He's a great guy and wonderful to work for."

"Okay, I guess we can make an exception for you. I do ask you not tell anyone what's in the file."

"Certainly. I can provide my security clearance if it would help you."

"Okay, I'll make a call. Can you come in tomorrow?"

Laura let out a scream.

Zack jumped and turned toward her. "Laura, what's wrong?"

She pointed, then lurched back. A long, black furry creature crawled out from behind the commissioner's desk.

Tomlinson laughed. "Oh, that's Homer, my pet ferret. I'm sorry he scared you. He's really quite harmless and thoroughly enjoys people."

Laura took a deep breath. "Okay, that's better. Can I pet him?"

"Certainly," Tomlinson replied. "He enjoys being picked up and petted."

Laura got down on her hands and knees and crawled toward Homer. She reached over and petted him, then picked him up. "He's so soft."

"Yes he is. I'm glad you like him." Tomlinson turned his attention back to Zack. "Look, I know you're upset, and I don't blame you. Please believe me we did everything we could at the time to ensure the truth came out. If you can come in tomorrow, I'll make sure the entire case file is available."

Zack stood. "Thank you, commissioner. Here's my cell number. Please call and let me know when to come in."

Tomlinson stood and shook hands with Zack. "I'll have my secretary call you. Again, I'm sorry for the way it turned out. I wish it could have been different."

"I do, too," Zack said. "Come on, Laura, say goodbye to Homer. We need to leave."

On the way out, Zack felt the cops could have done a better job of investigating his father's murder. *Did the police really have an undercover officer in the family? Why subject those police officers to a suicide mission?*

4

Manhattan, Monday, 4:30 p.m.

When they reached the sidewalk, Zack decided to change the pace. "How about we do something fun? After all, we're here on vacation."

Laura's face lit up. "Cool. What did ya have in mind?"

"We're in New York. Let's take in a play on the 'Great White Way'."

"Double cool. How do we make reservations?"

Zack tried to remember how it worked from the time he'd spent in New York before. "We head to Times Square. They have a place there where you can get Two-Fers."

"Two-Fers, what the heck are those things?"

"The theaters put out tickets priced two for one on the day of the play. There used to be an office somewhere in Times Square to handle those tickets. Let head over and check it out. We can eat dinner, then take in a play."

Laura gave him a hug. "Hey, pop, you're the greatest."

Good job, Kelly. "Okay, let's get over to the subway and figure out how to get to Times Square."

They hurried along Eighth Street until they reached the subway entrance, then hustled down the stairs and got tickets to go through the turnstiles. Zack checked the map and headed to the gate. "Travel in New York is really easy once you sort out the subway."

Laura looked at a map. "I just have to get used to it."

It took about ten minutes before the next train arrived. A short fifteen minute ride and they arrived at the Times Square station.

When they walked up the stairs to 42nd Street, the splash of color, lights, and the mobs of people announced they were there.

Zack spotted a police officer and asked for help to find the ticket office. Following his directions, they hurried across 42nd street and entered a building.

They checked the list of plays for that night and saw Jersey Boys was playing at one of the theaters. "I heard it's pretty good," Zack said. "How about if we go see it."

"Fine by me," Laura replied. "I could use a music and comedy hit about now."

"Me too. Come-on, let's get in line."

While they stood in line, Laura poked Zack's arm. "Look at the poster. It says Jersey Boys won best off-Broadway musical, and the best book and best music at the London Fortune Theater. It sounds really good."

"Keep your fingers crossed they still have tickets."

Zack purchased two tickets and checked his watch. "We have about two hours before the play begins. Italian or Chinese?"

"Let's do Italian. We're in New York. What say we live it up?"

Zack checked with another officer and got his recommendation.

When they entered the restaurant, the hostess seated them. Zack ordered a beer and Laura iced tea.

"Ya know, Dad, it won't be long before I'll be able to order a beer, too."

"I know, believe me, I know. What do you think about all of this?"

"You mean about what happened to Grandpa?"

Zack nodded.

"It bites at you all the time. You need to resolve what happened and accept it, or it will continue to gnaw away at you, not so good."

Zack took a sip of his beer. "How did you get so smart?"

"Are you just noticing these things? You're kinda slow, Kelly."

Zack had to laugh and reached over to give her a hug. "I love you, Laura. You're fun to be around. I gotta do more with you."

"Love you too, Dad."

Zack's cell rang. He checked, but didn't recognize the number. "I'd better take this. Hello."

"Hi Zack, it's Shelia."

"Who?"

"What the hell do you mean who? I thought I'd made more of an impression on you than that. Shelia O'Donnell. You know, the crazy medium from Galway, Ireland. It's been a while since we trooped around Ireland together."

"Shelia, for heaven's sake, where are you?"

"Here in New York. I had Colonel Garcia's cell phone number and called her. She told me you and Laura were here in New York on vacation. I thought maybe we could get together."

Zack felt a warmth all over and couldn't help but smile thinking about her. He remembered Shelia all right. Long jet-black hair, light blue eyes, and milky white skin. Oh, man, did he remember Shelia."

"Who is it?" Laura whispered.

"Just a minute, Shelia." He turned to Laura. "It's Shelia O'Donnell. You remember, the medium from Ireland. She's here in New York."

"Wonderful. Can we see her?"

"Shelia, Laura and I would love to see you again. Are you here for a while?"

"Silly, if I wasn't here for a while, I wouldn't be calling."

"Maybe we could get together for dinner tomorrow night."

"Great. I'm in a workshop tomorrow, but will be done by about five o'clock. Let me give you my mobile number, and you can call me tomorrow with the plan." She laughed. "I know how much you army guys like to make plans."

Zack loved her laugh. It sounded like tinkling glass. "Sounds good. I'll call you late afternoon."

She gave him her cell number. "Roger that, Colonel. Over and out."

Laura watched him. "Dad, you're smiling." She poked his arm." You liked her, didn't you? Didn't you? I mean really liked her."

"You caught me. Yes I did."

"Well I did too, and would love to see her again. So fun and so interesting. I'm trying to remember, what is a medium again?"

"A medium is supposed to be able to communicate with the dead."

Laura gulped. "Do you believe she can?"

"I'm not sure, but Shelia is pretty convincing. She's the youngest of ten brothers and sisters. Her parents are devout Catholics. They didn't like their daughter claiming to hear spirits. I guess her father tried to beat it out of her."

"Oh, my gosh, that's terrible."

"Yes it is. If I remember right, she attended Trinity College in Dublin, pre-law I think. At the time we worked together she was in law school. Maybe she has already graduated. We'll find out tomorrow. Her motivation is to show her father her special skill doesn't make her some kind of nut case."

Zack looked at his watch. "Guess we'd better get moving."

The smile slipped across his face again. He turned so Laura wouldn't see it.

"Caught ya." Laura poked him in the ribs. "It's okay. I remember her as a real looker. You really fumbled the ball, Kelly."

"What do you mean?"

"Here's this looker you really liked, and when she calls wanting to spend time with you, you say, 'who'? I mean, come-on, get real."

All Zack could do was smile and give his daughter a hug.

5

Newark Airport, Tuesday, 9:15 a.m.

Zack pulled his truck into the parking lot at the Newark Airport. Laura and Zack got out and walked over to catch the shuttle to the terminal.

I enjoyed the show last night," Laura said. "Did you ever see the Jersey Boys in person?"

"No. At the time I didn't even know about the Four Seasons. I certainly had heard of their lead singer, Frankie Valli."

"Can you imagine all their problems with gambling debts, Mafia threats, and family disasters?" Laura asked. "Must have been an awful time for them."

"Goes to show fame isn't always what it's cracked up to be."

As they waited for the shuttle, Zack's mind wandered back to Tomlinson. The guy had to be hiding something. The investigation didn't sound thorough. Nothing like he'd had to do in the military with statements, photographs and forensics. Zack figured Olney was probably right. Tomlinson used his father to cover up his own inadequacies.

"Dad?"

Zack's mind sprung back to reality. "Sorry, I was thinking about yesterday."

"I could tell," Laura said. "You were a million miles away."

I'm trying to process all we learned and how it fits. I can't get it together yet. After we pick up your grandmother, I plan to stop at police headquarters and go through the investigation file."

"I'm sure grandma would like to see Mr. Olney. I can take her to the hospital."

"Do you remember the way?"

She turned to look at him, hands on hips. "Dad!"

Zack had to laugh. "Okay, okay. One of these days I promise to quit being a father. Now, let's go find security for the Northwest gates."

The two only waited at the TSA gate for about fifteen minutes before Ethel Kelly came whipping down the passageway. Jet black hair and a slender, petite 5'2", she always carried a large purse over her right shoulder. Standing ramrod straight, her brown eyes emphasized a fetching smile. Today she wore navy pants with a lime green short-sleeved blouse, a coat hanging over her left arm.

Zack waved to his mother and she waved back. Once she passed security, Laura ran up and gave her grandmother a hug. "I'm so glad to see you."

"It's great to see you too, Pumpkin." Ethel smiled. "Guess I'd better not call you Pumpkin anymore. You're way past that."

"It's okay," Laura said, "when it's just the two of us."

Ethel reached over and hugged Zack. "Hi son, thanks for driving over and getting me."

Zack laughed. "No way would I ever consider letting you loose in New York City all by yourself. You'd set all the guys on their ear."

"Yeah, right. How's Chester?"

"I called this morning and apparently he had a restful night and is awake. What I thought we'd do is head back to the Navy Lodge where we're staying, and leave your bags. You can share a bedroom with Laura. After that, we'll catch the ferry to Manhattan, then the subway to the hospital."

"That would be great," Ethel replied. "Does his memory seem okay to you?"

"Seemed okay at the hospital yesterday," Laura replied. "After we left the hospital, we met with Commissioner Tomlinson. He said dad could review the investigation report concerning what happened to grandpa."

"Frank was always the politician," Ethel said. "So now he's the police commissioner for New York City. I'm not surprised.

I'll have to admit I never cared much for Frank, and I don't think your father did either."

"I thought he was a creep," Laura said. "Although he does have an adorable little ferret in his office."

"A what?" Ethel exclaimed.

"Grandma, you don't know what a ferret is?"

"Well, I guess I do. I didn't know Frank had one in his office."

Laura took her grandmother's arm as they walked. "And he's so cute with such soft fur. At least I think it's a 'he'."

"I'm going to reserve an opinion on Tomlinson," Zack said. "But so far, don't think much of him. His secretary called earlier. I can review the investigation report and see what I can figure out. You two head straight out to the hospital to see Olney."

Ethel reached over to hug Laura. "Watch out, New York, the Kelly chicks are on the loose."

Laura raised a closed fist into the air. "Yes!"

Zack had to cover a smile. "Oh, boy. What have I unleashed?"

***

Today marked Casey's day off from flipping burgers. He slipped out to get a copy of the New York Times and as always, kept his TV tuned to the news with the sound muted. He stayed alive by making sure he knew all the events happening around him in New York City.

Living in the city was much better than out west. Here he used the subway to move around. No need to own a car like in Montana. Registrations and insurance were always a problem. Even name changes were not a safe way to live. Here, no one could trace him since he didn't own anything. Burger flipping was a good way to be paid on the underground economy. The grubby owner didn't need to report him and he didn't need to report to the government. Good.

He spotted a short article in the local section. A retired police officer, Chester Olney, had been assaulted in his apartment and admitted to the hospital. The police were investigating the circumstances. What the hell was Chester into now? Why would someone beat up an old fart police detective? It might be worth checking out. Always checking. That's how Casey Matheson stayed alive.

Thinking about it for a moment, he decided it was worth the risk. There was always a risk in going outside, but he couldn't sit here all day when he didn't go to work. He got up, pulled on his favorite blue jacket and Yankee baseball cap, adjusted the dark glasses and went outside, stopping to paste up the string and lock the two dead bolts. Can't be too careful.

He walked down the stairs, thankful he didn't meet anyone, and stepped outside. Stopped and soaked in the surroundings. Nothing out of place. Heading over to the subway, he'd take the yellow line first, then transfer to the red line. Never hurts to transfer a couple of times. After all, Casey Matheson was never in a hurry. That's how he stayed alive.

***

Zack stepped off the subway at the Chambers Street station, leaving Laura and his mother to travel on to see Chester Olney at the hospital. After a short walk to the City Hall, he headed inside and worked his way through security.

He couldn't stop thinking about Shelia, the time they'd shared a room in Gettysburg and she'd locked herself out in the hallway in a sheer nightie. What a sight to behold.

Zack took the elevator up to Tomlinson's floor and hurried to his office, anxious to see the file.

The receptionist smiled up at him. "Hi, Colonel Kelly. Commissioner Tomlinson had to leave for a meeting across town, but he left this for you." She handed him a blue folder. "You can sit over there at the desk. I do ask you not take it outside this office and not take any photos of what's inside without permission."

"Okay." Zack had thought about the file for years and here it sat, finally in front of him. What he'd been looking for all these years. Finally answers to his questions.

He took a deep breath and opened the folder. On the left side lay an event summary. He took about thirty minutes to read through the summary, realizing he already knew most of these details. He read through the names of the fourteen member police unit and the timing of all that had happened. He didn't know any of the officers other than Tomlinson and Olney.

On the right side of the folder was a schematic of the site, the positions of the fourteen officers and the suspected location of the seven drug dealers. According to the report there were a total of forty-seven rounds fired by the dealers. His father died and three others were wounded. He wrote down the name of the wounded police officers as well as the names of all the dealers. He scanned the statements, making a few notes.

He'd need a copy of each one because he wanted to talk to them, face to face. He also made a note of the exact address of the warehouse where his father died. He'd want to go later and see the site for himself. See where some bastard had gunned down his dad.

It surprised him there was no forensics summary in the file. He had no way of knowing which dealer had killed his father.

He got up and walked over to the receptionist. "There doesn't seem to be any forensic material in the folder. You know, types of weapons, which weapon hit which person. Is this the complete file?"

"As far as I know it is, Colonel. I can check with Commissioner Tomlinson when he returns if you'd like."

"Thank you." Zack walked back to the table and sat, looking out the window at lower Manhattan. He could see the Statute of Liberty in the distance. *Was this the headquarters of the police when his dad was on the force? Did his dad look out this window, see the very same statute?*

Zack read through the event summary again taking careful notes. Then he drew a copy of the site schematic, closing his eyes and visualizing how it had taken place. He'd led a number of attacks in Afghanistan and thought through how he would have done it. Sure as hell not like Tomlinson. Head on seemed pretty stupid. Of course, hindsight was always 20/20.

He stared for a long time at the spot on the map where his dad had fallen. He needed to see the report of the entry and exit wounds to compare to the position and get a fuller picture. Something itched in his brain. But what?

Zack pulled together the folder and returned it to the receptionist. He folded his notes and took the elevator back to the lobby.

It was only a couple of blocks to the subway station. He stopped at a food stand and picked up a sausage in a hot dog bun, put onions and mustard on it, then sat down to enjoy it with a cold soda. While he sat, he called Laura to let her know he would be getting on a subway to come out to the hospital.

6

Staten Island, Tuesday, 12:30 p.m.

"Kitten wiped perspiration from her face after the walk back from the ferry terminal. The summer day temperature on Staten Island had heated up after lunch.

She looked around at her seven teammates, watching her from their chairs. "All right, listen up. There are a number of police at the terminal, but like all guys, they have one problem. They love to watch and talk to the ladies, particularly if the lady is smart enough to wear a low-cut blouse. I had my hat and sun glasses on and leaned forward a couple of times and could almost feel the cop's eyes boring a hole through my boobs. I don't think they'll be much of a problem."

Eagle smiled at the chuckles around the room. "What else did you discover?"

"There are two bomb-sniffing dogs in the early morning, but by mid-morning, it drops to one. Once you're through the metal detectors, one of the officers may bring a dog over to check a backpack or a roller bag. The dog sniffs the bag. If you're clean, the cop pulls him back, then returns to his original position. This is important because we'll have the plastics and the masks in the backpack."

"How much of a problem will his review be?" Eagle asked.

"Not much at all. There are two options. If you enter on the far side from where you enter the terminal building, the cops don't seem to come over with the dog if you head right into the can."

"Okay," Eagle replied. "That sounds good. Can we depend on it?"

"To the best of my knowledge we can, although nothing is failsafe. The second and I think a better option, is if you wait until the ferry is ready to go, then you can run right past the guard, looking harried. He doesn't seem to stop those people. I think our plan should work. We just don't want the cops to open our bags."

"Anything else?" Eagle asked. "Remember our on-board contact can help us."

"I rode two of the ferries, the Andrew J. Barberi Ferry and the Senator John J. Marchi. Up until 9:30 they depart every fifteen minutes, then thirty minutes after that. There are two decks with pushbutton locks to open the doors between the deck and the control towers. There are two control towers, one at either end of the ferry. We need to control those two towers and we'll control the ferry. No one stopped me even though I had sunglasses on and a ball hat pulled low for cameras."

"Very good," Eagle replied.

Kitten raised her hand to silence him. "Let me summarize what I believe we need. One of our team, a woman, will be needed to talk to the officer with the dog. Another team member with a backpack can arrive a second later and cut right and go into the bathroom, then right on to the ferry. A couple with backpacks can run in at the last minute and onto the ferry. They'll have on ball caps and sun glasses for any cameras.

"What else?" Eagle asked.

"We need to know which ferry our inside man is on so there will be no confusion. We'll depend on him to know the code for the locks to get us inside the control towers. Then our ex-captain needs to be there to steer the boat. The crossing only takes 22 minutes so we must take over within the first seven minutes."

"Great job." He laughed. "You'll be the perfect candidate to go early and throw your chest around. It will tie any guard in knots. I think it's best if you go back tomorrow and see what else you can find out."

Kitten frowned. "I thought we'd go tomorrow. That was the plan."

"I need to talk to our inside man one more time. Make sure he fully understands our plan and is ready."

Kitten leaned forward. "But . . ."

Eagle held up his hand. "I said we wait for another day. Too much is at stake. We need to be sure."

Kitten looked away. *Chickenshit Eagle. He'd wait too long and fuck everything up.* She thought back to all those flights on the U.S. Air Force Boeing 757. It was fitted with all of the advanced communications gear money could buy. She handled it with no problem. Now a simple maneuver and he wanted to keep pushing it back. "Do you want me to call the other team?"

"Yes. I'd appreciate if you would. Tell them I need to do more coordination."

"Oh, one last thing," Kitten said. "The Coast Guard station is next to the Whitehall docking station on the Manhattan side of the ferry crossing. We must gain control rapidly as they'll be able to react quickly."

"We'll be ready," Eagle replied.

They all stood and clasped hands. Eagle led them in their mantra. "We served our country and now our country has forgotten us and so many of our comrades. But we will be forgotten no longer."

***

Zack reached the hospital and took the elevator up to Olney's room. He stood outside the door for a moment, looking in the room. Olney leaned back against a pillow. Laura and his mom sat on one side of the bed, Sergeant Huna on the other.

It surprised Zack to see Huna in the room.

He stepped inside. "Hi everybody." Glancing at Huna, he asked, "What brings you here?"

Huna looked up from her laptop. "Just following up on a couple of things."

"Any particular problems?"

"Nope. Gathering information."

Zack pulled up a chair. "Say, I'm interested in your background. Did you say you're from Alaska?"

"That's right. I always wanted to be a cop, but life here is very different from my home. In my tribe, I'm an eagle, so I'm supposed to marry a raven. My parents are upset with me that I moved away and didn't follow tradition."

Zack leaned forward in his chair. "Must be hard on you. Do you get home much?"

"Not as much as I'd like."

"Tell me a little about your tribe. I know Laura and my mom would be interested, too."

"Okay. Let's see. Well, there are fifty letters that make up our alphabet as opposed to your twenty-six. Makes it difficult for me to translate. When I'm telling people about my tribe, I have to remember that if it's not my story then I can't tell it."

"How can you share background on your friends with other people?"

"That's the point. I can't. Only those people can tell their story."

Laura's face lit up. "I guess there's not much gossip in your world. Would be a huge improvement in ours. So many of my friends gossip. I call it 'Dishing Dirt.'"

"There are only about 800 people who live on my island. As a matter of fact, there are more brown bears on the island than people."

Ethel laughed. "I think even more brown bears than we have in all of Minnesota."

Huna wore a sad smile. "It was hard to leave, and sometimes I miss it terribly."

"I understand that," Zack said. "I grew up in Minneapolis. Loved spending time outdoors. We used to go fishing in northern Minnesota, up by Brainard. So peaceful on the lake, just me and the fish. It's hard to go back to the city and reality."

"How did you happen into the military?" Huna asked.

"Well to be honest, I wasn't doing well in college. My girlfriend and I decided to get married and jobs weren't very plentiful. So, I enlisted. Kept going to school when I could and finally received approval to go bootstrap. The military will give you six months full time to finish your degree. After I finished my degree, I applied for officer candidate school and made the cut. From then on, it was a lot of work and also a lot of fun. I really enjoy the military."

"Must have been hard losing your father at such a young age."

Zack glanced at his mother.

Ethel brushed a tear from her eye. "Zack came home from school one day, I think he was in the first grade, and saw me sitting in a chair, holding my daughter and crying. He thought his kid sister had been hurt. I've always been straight with my kids, so I lifted him onto my lap, and told him his father had been shot and killed in the line of duty."

Zack sat staring out the window. "She said we needed to be strong, but I didn't feel strong one bit. All I could think of was my dad and I were going to a Yankees game that night. That's what we did almost every Wednesday night. He was a big baseball fan. I still don't go to ball games."

Huna stood and walked around the room. "Must have been an awful time."

"Well, enough of that." Zack turned to Olney. "When will you be able to go home?"

"The doc said tonight if I have someone to help me."

"You do," Ethel spoke up. "I'd be glad to help." She glanced at Huna. "Would that be okay? I guess his apartment is still a crime scene. I imagine he has a second bedroom."

Huna stood. "I think you're helping him would be fine."

Ethel glanced over at Zack and Laura. "What about you two?"

"I'm not sure." He looked at Laura. "What do you think?"

"We're supposed to be on vacation. I vote we go out on the town and taste New York. Do some sightseeing. I hope we can catch up with Shelia."

"Shelia?" Ethel asked.

Zack nodded. "I met her on a prior case. She called last night and told me she was in New York. Apparently she's taking some workshop."

"She's a medium," Laura said. "Isn't that exciting? She's really fun."

Zack saw that Sergeant Huna seemed to pull back. "Does it bother you?"

"Mediums communicate with the dead. Be careful in dealing with spirits. You can get hurt."

Laura eyes widened and she looked at her dad.

"It'll be fine. Shelia would never hurt anyone."

"Just be very careful," Huna said.

"Oh, we will," Zack said. "Now, Laura, what would you like to see first?"

"Tomorrow, grandma and I have tickets to go see the Statute of Liberty. What I'd like to do this afternoon more than anything is see the Metropolitan Museum of Art, then head over and see where the Twin Towers were. If we have time, wouldn't it be fun to see Grand Central Station? Those are my big three."

"Okay, then it's what we'll do," Zack said. "We'd better go see the Metropolitan Museum of Art first. I'm told it'll take about two hours and the museum is over in Central Park West."

Laura jumped up. "Wow, you're starting to sound like a local."

"Well, maybe a little."

7

Manhattan, Tuesday, 3:00 p.m.

After a quick lunch of a sausage and soda from a street vendor, Zack and Laura caught the red line to the 79th Street Station, then walked over to Central Park and the Metropolitan Museum of Art.

Laura looked around. "I'd like to see the dinosaurs first. I read they have an exhibit of the Barosaurus, the world's largest free standing dinosaur, right here at the entrance. Then we can walk up to the fourth floor and see all the dinosaurs."

It took them about an hour and a half to see the dinosaurs and some of the other smaller exhibits before they wore out. They walked down the stairs and out the front door.

Zack took her arm. "What say we take a break and get something to drink?"

They found a vendor with scones and iced tea, then located a shady park bench in front of the museum and sat.

"Laura took a bite of her scone and chewed it down before saying, "This is what I think of when I hear Manhattan. Drinking tea, eating scones and people-watching in Central Park. I love it, Dad. Thanks."

Zack enjoyed watching her, so animated. "I'm glad you had fun. I did too. And I most enjoy spending time with you."

She reached over and gave him a kiss on the cheek. "Now eat your scone so we can head down to the site of the World Trade Center. We don't want to become old farts sitting around here all afternoon."

Zack had to laugh, although he would be very happy to sit a little more. "Okay, I've got the word. I'm ready to roll."

They headed back to the subway stop on 79th Street, then caught the red line to the exit for the World Trade Center. The two hopped off the subway and walked south toward the site.

As they walked, Zack said, "You know, the enormity of the September 11ᵗʰ tragedy is really driven home by the size of the massive bathtub that held the World Trade Center. The 'Twin Towers' once dominated the city skyline. Visitors from all over the world now make a pilgrimage here to see the site."

"It's so sad," Laura said. "And it seems to me so unnecessary. Why do people do stuff like that? All those people who died. Makes me shiver."

When they arrived at the site, they entered the National 9/11 Memorial Museum, located within the archaeological heart of the original site.

Zack read the inscription along the wall, "*The Museum serves as the country's principal institution concerned with exploring the historic implications of that tragic date, through state-of-the-art multimedia exhibits, archives and monumental artifacts. Paying reverent homage to the nearly 3,000 victims of the attacks, the museum also recognizes the thousands who survived, and all who showed extraordinary courage & compassion in the catastrophe's aftermath.*"

The two sat down on a bench and enjoyed the beauty and the silence.

"It's really eerie," Laura said. "I almost feel like I can sense the ghosts of those people. It makes me want to cry."

"Me too," Zack said. "All those people and they were just going about their every day business. Doing their job, maybe thinking about their daughter's afternoon soccer game when bang, it happened."

After they finished walking around the site, they sat on a bench along the street, drinking a soda. "You know what, Dad, I'd like to see where they shot grandpa."

Her comment caught Zack off balance. But then he thought, here they were. She had every right to see where her grandfather had been killed. She sure as hell had heard enough about it.

Zack pulled the map he'd drawn out of his pocket to get his bearings. They walked along Sixth Street and found the site where Roger Kelly had been gunned down.

Laura put her hand in Zack's. "It's so awful, Dad. You'd better not let anything happen to you. I don't think I could stand it."

"Okay, enough of memories," Zack said. "Let me call Shelia and see when she can meet us for dinner. Have some fun."

"Can we do more Italian? That meal last night was really good."

"You bet."

*****

Zack and Laura hurried along 44th Street until they arrived at 200 West 44th Street. "Here it is," Zack said. "Carmine's Restaurant. Supposed to be one of the best Italian restaurants in Midtown."

The host led them to a table and held a chair for Laura.

As Zack sat, he said, "We're meeting a young woman who should be here shortly. Her name is Shelia."

"Yes sir. I'll bring her over as soon as she arrives."

"Wow, look at this place," Laura said. "It's huge."

"And I understand the portions are also. They call them hearty portions."

"Great," Laura said. "I'm feeling hearty."

Zack glanced up to see Shelia approaching their table. She still had the same slender figure, the long black hair and light blue eyes. Her milky white skin was accented by the short black, sleeveless dress. A colorful scarf wrapped around her neck set off the package.

Zack almost tripped when he rose to meet her. Tongue-tied, he managed to squeak out, "Hi, Shelia. You look beautiful."

She walked up to him and gave him a hug. The touch of her soft breast sent an electrical shock through him. It had been almost eighteen months since their last time together in Ireland and Gettysburg. What a time they'd had. *Why hadn't he followed up with her?*

She leaned back, looked up, then kissed him on the cheek. "Hello Laddie, nice to see you again."

He loved her Irish accent, it almost sounded like music. "Shelia, it's great to see you. You remember my daughter, Laura."

Shelia bent over to hug Laura.

"Hi Laura, I remember we met after your father and I returned from Ireland. What a crazy time we had over there. I do love my home."

Laura smiled up at her. "Wasn't it nuts? Cool to see you again. I'd love to hear more about what it's like to be a medium."

Shelia laughed. "I'd be glad to tell you some stories."

Zack pulled out a chair for her and Shelia sat.

"Oh, my," Shelia said. "I'm so glad we could get together and catch up. Have you ordered drinks yet?"

"Nope," Zack said. "Your timing is perfect."

Shelia flashed her beautiful smile and winked at him. "I'd love a pint of Guinness."

Zack motioned for the waiter who hurried over. "Yes, sir."

"Do you have Guinness, Lad?" Shelia asked.

"We do. And for the young lady?"

"Oh, I guess I'll have iced tea."

Zack put his hand on Laura's arm. "Won't be long and you can order a beer, too. I'll take a Blue Moon."

"Very good sir." He hurried off.

"Won't be just a beer, but I'm not sure what I'll celebrate with." Laura glanced over at Shelia. "What brings you to New York?"

"Guess what, I graduated from law school. I'm a real lawyer. A pain in the butt and lots of work, but now I'm an official member of the bar in Ireland." She laughed. "Our law firm has an office in Manhattan, so I'm doing an internship here to learn the ways of your goofy legal system."

Zack couldn't help but smile again at her laugh. He looked up to see the waiter headed their way. They all ordered the pasta special which turned out to be delicious.

During dinner, Zack shared with Shelia what had brought them to New York. He told her about the death of his father and his frustration about the dirty cop stigma.

While they drank their coffee, a cloud seemed to drop down over Shelia's eyes.

Zack put his hand on her arm. "What's wrong?"

"Hey," Laura chimed in, "you look down all of a sudden."

"This is really hard for me."

"What's wrong?" Zack leaned forward. "You know us. Just spit it out."

"Sometimes I hate being a medium." She lapsed into silence, then she said, "You'll probably think I'm a nut."

"I would never think that," Zack said.

"Me neither," Laura said.

Shelia sighed. "All right. As you've been talking, I've been getting messages."

Zack now realized what Shelia was talking about. She's sensed messages from the other side. Should he hold her back until they were alone? Was Laura ready for this?

"I know what you're thinking, Kelly." Laura pointed her fork at her dad. "I'm not a little kid anymore. Whatever Shelia has to say, I want to hear it, too."

Shelia looked at Zack, who nodded. "Okay. As you've been talking, I've been receiving messages. I don't know for sure, but they could be from a friend of your father's."

Zack felt as if someone had punched him in the chest. He stared at her, mouth open.

"Zack, you're in terrible danger. You should quit what you're doing and not probe any further. You're running a risk not only for yourself, but for your mother and for Laura."

***

Zack and Laura walked Shelia back to her hotel located only four blocks from where they had eaten. Horns honked and buses rumbled by them as they worked their way through the crowd of people. Zack marveled at how many people walked the sidewalks of New York in the evening.

"I love all the people and activity," Laura said. "It's so exciting."

"It is that," Zack replied. He was still troubled by what Shelia had told them. Could she be in communication with a friend of his father's? He knew she had a special gift, but now when it might include him, he wasn't sure what to think.

When they arrived at the front door of Shelia's hotel, she took a step up the stairs, then turned to give him a peck on the cheek and a hug to Laura. "What are you two doing tomorrow?"

"I'm meeting grandma at nine thirty, then we're taking the ferry over to the Statue of Liberty and Liberty Island."

"Oh, that'll be fun," Shelia said. "I've never done that."

"When we get back, we'll hit one of the restaurants for lunch. I imagine grandma will want to go back to spend time with Chester in the afternoon. I'm not sure what I'll do. Do I need to be a chaperon?" Laura laughed. "I mean, I don't want you two kids to get in trouble."

"I don't know, Zack?" Shelia chuckled, a throaty chuckle. "Do we need a chaperon?"

Zack wasn't in the mood for laughter. "I'm going to continue poking around about my dad. I know you said to be careful and I will, but I can't leave it alone. At least not yet."

Shelia put her hand on his arm. "Well, I'm off tomorrow so if you want some company, let me know. I'd love to tag along with you. I thought we made a hot team in Ireland."

Zack had to smile. They had made a great team both during the day and at night. "Thanks for the offer, Shelia. I'm thinking of a couple of things I need to do and it might be fun to have you along. I could use a little medium brain power. How about if I call you in the morning?"

"That's a deal. I look forward to it."

As she walked toward the elevator, Zack thought, what a beautiful woman.

8

Staten Island Ferry, Wednesday, 6:30 a.m.

Zack leaned on the railing of the Staten Island Ferry and marveled at the beauty of the Statue of Liberty as they cruised past it. Puffy white clouds framed the view, and the sunrise reflected on the water of the Hudson. He loved the early morning. Everything fresh. A new beginning.

Laura had given him a ride to the terminal, then driven back to get herself ready to meet her grandmother for their tour. She planned to leave the truck in the parking lot for a later return.

Today he hoped to catch up with the Mafia boss as well as the retired cops who had been part of the task force and thus involved in the operation. It would be interesting to see what each of them had to say, then compare their statements to what Tomlinson had told him and what he'd read in the after-action report.

As the ferry closed in on the Manhattan side of the river, he pulled out his cell and pressed in Shelia's number.

"Hey, Kelly, I wondered when you'd get it together enough to make the call. I'm all dressed and ready to go. All I need is a cup of coffee to get the fires burning."

"I'm just arriving at the Whitehall Terminal and can be at your place in probably thirty minutes."

"I'll be down in the coffee shop, Laddie. Better hurry or I'll be two cups ahead of you and you know what that means. You'll never catch up."

"I remember. I'll hurry."

After disembarking, he walked across the street, then down the stairs into the subway station. He checked directions, then headed up town on the red-line. An easy way to travel around New York, and no parking problems.

As promised, Shelia waited for him at the coffee shop. Dressed in a pair of black slacks and a red shirt, with a white sweater over her shoulders, she looked lovely.

She stood to give him a hug. "Hi, Zack."

Zack hurried over to her. "Hi yourself. You look terrific."

"Are you putting the make on me before you've even had a cup of coffee?"

Zack had to laugh. "No, but I should have thought of it. I'd like to meet with the Mafia boss Tomlinson talked about. The one who my dad supposedly worked with."

"Oh, Zack, is that a good idea?"

"Maybe not, but I think it'll give us a lead. Let me call Tomlinson and see if he'll give me an address."

Zack pushed in Tomlinson's number on his cell and got his secretary. Soon, Tomlinson came on the line. "Good morning, Zack, you're at it early."

"Yep. First, I wanted to thank you for letting me look at the case file. It helped me cement in my mind how everything went down.

"You're welcome."

"I've got lots to do today. I'd like to start with a visit to the Mafia boss who supposedly got my dad to work with him."

"Look, Kelly, I know you're upset about your dad's death, but Angelo is a killer. I don't want you to end up dead, too."

"Hell, I don't either. It's not my dad's death that's so bad, it's the fact that some bastard smeared his name. I'd like to figure out how it happened and why."

"Kelly, I don't think you know who you're dealing with. Angelo puts people in the river. Dead. At least you should let me send someone with you."

"If you send someone along, Angelo probably won't see me. Just give me his address. I know I can get it myself if I have to."

"All right. I'll give you his address on Long Island. I doubt he'll even see you, but I sure as hell can't stop you."

"True enough." After Zack got off the phone with Tomlinson, he said, "I can't ask you to go with me all the way out to Long Island to see this guy. He's pretty dangerous."

"You'd better not try and stop me or I'll punch your lights out," Shelia said. "Now on the brighter side, I have a friend at work who owns a car and her garage isn't too far away. Let me see if I can borrow it. That would be a lot easier than taking the train."

After a short call, Shelia disconnected. "Let's go. She told me where she hides the key."

"Wow, that was nice. She must trust you."

"I'm not sure about that, but she did say okay and where she keeps a spare key."

***

Holding the door to the building open, Ethel Kelly helped Chester Olney walk outside. She held his arm, then gave him his cane. Together they began walking along the sidewalk.

"Take your time, Chester, we're not in any hurry. I've got a couple of hours before I need to meet Laura, and I don't want you to fall and hurt yourself."

"Thank you, Ethel, it's so good of you to do all this."

"You helped me when Roger died. This is the least I can do to repay you. Makes me feel needed again."

They walked a few steps across the sidewalk, then they turned around. Ethel held the door open again as Chester limped up the two stairs and into the lobby.

When they arrived at the eighth floor, Ethel slid the wooden door open and helped him out. "I haven't seen elevators like this since I lived in New York years ago. Doors you have to push open when you reach the right floor. A real touch of history."

She helped him across the hallway to his door. He gave her the key and she slid it in the lock, then pushed it open.

She helped him off with his sweater, then balanced him as he sat on the couch.

"Whew, I feel like I just ran a race."

"You've been through a great deal. Now, let's see about your medications. You're supposed to get one of each of these every four hours. I'll get you water. How about some tea or coffee?"

Olney wiggled around to get comfortable. "Coffee would be wonderful."

As she got the medications ready and started the coffee, Ethel found herself humming a tune. It felt good to be needed. Really good.

She remembered most of her clothes were still in her suitcase on Staten Island. Luckily she had toilet articles in her smaller bag.

Chuckling to herself, she thought maybe she'd just borrow one of his shirts like they do in the movies. A slight twinge of heat blossomed up from somewhere deep inside her. She hadn't felt anything like that in years. Darn, it felt good.

***

Laura watched from the front of the ferry as it pulled into the Whitehall Terminal on the Manhattan side of the Hudson River. When the gates opened, she walked down the gangplank, then across the waiting area and down the stairs.

She had made arrangements to meet her grandmother at the ticket booth for the ferry to the Statue of Liberty and Ellis Island. They'd agreed to go to both sites and Laura was excited to see each of them.

Grandma Ethel said her father and mother came through Ellis Island from their home in France. After they processed all the paperwork, they found a tiny apartment and began their new life. What guts to leave everything behind. Laura wasn't sure if she could do it.

At the base of the outside steps, Laura turned left, crossing the street, then walked toward Battery Park. She had made arrangements to meet her grandmother at the ticket booth at 10:30.

Her grandmother came hurrying up, waving, "Laura, here I am. Thank you for bringing my small bag. It'll keep me stocked with a few things anyway. Another trip to the store may be in order."

Laura hugged her grandmother and together they went to the ticket booth where they had to wait in line for a few minutes. Grandmother Ethel paid for the reserved tickets, then they followed the sidewalk to the boat, reading the information on the small bulletin boards posted along the way.

"We've got about twenty minutes to kill, so what do you say we get a coffee and scone."

"That would be perfect," Laura replied. "I didn't eat much breakfast."

"I took Chester for a short walk and he doesn't move very fast. Poor dear."

The two walked over to a small vendor wagon. "We'll have two of those," Ethel said, "and I'd like a cup of coffee. What about you, Laura?"

"Iced tea."

Laura sat and put the straw into her iced tea. "How are things going with Chester?"

"Each time he can go a little farther. A really sweet guy."

"Ah, ha. Are you getting close? I mean, you know."

Grandma Ethel laughed. "I'm enjoying him, but no, we're not close. Certainly not that close."

Laura smiled. "Inquiring minds want to know. I'm really looking forward to seeing the Statue of Liberty."

"I am too," Ethel replied. "And I'm also looking forward to spending the day with you. Oh, look, they're beginning to board. Let's go."

The two got up, put their cups in the trash, and hurried toward the gate.

9

Long Island, Wednesday, 10:30 a.m.

Shelia and Zack picked up her friend's Honda about a block from the hotel, then took the FDR Drive along the east side of Manhattan, and cut across the Queensboro Bridge. Neither had been on Long Island before, so they plugged Angelo's address into the GPS. Fortunately, there was not much traffic to contend with. You could never tell in New York City.

Once on Long Island, they followed the South Shore Road, which paralleled Fire Island, toward the Hamptons. The address Tomlinson had given them was a four-story mansion with a dark red-brick wall around it. With stately columns in the front, the house had a number of balconies around the third story. Stately oak trees spanned what Zack could see of the property. A captain's walk decorated the top of the roof, and the compound seemed tightly secured with closed-circuit cameras and what looked like an electrified fence above the wall.

Shelia pulled up to a wrought iron gate and stopped. Zack could see a circular driveway inside the fence leading up to the front door of the mansion. The door looked as if it might be made of gold.

Zack shook his head. "This place is really something. I wonder if Angelo gets lost walking from one end of the house to the other?"

Shelia shuddered. "I'm getting really bad vibes here. This guy sounds like one bad dude."

Zack kept gazing out of the passenger window. "Maybe it's best if I go in alone."

"Not on your life. It's just dark here. Very dark. We must be careful. Protect ourselves."

The two got out of their car and walked up to the gate. A bell stood about half-way up the wall off to the right of the gate. Zack pushed the bell and waited. A voice through a speaker asked him to state his business.

"My name is Colonel Zack Kelly. My father was a New York City police officer who was killed thirty-plus years ago. He was accused of working for Mr. Angelo and this tarnished his reputation. I'd like to speak with Mr. Angelo for a few minutes and ask him if he knew my father."

"Wait."

Shelia put her hand on Zack's shoulder. "Oh, Zack, this place feels dark. Many bad things have happened here."

"Are you sure you want to come in with me?" Zack whispered.

She smiled at him. "Yeah, let's do it, Laddie. Besides, it could be exciting to be frisked by a mobster. Hope he's pretty thorough."

Zack almost bent over he was laughing so hard.

In a moment a buzzer sounded and the gate swung open. Zack took Shelia's arm and together they walked up the circular drive and waited at the front door. The door opened and they stood face-to-face with a huge man, probably one who could play left tackle for the Washington Redskins. Easily six foot, five inches with broad shoulders, the man was dressed in a dark suit. Zack spotted a bulge under his left arm which undoubtedly meant he was packing.

"Please turn around," the man said. "I need to pat you down before you see Mr. Angelo."

They turned and after the mobster frisked him, he moved to Shelia. When he finished, they followed him into an anteroom easily twenty feet by twenty feet. A glass chandelier hung in the center of the room. Paintings decorated the walls. Zack didn't know much about art, but these paintings looked expensive.

The monster beckoned with his arm. "This way."

Zack and Shelia followed him into a den which looked as if you could play a pick-up game of basketball and still have room along the sides for fans. Book shelves circled the room.

Behind the mahogany desk sat a man who pushed himself up and walked over to Zack. Slightly taller than Zack, he appeared to be in excellent shape. His silver gray hair was brushed back on his head. French doors opened onto a patio with wicker chairs placed around the area with a table spotted in the middle. A large pool swept across the back yard with a tennis court behind it.

The man reached out his hand. "Welcome, Colonel Kelly. My name is Sonny Angelo."

"Zack Kelly." He turned to Shelia. "This is my friend, Shelia O'Donnell."

Angelo shook her hand. "And a very attractive friend you have." He motioned toward a grouping of chairs. "Can I offer you something to drink? Maybe a scotch or coffee?"

"Coffee would be great," Zack replied. "Thank you. Shelia?"

"Yes, coffee, please."

Anglo motioned to the monster who left the room, then he sat in a leather chair a few feet across from them. "Now, how can I help you?"

Zack repeated the story of what happened to his father. When he finished a young woman brought in a tray with three coffees. She gave one to Shelia, then Zack, then Angelo.

Angelo took a sip of coffee. "Being a police officer in New York City can be a very dangerous business."

"I understand police work can be dangerous as I'm with the army rangers and have served three tours in Afghanistan and one in Iraq."

"I didn't know." Angelo tipped his cup in a salute. "Thank you for your service."

Zack drank to that. "My dad was an honorable man. He died in the line of duty. I've come to grips with the fact my father died when I was six, but I can't get past the fact his reputation was soiled by the claims he was a dirty cop. I don't believe it. That's why I'm here. To find out what happened."

Angelo set his coffee on a small table next to his chair. "How old are you, Colonel?"

"What does my age have to do with anything?"

"We're close to the same age. You must have been in grade school when your father died. I was too. What happened over thirty years ago is ancient history. What our fathers did or didn't do can't be changed."

"Well, that may not be true," Zack said. "Since you were young, your dad would be the one to know what happened. Is he still alive?"

Angelo shook his head. "I'm sorry to say he died about twenty years ago. Shot down while he ate in a restaurant. Can you imagine; all he was doing was eating some pasta."

Zack took a sip of coffee to figure out what he wanted to say. "I'm sorry to hear about your father. But what happened to my dad is not ancient history for me. Not a day goes by I don't think of him. And goddamn miss him."

"I can understand. You may not realize it, but I miss my dad, too. Other kids in school had their dads, but mine was gone. I played a lot of football. He never attended any of my games."

"My dad made a career choice to be a cop," Zack said. "All fine and good. He died. Happens to cops. But some son-of-a-bitch set him up. He wasn't a dirty cop. I'm going to try and prove it, and I'd like you to help me."

Angelo picked up his cup and took another sip. "What do you want me to do? I'm a businessman."

Zack sipped more coffee, knowing he needed to be more careful here. "Someone in your organization may know the truth of what happened. I'd like you to help me find the truth."

Angelo put his cup down on the table with a clank. "What do you base that on?"

"My dad's partner, Chester Olney, told me my dad wasn't a crook. He was set up by someone. I heard the accusation was based on what one of the drug dealers said. There is very little information in the official file. Almost like someone cleaned it out. I believe someone in your organization may know something to help me."

"You certainly don't believe my father had anything to do with those events."

Zack thought for a moment. More coffee. "To be honest, maybe not your dad, but perhaps someone who worked with him."

Angelo leaned forward, his eyes bright. "I'll have to say I don't appreciate your comments. I'm hosting you as a friend. Are you accusing my dad of organizing this?"

Oh, oh, be careful. "I don't know for sure what I'm doing. I just know someone has got to know something because I'm sure as I can be that my dad wasn't a crooked cop."

Angelo stood and glared down at Zack. "Just so we're clear, if my father had been out to get your father, there wouldn't have been any body to discover. He never left a body. There wouldn't have been any question. Am I clear?"

Zack gulped and glanced a Shelia. "Yes. We're clear."

Sitting back down, Angelo said, "Okay, I appreciate what you've done for our country, Colonel Kelly. Let me see what I can find out."

"Thank you. Now if your offer is still good. I'd like a beer instead of a scotch, and I think Shelia would too."

Shelia nodded. "Guinness if you have it. Gives me a little touch of home."

Angelo laughed. "How about if we add sandwiches. Getting close to lunch. Won't take long."

"That would be great," Zack said. "Thanks."

Angelo turned to Shelia. "Do I detect an Irish accent?"

"Aye, you do, Laddie. That you do."

"All right," Angelo said. "Let's drink a toast to Ireland. Then to Italy."

And they did.

***

After lunch, Sonny Angelo watched Zack and Shelia walk down the front sidewalk toward their car, an old Honda. He waved goodbye, then pulled his cell out of his pocket and pushed in a number.

"Yes?" They never used any names. No need. Only two people had access to the line.

"I had a visit from a Colonel Kelly. He's looking into what happened to his father, Roger Kelly, years ago. Seemed like a nice chap, but unfortunately pretty sharp. Strikes me as someone who will keep at it until he finds out what he wants."

"What do you suggest?"

"He is planning to interview some of the officers who were involved and are now retired."

"I'd heard that."

"Probably shouldn't let it happen."

"Take care of it."

"I plan to." Angelo disconnected and put the phone back in his pocket.

10

Lower Manhattan, Wednesday, 1:00 p.m.

Laura and her grandmother arrived back at Battery Park from Ellis Island and disembarked. "I'm thirsty," Laura said. "Let's get some iced tea. I'll pop for the drinks."

Her grandmother pointed. "There's a bench. You get the tea and I'll save us a couple of seats."

Laura brought the tea over and the two sat together. She toasted her grandmother. "I received a text from Dad wondering how we're doing."

Grandma Ethel sipped on her tea and looked out across the bay. "To be honest, it's easy to be uneasy. The attack on Chester. The police don't know who did it. Makes me scared shitless."

Laura laughed. "Grandma!"

Her grandmother smiled. "Well, it does."

"Dad could be stirring up something with all of his inquiries," Laura replied. "Guess we'll have to wait and see."

"I agree. We need to be watchful." Ethel glanced at Laura. "Are you done with your tea? Maybe we should head out to Chester's condo. I told him we'd be there for a late lunch."

"Sounds like a plan. Let's hit it."

When Laura stood, she glanced around. A man in a dark brown hat and trench coat caught her attention. She whispered to her grandmother, "Take a look at the man in the coat sitting on a bench and reading his paper.. Don't you think it's odd he wearing a coat on such a warm day?"

Ethel moved her gaze toward the man. "Let's get out of here."

They hurried to the South Ferry station and waited for a red line train to take them to Chester's.

Laura kept watching for the man, but didn't see him. She leaned close to her grandmother. "Whew, looks like it was just my imagination. No man in a trench coat." She followed her grandmother onto the train and sat down, glad for the air conditioning. She looked around, then lurched back. "Grandma, it's him."

"We'll be okay on the train. It might just be a coincidence."

"I'm like my dad, Grandma. I don't believe in coincidences."

As they rode, Laura watched him. Still reading his newspaper.

At the 116th street station, they got off the subway and hurried up the stairs. Laura looked back. "Good, he didn't get off the train. I was starting to worry."

"When they reached Chester's building, Ethel rang the bell then heard a buzzer. Laura reached over and opened the door, holding it for her grandmother.

At the eighth floor, they slid the metal elevator door, pushed open the heavy wooden door and walked the few steps to Chester's door.

Chester waited, holding it open for them. "How was the Statute of Liberty? I assume it's still there."

Laura laughed. "Yep, still there and so is Ellis Island. No one moved either one of them. Fun to read the stories of those who passed through Ellis Island. I'd be so scared coming to a new country, but it must have been exciting for all those people to get a fresh start."

Laura told Chester and her grandmother about Shelia. "She's a friend of Dad's. He met her on a case he worked a year or so ago. She's quite a lady. Just finished law school and also is a medium."

"A medium?" Ethel said. "I'm not sure I like that. Never believed in mediums."

"She is really lovely," Laura said. "I think you'll like her."

Laura walked over to the window and looked out. Leaning against a tree on the river side of the street stood the man in a trench coat, watching their building.

***

Next on Zack's list was a visit to one of his father's partners, Sergeant Curly Frost. He'd set up an appointment for one thirty.

The Frosts lived in Brooklyn, about a thirty minute subway ride from Shelia's hotel on the orange line. Zack watched the people on the subway. From homeless persons to Wall Street executives, everyone depended on the subway to travel around Manhattan. Driving was a nightmare and parking impossible.

Their house was a two-story bungalow with a chimney on one end and an attached double garage on the other. The garage door stood open, revealing an older model Buick in one stall and piles of stuff in the other. The exterior walls of the house looked freshly painted, white with gray trim.

Zack knocked on the door. When Frost opened the door, Zack introduced himself and Shelia. A short, puffy man with thick glasses, Frost seemed ready with a smile. "Welcome. Please come in."

They entered a short hallway with a stairway ascending from the other end. Off to the right stood a dining room with a mahogany table surrounded by six chairs. A number of knickknacks decorated the glass shelving in front of the windows.

Frost led them into the living room, a comfortable sized room with two over-stuffed chairs, a couch with a coffee table in front of it, and a few miscellaneous wooden chairs scattered around. All of the furniture had slipcovers placed neatly over them, reminding him of his mother's home back in Minneapolis.

A gray-haired woman with a flowery dress entered from the hallway. "Good afternoon, I'm Amanda Frost. I've made coffee and fresh blueberry muffins. Can I interest anyone?"

"Oh, my goodness, yes," Shelia said. "They smell wonderful."

When they were seated and each had coffee and a muffin, Amanda excused herself.

"Thanks again for the coffee," Zack called, then turned to Frost. "You were with my father when he died. Can you tell me what happened?"

"Your dad was one hell of a great guy and a balls-to-the-wall cop." He glanced at Shelia. "I'm sorry. Shouldn't have said that."

"Why not? It describes Zack's dad. And believe me, I've heard it all so don't think a couple of balls are going to bother me."

Frost laughed. "Okay, we're going to get along great. Zack, your dad and I worked a number of drug busts together."

"Please provide all the details you can."

Frost repeated the story, most of which Zack already knew. "I'll never forgive Tomlinson for rushing things. I think he did it because the mayor was on the chief's ass due to all the damn drugs in the city. The crap filters downhill fast."

Shelia shook her head. "An unforgivable loss of life. All for politics."

Frost leaned back in his rocker. "Let me think for a minute. Roger died on a Wednesday night. They held the memorial service the following Saturday."

Zack remembered it vividly. He'd held his baby sister's hand, both of them crying during the service. His younger brother stayed with a neighbor.

Frost snapped his fingers. "It was almost a week after the memorial service, a Thursday morning. Tomlinson called us all into his office."

The emotions roiled inside of Zack. He'd handled Afghanistan, a mountainous country locked between Pakistan and Iran. Some of the least educated and most war-weary people in the world. He had worked with them, managed everything he was asked to do, and now the frustrations from the death of his father threatened to overwhelm him. He had to swallow his anger. *Don't let the PTSD grab hold of you. Take deep breaths.* What his doc had said. Take deep breaths and relax. Hard to do. "Was Tomlinson injured in the attack?"

"Nah, he hung back. Said he needed to coordinate things." Frost paused as if to organize his words. "Sorry, I want to make sure I remember it accurately. I know this is important to you."

"Thank you. I appreciate your time."

"Listen, Roger Kelly was my friend. A good guy. I never believed he was dirty. I remember now. Tomlinson called us into his office. There were nine of us sitting around his conference table. He said there had been concerns about the way the operation went down, and we all would be called individually for questioning. He assured us there were no problems. Just routine."

Yeah, Zack thought, routine my ass. "Did you believe him?"

"To be honest, I had no reason not to."

Amanda walked back into the room and poured a second cup of coffee for each of them. "You know, Zack, I met your father a number of times. He was a good man. Always pleasant, always nice. A handsome man. You look like him."

Her comment made Zack blush.

Shelia laughed. "Now Zack, don't get all prissy. You're a good looking hunk, so enjoy women telling you that."

Zack took another sip of coffee. "Well, since you put it that way, I guess I'd better."

Amanda walked out, then she turned back, "Always remember, your dad was a good man. He did his job well and everyone liked him."

"Thank you." Zack sighed. "You started to tell me about the meeting in Lieutenant Tomlinson's office."

"There wasn't much more to it," Frost replied. "The lieutenant said no one had anything to fear. Just tell the truth."

"Who would conduct the inquiry?"

"Internal Affairs."

"Didn't that signal something wrong?"

"Not really. To be honest, I hated those assholes. I knew a couple of my friends who had problems with them. But after an incident where an officer had been killed, it didn't seem unusual."

"What happened next?"

"The next day I got called in. The Internal Affairs guys turned on the recorder and asked me about the operation. I told them what I told you. I was behind the building, so I didn't see your dad get shot. Then they asked me what I thought of Roger Kelly."

Shelia took a bite of muffin. "Had he explained your rights before he questioned you?"

Zack put down his coffee cup. "Shelia's an attorney."

"Yep, they covered all the bases."

"Didn't the question make you suspicious?" Zack asked.

"Set off all kinds of alarm bells. I told them I liked your dad. Thought he was a good cop, and it pissed me off he'd been killed."

"What else? Please be honest."

"There were two of them. The one I'd had trouble with, in another interview, said something like, 'Is there any chance Kelly could have tipped off the dealers?' "

Here it comes, Zack thought.

"I told them hell no. No way Roger would do anything like that."

Zack paused for a sip of coffee. "Why did they ask you?"

He looked away for a moment, "I overheard one guy say something like 'I wonder if the tip could have been wrong'?"

Zack took another deep breath. "I don't get it. If it was just a shot-in-the dark by one of the drug dealers, why would they go with it without confirmation? Did they have any more proof to go on that you know of?"

"Shouldn't all of the information be in the file?" Shelia asked.

"Yeah, but you probably didn't see the IA files. They keep them separate."

Zack felt like he'd stumbled onto his first real lead. But why wouldn't Tomlinson let him know about the IA file? He must have known. Then it dawned on Zack. Maybe Tomlinson wanted to keep it all quiet.

Zack stood and Shelia followed suit. "Well, we've taken enough of your time and better get going. I need to see if I can find the Internal Affairs file."

"Good luck. They may try and keep it under wraps. But, be careful. Bringing up old things can cause problems. Be alert."

Shelia pointed at Zack. "After all this time, you should be able to access the file."

Frost opened the door and stepped out onto the porch. As Zack reached over to shake Frost's hand, he glanced up the street. A black sedan pulled out from the curb two houses away and drove down the street much too slowly for the speed limit. The windows were tinted dark. Shelia's comment burned through his mind. Be careful.

A rifle barrel pointed out of the rear window.

"Watch out," Zack called and dove toward the bushes, pushing Frost and Shelia ahead of him. Three shots rang out, then a squeal of tires as the car drove off.

Zack poked his head up and reached for Shelia. "Are you okay?

She shook her head as if to clear it. "I ... I ..., I think so. A couple of scrapes."

Zack's gaze switched to Frost. Blood flowed from his head. "Frost, Frost, speak to me." Zack checked for a pulse. Faint.

"Listen to me," Frost whispered, his voice hoarse. "Listen. You need to be careful. You have no idea what you're up against. Get out now. Leave this alone."

Frost fell back, his breathing labored.

Zack grabbed his cell and dialed 911.

11

Brooklyn, Wednesday, 2:30 p.m.

About seven minutes after Zack's call, a police car squealed around the corner, siren wailing, followed closely by an ambulance. The two vehicles stopped at the curb and an EMT jumped out and hurried up the sidewalk. One of the two police officers got out and began to string yellow, crime-scene tape around the area. The other directed the crowd, which had been forming, to get back.

The EMT reached Zack and knelt beside him. "What happened? Are you hurt?"

"Someone shot at us while we were standing on the porch," Zack said. "I saw what looked like a rifle barrel sticking out of the back window of the car, which I think was an Oldsmobile, and pushed everyone down into the bushes. The older man has been hit. Take care of him first."

"I'm all right," Shelia called, "just some bruises and scratches."

The EMT moved over to Frost, still laying in the bushes. "Where does it hurt?"

A loud moan sounded from Frost.

Zack leaned over and put his arm around Shelia. "Sure you're all right?"

"That son-of-a-bitch could have killed us."

"I think that was the idea. Or, at least to scare us off."

She pushed herself up and stood. "What do you mean?"

Zack brushed himself off. "Frost whispered to me something like 'You don't know what you're dealing with. Stop messing with this.'"

Shelia turned, wide-eyed. "What?"

Zack heard more sirens and looked down the street. "Police."

The police rolled in like a wave of blue, flashing red lights, officers shouting to one another. The first officer continued to spread crime scene tape around the yard. A second held back a couple of reporters who had just arrived.

An officer hurried up the sidewalk. "I'm Sergeant Jefferson. Are you both all right?"

Zack pointed toward where the EMT leaned over Frost. "He's the one who got shot. Could be in pretty tough shape. Shelia and I are scratched and bruised from diving into the bushes, but otherwise seem to be okay." Zack turned to see Amanda crying. "She's his wife. Probably scared to death."

The officer opened the door. "Let's go inside so I can take your statement. The crime scene guys need to do their work out here. After that, both of you need to be checked by the EMTs."

When they were seated, the officer said, "Okay, tell me what happened."

As they talked, a tall man in a suit wandered in the front door. "My name is Detective Inspector Hooper. Please finish."

It took about thirty minutes for Zack to finish the story, Shelia adding comments as he talked.

Hooper looked down at his notebook, obviously trying to piece together his next questions. "So your father was killed in the line-of-duty thirty years ago, and now you're looking into it?"

From his tone, Zack could tell the detective wasn't sure what to make of his story. "That's right. There was a drug raid and my dad was shot and killed by one of the dealers. Later, they accused him of being a dirty cop. My daughter and I are here in New York trying to find out anything we can."

Hooper made a note in his book. "Roger Kelly. I don't believe I've heard that name. Do you think what happened here is tied to the old case?"

"I have no idea," Zack replied. "Look, I visited Commissioner Tomlinson yesterday and read the case file. Mr. Frost was one of the detectives on the scene. I wanted to talk to him and find out what he remembered."

"Was he helpful?" Hooper asked.

Zack took a sip of coffee, pondering his reply. "Not as much as I'd hoped. He shared with me pretty much what I already knew from the file." Zack decided to not say anything about the Internal Affairs folders. He needed to be careful who he told what.

Zack's cell rang. He looked at it, then at Hooper. "It's my daughter. I'd better take it." He pushed on his cell. "Hi."

"Dad, it's me. I think someone is following us."

"What? Who?"

"When we got off the boat at Battery Park, I noticed a man in a light-brown trench coat. I thought it was kinda funny to see a guy in a coat as warm as it is. Then he was on the subway in the next car."

He'd never forgive himself if anything happened to them. "Was that it?"

"I thought so because I didn't see him when we got off the subway."

"Good."

"Not so good. We're at Olney's apartment. I just looked out the front window. There the guy is. Sitting on a park bench reading his damn paper."

"Okay, stay inside and don't move. I'll get you help. I'll call you right back."

Zack disconnected. "Look, someone may be following my daughter. I'd better call Tomlinson." He dialed the number. When his assistant answered, he said, "This is Colonel Kelly. I've got to talk to Tomlinson right away."

"He's in a meeting."

"Please get him on the phone. Someone is following my daughter."

"Oh, my, just a minute."

Soon Tomlinson's voice sounded on the phone. "Colonel Kelly, what's going on?"

Zack explained what Laura had told him.

"Don't worry. After what happened to Chester Olney, I have one of my detectives following your daughter and mother. I wouldn't want anything to happen to them."

"What a relief. Thank you."

"Actually, I coordinated it through Chester Olney. He told me the two were at the ferry to the Statute of Liberty. He should have shared the plan with them when they arrived at his place."

"Okay, I'll let them know. Look, we're at Detective Frost's house. As we were leaving, someone shot at us from a black Oldsmobile. Shelia and I are okay, just a few bruises, but Detective Frost is in tough shape and on the way to the hospital."

"What?"

"Yes. I'm meeting with Detective Sergeant Hooper summarizing what happened for him right now."

"Let me talk to him."

Zack handed his cell to Hooper. "Commissioner Tomlinson wants to talk with you."

Hooper spoke with Tomlinson for a few minutes, then handed the cell back to Zack.

"Look Zack," Tomlinson said, "I can't think of a reason anyone would go after Sergeant Frost after all these years. Someone may be after you. What about Angelo? How did your meeting go?"

"He was a gentleman except when he thought I was blaming my dad's death on his father. He told me if his father had been involved, there wouldn't have been any body left."

"That's probably true."

Zack thought for a moment. "The only thing that seems to make sense to me is someone is concerned about what he might tell me."

"Well, be careful. Would you like me to put someone on you and your friend?"

"I don't think it's necessary. We'll be careful."

After Zack disconnected, he pushed in Laura's cell number. When she answered, he said, "Don't worry. The man outside is a police officer. After what happened to Chester Olney, Tomlinson put a tail on you to make sure you're safe. Olney should have mentioned it to you."

"Well, I guess I never said anything to him. Oh gosh, what a relief. I'll tell grandma. She's really worried."

"What are you planning to do?" Zack asked.

"I think I'll stay for dinner, then head back to Staten Island for the night. Grandma is going to stay here."

"I'm not sure it's wise with all the things going on."

"Look Dad, I'm out of clean clothes and really need some of my stuff. I'll be careful. Just on the ferry, then back to the Navy Lodge."

"Be careful. Call me before you leave. Love you."

After she disconnected, Zack turned back to Hooper. "I'm sorry, but with what's been happening, I needed to help my daughter."

"No problem. I have a daughter, too. Besides, I had a couple of details to check out. So after you talked to Detective Frost, the three of you were standing on the front porch."

"That's right."

"And you saw a black Oldsmobile moving down the street and slow down in front of the house. None of you thought it was strange?"

"It did have tinted windows. I remember wondering why. Mr. Frost didn't say anything. Like I told the other officer, I didn't think much more about it until I saw the rifle barrel sticking out of the window. Then I dove into the bushes taking Shelia and Frost along with me. Unfortunately he got hit. Happened so damn fast."

"Did you get a license number?" Hooper asked.

Zack shook his head. "No. Wish I had. Do you have any information about Detective Frost?"

"I understand he will require surgery. Hopefully he'll come out of it okay. So you're free to go, but please don't leave New York City. I may have more questions for you."

"I'll be here at least a few more days."

Hooper walked outside and began to confer with the other police officers.

Zack put his arm around Shelia. "How are you doing?"

"The dark energy is really strong. I'm ready to get out of here. Like now."

"Let's go find some coffee and figure out what to do next?"

"Great plan. I'm shaking like a leaf. Let me stop in the kitchen and say goodbye to Mrs. Frost if she's still here. I suspect she's already at the hospital."

12

Brooklyn, Wednesday, 5:30 p.m.

When Zack and Shelia walked down the front sidewalk of Frost's house, they were both still shaking. An unmarked police car waited in front. Sergeant Huna got out of the driver's side and waved to them. "Get in the car, please."

Zack held the door for Shelia, then got in. "What are you doing here?"

"Commissioner Tomlinson asked me to drive over here. He's concerned about your safety and thought someone better check on you."

Zack took a deep breath. "I'll have to thank him. What a day. Mr. Angelo was very nice to both of us this morning, but someone shot at us a little while ago. Detective Frost has been badly hurt. We got out with just some scratches and bruises."

Huna looked out the window for a moment. "Oh, how awful."

"You're right," Zack said. "The Frosts were both very friendly and helpful to us."

"Did you find out anything interesting?"

Zack wasn't sure what to answer.

"Don't worry, colonel, I'm not going to run back and squeal. To be honest I volunteered to check on you to make sure you were okay. It sounds like your dad got a raw deal and I'd like to help."

"Thank you," Zack said.

"Plus, I like Sonny Angelo. He's an upright guy."

"How do you know him?" Shelia asked.

She leaned back in her seat and put her hands on the wheel. "As I told you, I'm from a small island in Alaska, the home of my tribe. Shortly after I arrived here, one of the men came here and demanded I go back home. We had dated briefly before I left. Many males think they own their women. Tradition, you know."

"If he doesn't, I do," Shelia said. "Men can be massive pains in the butt."

"It so happened Sonny heard the threats at a restaurant. He came over and asked if everything was okay. Before I could answer, the guy told Sonny to get the hell out of there. I was his woman and he'd handle it."

"Oh, oh," Zack said.

"Yeah, oh oh. The guy ended up on the floor with two cracked teeth, a broken arm and a black eye. Sonny told him to get the hell out of town and never come back."

"Did he ever come back?" Shelia asked.

A big smile. "He never did. Sonny reached in his pocket and pulled out a quarter. He told me if I ever had another problem with one of those guys to give him a call."

"Have you ever had to use that quarter?" Zack asked.

"No, but I still have it."

"He seemed like a pretty cool lad," Shelia said. "Smart, entertaining, and appeared to be a real gentleman. I don't know I'd trust him, and he's definitely worth checking out. During the time of 'The Troubles' in Ireland, many of the Irish blokes could appear to be super guys, but wouldn't hesitate to stick a knife in your back if you crossed them."

"What do you mean, checking out?" Huna asked.

"I could run his name through our business and economic locater and see what I can find out about him. I'm curious where he gets the money for his mansion and all the stuff we saw. I'm sure he has a number of interesting businesses."

"Good idea," Zack said. "I suspect he's still in the rackets, but he's probably got several credible front organizations. It would be fun to see what they are."

"Okay. I can do that."

"Well, I have to get back," Huna said. "Can I give you two a lift?"

"Maybe just to the nearest subway stop," Shelia said. "We're headed back to my hotel."

"I'd be happy to give you a ride."

Shelia looked at Zack who nodded. "I'm still pretty shook up. Thank you."

When they reached the hotel, Huna said, "Keep me in the loop. If I can be of help, let me know. Somehow, I think you're getting the run-around."

"If you find out anything," Zack said, "let me know how Detective Frost is doing."

"Will do."

Zack opened the door and started to get out when he turned back. "Oh, one more thing. What's going on with the investigation of Olney's beating? Any suspects?"

"Chester said he heard a knock. He thought it was you. When he opened the door, two men pushed their way in and beat him up. One did have a gun."

"What I can't figure out is how they got into the building," Zack said. "They must have had a key or someone let them in."

"We checked with everyone in the building and no one remembers two men and no one said they let these guys into the building. It's like they had a key."

"But how ...?"

"I don't know how they got the key and no one else does, including Olney."

"End of investigation?"

Huna shrugged. "Unless we get more information."

Zack reached over and shook her hand. "Anyway, thanks for driving us here and for helping. I appreciate it."

"You're welcome. Take it easy and be careful."

When Zack and Shelia got out of the car, Huna drove off.

Shelia watched after the car. "I really like her."

"I do too." Zack pulled out his cell. "I'm going to call Laura. See what she and my mom are up to."

Zack pushed in her cell number and heard the familiar voice. "Hey Pops."

"How are you and your grandmother doing?" Zack asked. "Is the man in the trench coat still there?"

"Yep. After you told me who he was, I hustled downstairs and invited him up for dinner. He was a little embarrassed to be spotted, but he came up and is enjoying some of grandma's spaghetti."

"Are you still thinking of going back to the Navy Lodge?"

"Look, I'm pooped after all our running around and would like to take the ferry back to the truck. My clothes are a mess and I am too. Plus I want a run in the morning."

"I'm concerned for you."

"I'll be careful. The police officer agreed to ride with me on the subway and walk me to the ferry. What sounds great to me is a hot bath, some TV and junk food, then hitting the sack early. I've got to get some more clothes. Maybe call a couple of friends. Dad, I'll be fine. How was your day?"

"Kinda crazy. First we drove out to Long Island and met with Sonny Angelo." Zack shared some of the discussions with him. Then he talked briefly about their visit to Sergeant Frost. "So it's been pretty busy, but I think productive."

"Sounds like it," Laura replied. "Let me know if you need a ride back to our pad from the ferry later on."

"Will do. We'll coordinate on a plan for tomorrow. I haven't had a chance to think much about it yet."

"Okay. We'll talk later. Love you. Say hi to Shelia."

"Will do." Zack disconnected his cell.

Shelia touched his arm. "You didn't say anything about the shooting."

"I didn't want to scare her. She'll be safe with the police officer."

"How about if we think about our day over dinner near my hotel."

"Great idea."

Zack held the door for her and they strolled into the hotel lobby. People hurried around, talking, reading newspapers, whispering into their cell phones. "Let's trek into the bar?"

Shelia wiped her brow. "I'm a sweaty mess and need a few minutes to freshen up."

"You look wonderful to me. No sweaty mess there."

"Thanks, colonel. You are so sweet. Zack, I still have the shakes and need to settle down."

"I'll wait in the bar for you."

"Not on your life. I can't let you get ahead of me with a beer. Won't take me long."

"Are you sure?"

"Don't be silly, Mister Colonel. You are so backward. I won't bite. I promise."

"I know you don't bite." Zack had to laugh. "Okay, I just don't want to be in your way."

"If you were in my way, I'd say so. Lad, you're not in my way. So cool it. Now go over there and push the button to get us an elevator. Now."

Zack snapped to attention. "Yes sir."

13

Staten Island, Wednesday, 7:30 p.m.

Eagle paced around his motel room, driving Horse crazy. "Have we thought of everything? What else is there?"

"Relax," Horse said. "We're set. We have gone over every step several times, too many times if you ask me. We know exactly what we need to do."

"Listen, do you have any idea how long we can spend in jail if we get caught. They'll throw the key away and we'll never be heard from again."

"Stop. Just stop thinking like that. Kitten said our other group is all set. With the two operations going on at the same time, the Feds will be all fucked up. Is our inside man all set? Do we know the ferry he'll be on? Exact times. I don't want to be sitting there with my dick in my hand."

Eagle sat on the bed. "I talked to him today. He's all set and has a getaway plan."

"Okay. It'll be fine. Now get some sleep."

"Sleep. How the hell am I supposed to sleep?"

Horse laughed. "Lay down and close your fucking eyes. That should do it."

Eagle smiled. "I know you're right. But I still can't help ..."

"Stop. Just stop."

"Okay."

***

When they reached her door, Shelia unlocked it, then pointed toward one of the two chairs near the television set. "Give me a hug first. I'm still scared from what happened today."

Zack hugged her. "I'm sorry I got you into a shooting. I should have been more careful."

"I chose to go with you, Laddie. My decision. My responsibility. Now, I'm headed into the bathroom and will be out in a few minutes. We can go down and eat in the restaurant which is very nice, or if you want we can order room service. Why don't you check out the menu?"

Zack sat, stretched out his leg, then glanced around the room. A standard hotel room, two double beds, large screen television, a desk with a few chairs scattered around. Zack got out his cell and checked for messages. He needed to compose an email updating Admiral Steele on the day's actions. The admiral's connections would be helpful to cut through any red tape.

Nothing from Laura. He sent her a text telling her he would have dinner with Shelia and might stay over as it would be pretty late.

In a few minutes, Shelia opened the bathroom door a bit and tossed out her blouse. Then she shut the door again.

Zack started to smile. Shelia didn't stand much on protocol and Zack loved her for it.

The bathroom door opened a second time and out came her slacks. Zack found himself getting aroused. He decided as tough as it was, being cool was definitely the right course of action.

The door opened again and out came her bra. Oh, man, this was really getting good. Zack sat back and watched the door, nothing else interested him.

The door opened again and out came a pair of blue panties. Zack remembered she always preferred blue panties. Zack was definitely standing at attention.

The door opened again and out came Shelia, dressed in an oversized jersey with "Irish Lass" on the front and it didn't look like much else.

As she slipped the jersey down from the top, the curves of her breasts peeked out. The tail of the jersey brushed against her bare thighs.

His heart thumped in his chest. He couldn't talk.

She raised her arms. The jersey slid slowly down her chest fall to the floor revealing a beautifully naked Shelia.

He couldn't move. Just watched.

She walked over to him and sat on his lap. Kissed his cheek. Then she brought her lips to Zack's, her kiss soft and gentle. His fingers ran through her hair as they kissed. He gently ran his other hand down the curve of her back, hips, reveling in the softness.

Shelia leaned back and looked at him. "This has been a terrible day. So much pain and darkness. I need to celebrate happiness. And with you it would be perfect."

Zack just stared into her eyes for a minute. "You are the most beautiful woman."

She laughed, that lovely Irish laugh of hers. "Very nice, Laddie. Now are you going to sit there all afternoon or join me in the bathroom under a nice warm shower?"

***

The darkness surrounded him like a blanket. No moon light. No stars. Off to the west he heard the rockets hitting around him. He needed to pull in tighter to the wall, but he had trouble seeing. Why couldn't he see? Where the hell were his night vision goggles?

Then, a shadow moved, coming straight toward him. A tall shadow, hell, an outline of a gun. Zack reached for his rifle. No rifle. Where had he left it? Think, dammit, think.

The figure took aim and shot at him. Must have missed. No pain. He kicked out, but couldn't reach the shadow. Kicked again. The shadow took aim again. Zack kicked as hard as he could. Hit something. Damn, his foot hurt.

"Zack, Zack," a voice called. "Zack, wake up. Wake up."

Zack shook himself. Tied up in the blankets. He couldn't move.

A hand reached over and pulled down the blanket, unwrapping him. "Zack, wake up. You're having a terrible nightmare."

His heart pounded in his chest. His breathing raced. Head felt like it would explode.

The hand stroked his forehead until his breathing began to return to normal. The dream was familiar. Won't let him go. All the memories came flooding back. The losses. The bloodshed. The pain.

The bedside light came on. Shelia stared at him, concern in her eyes. "Oh, Zack, I'm so sorry for what you've been through. It must have been terrible. Are you okay?"

Zack couldn't speak for a moment. His head pounded. Then it came flooding out. "I joined the army one year out of high school. Airborne, ranger training, but nothing prepares you for what you meet in combat. You have to prepare yourself with the help of your buddies. Then when you lose one of those buddies, it's goddamn awful."

She reached up and shut off the light. Cuddled him under the covers. "Come over her. Let's try and go back to sleep. I'm still thinking about today. Oh, Zack, it was so awful. I need you to hold me."

14

Staten Island Ferry Terminal, Thursday, 8:00 a.m.

Laura parked in the pay lot next to the terminal. Since it was a nice day, she skipped the courtesy shuttle and walked past the ballpark at St. George and along the water, then up the stairs toward the terminal. A slight breeze blew in from the water and clouds dotted the sky. It would be a perfect day to take the ferry. After her tour yesterday, the Statue of Liberty had much more meaning.

She followed the crowd into St. George's terminal, past the Au Bon Pain restaurant, her stomach starting to growl. She noticed a sign reading Marsec Security Level 1. She wondered what it meant. Terrorism had become such a big deal now. It scared her to think about all the things that could happen in Manhattan. She worried about her dad and was happy to see the police presence wherever she went.

Laura felt happy her dad had decided to stay over in Manhattan with Shelia. She really liked Shelia and thought, what would it be like to have medium for a stepmother? Then she laughed and pushed the thought to the back of her mind.

She passed a NYPD officer in the hallway talking to a young woman, turned left and walked into the main waiting room. Lifting her backpack, she made her way through the security detectors. When she got through the two waist-high detectors, two police officers with bomb sniffing dogs waited for her.

One walked up to her. "Excuse me," he said. "Please set down your backpack so my dog can check it out."

"Sure, no problem," Laura said. "Beautiful dog. Is that a Lab?"

"Yep," the officer replied. "She's really a sweetheart."

"I imagine there's a lot of training that goes into her program."

"You bet. All of these dogs are very valuable."

Laura waited for the dog to circle the backpack. "Do you get many alerts from the dogs?"

"Thank you. You may move ahead."

She figured he might not answer that question. Too sensitive.

Picking up her backpack, she walked over to one of the rows of chairs, selected one with no one on either side and sat. Checking the schedule, she had about fifteen minutes before boarding. She reached into her backpack, pulled out the latest James Patterson novel. People watching was great sport. She loved to sit in bookstores and watch people. Try and figure out who they were and what they were doing. But, looking around, she didn't spot anyone she knew so she opened the book and started to read.

A few minutes later, something caused her to glance up. A woman in a baseball cap and sunglasses came through the metal detector, holding her bag up. The police officer walked toward her, the dog on his right.

The woman looked familiar. It was hard to tell who because the cap sat low over her face. With the sunglasses and her hair up under the hat any identification was tough.

Laura ran names through her brain. Did she know this woman? The way she carried herself she looked to be in excellent condition and only a year or two older than Laura.

Then it hit her. The woman looked just like Kinsey Cartwright. Damn, it was Kinsey. Kinsey was a junior at GW and a member of the varsity soccer team. Laura had met her during spring practice, but didn't know her very well. They would start the summer workout in another week. Seemed really nice, but a little standoffish.

Apparently from what she'd heard, Kinsey's twin brother had been wounded by an IED in Iraq and had to spend time in a VA hospital. If she remembered right, the brother was still in a wheelchair.

Laura closed her book, put it in her backpack, then got up and walked over to the woman. "Hey, Kinsey, is it you. It's me. Laura Kelly."

Kinsey jumped when Laura called her name. She whirled and stared at Laura. "Kelly, what are you doing here?"

Laura laughed. "What do you mean? I'm standing here waiting to take the ferry to Manhattan. What do you think?"

The police officer had finished with Kinsey, so he pulled on his dog's leash and the two walked over to an older man. "Excuse me, sir, would you please set your backpack on the ground? We'd like to give our dog a chance to check it."

The man set it down and backed up a step or two.

Kinsey seemed to regain her composure. "Pretty stupid question. You surprised me."

"I could tell," Laura said. "I didn't know you were visiting New York. I'm here on a vacation with my dad. A little break before practice starts."

Kinsey looked around, seeming a little distracted. "Aw, only another week before we start the two-a-days."

Laura wanted to get to know Kinsey better. She didn't know many members of the varsity team. Take advantage of it. "Are you visiting here with someone? Maybe we could get together for a drink later today if you're not busy. I'd like you to meet my dad."

Kinsey was watching the sliding glass doors to the ferry so didn't respond.

Laura asked again. "Any chance of getting together? To be honest, I'd really like to know some of the senior members of the team a little better."

Kinsey glanced around again. "I'm, ah, I'm with a group. We've got a number of things planned for the next day or so. The way it looks now, I don't think I'll have any spare time. See you back at school. Sorry."

"Well, okay," Laura said. "My dad and I are staying at the Navy Lodge here on Staten Island. I'm headed into Manhattan to meet him. We'll be here for another three days. Let me give you my cell."

"Ah, yeah, sure." After getting her cell number, Kinsey hurried across the terminal toward the bathrooms.

Kinda strange, Laura thought. She seemed pretty jumpy.

While she had her cell out, Laura thought she might as well text her dad. She smiled. Late enough so she shouldn't wake them up. She knew it was a *them*. But that was good. Shelia seemed cool. Laura would like to get to know her better. A medium. Damn, that was really something and she seemed so nice.

Laura thought for a moment. She texted her dad she was leaving Staten Island now and planned to take the ferry to Manhattan, then travel by subway to Chester Olney's. They had planned to meet for lunch so she wanted a confirmation of when and where.

***

Ethel Kelly helped Chester balance as the two walked out of his apartment. He reached back and locked the door, then they took about the twenty-some steps to the elevator.

Ethel held his arm to balance him and reached for the bell to summon the elevator. "It's nice you're so close to the elevator."

"I never thought it would be, but now I'm glad."

"Pretty interesting elevator," Ethel said. "I bet folks who are new to the building complain they wait and wait and don't realize the elevator is already there."

Olney nodded. "I had some problems with it at first."

As they waited, a gray-haired woman stepped out of her apartment. "Why hello, Chester, how are you doing? I heard the police were here, and you had to go to the hospital."

Olney nodded. "Kind of scary. I was expecting some visitors so when the doorbell rang, I answered it. Two men, with masks over their faces pushed their way into my apartment and roughed me up. I guess they were looking for drugs or guns so they didn't stay long. Took a few dollars in cash, but fortunately they left my billfold."

"How in the world did they get in to our building?" the woman asked.

"No idea," Olney replied.

She glanced at Ethel. "I'm Evey Morrison."

"Hello, Evey, I'm Ethel Kelly. My son and granddaughter are here visiting and they are the ones who found Chester. Chester and my husband were partners years ago. When I heard he'd been hurt, I thought why not fly out and help, then visit some with my son and granddaughter."

"That was certainly nice," Evey said.

"Chester and his wife were so nice to me when someone shot and killed my husband."

"Oh, my," Evey said, "how terrible. Did it happen recently? I don't remember reading about police shootings in the paper."

"Oh, no, many years ago." Ethel decided to let the subject drop. Evey didn't need to know about what happened after the funeral and how it made Ethel leave New York and move to Minneapolis. Too painful.

The elevator arrived and the two women helped Chester on, one balancing his arm, the other holding the door. Evey pushed the button for the lobby and the elevator lumbered down to the first floor.

When they reached the ground level, the two women helped Chester out to the sidewalk. Evey said she had to run some errands so she started off.

Chester's building stood directly across Riverside Drive overlooking the Hudson River. The humidity seemed low for this late July day, but Ethel figured it would soon build. Ethel looked back up at the building as they started to walk and smiled. "My goodness, a pretty nice place for a retired NYPD cop."

"Yes, I was really lucky. My wife was a professor at Columbia University. These three buildings are owned by the college, and even though she died, I can still live here. It gets gradually more expensive each year, but thanks to rent control, remains so much cheaper than other buildings along Riverside Drive. So, it's worked out well for me."

Ethel took his arm and the two started walking.

Olney leaned down and whispered to Ethel. "I really appreciate all your help. You're a pretty special lady."

"Well, thank you. I'm glad to be able to help out. It's been a long time since we've been able to spend some time together. I can't imagine why someone would come to your apartment and attack you. Makes no sense. Could it be a result of an old case?"

"I don't think so. And believe me, I've been racking my brain trying to figure it out. I don't think it was random. Not picking me out on the eighth floor. But as Evey said, how did they even get into the building? Really a mystery."

"I hope Sergeant Huna can come up with something. She seems nice."

Chester nodded. "And what an interesting background. I'd like to sit down with her and hear a little more about Alaska and the Inuit population."

"Maybe we can have her over for coffee some afternoon. She's very nice."

Olney stopped and took a deep breath. "I can't believe how slow I am. I love to walk and normally walk a mile or two each day."

"Now, Chester, don't be so hard on yourself. Just be happy you're able to do what you are doing. It'll get better every day, and I'll be here to help you."

"That's what I like about you, Ethel. You're an optimist."

As they started to cross the street, a black sedan pulled up to the curb in front of them. A heavy set man, his hat pulled down over his eyes, stuck his head out of the passenger side window and called, "Hey Olney, come over here."

Ethel leaned over and whispered, "Who are those men? I don't like the looks of them."

Olney's hands seemed to tremble a little. "Just a couple of guys I knew from my days on the force. Their bark is much worse than their bite. Let me go over and see what they want. It won't take a minute. It's probably best if you wait here."

"Can you make it okay? I'll be glad to walk with you."

"No thanks, Ethel, I'll be okay. Can't look weak. You know, it's a guy thing."

Ethel laughed. "Men, what a pain. Roger was the same way. Had to be the tough guy all the time."

"Probably tied to being a cop."

He walked over, using his cane for balance. Putting his hand on the roof of the car, he leaned down and whispered to the man.

Ethel couldn't hear what they were saying, but Olney gestured with his hand and she heard both men raise their voices. She was a little ashamed for trying to listen to what they were saying, but she couldn't help herself. She didn't like the looks of the man in the car and she couldn't see what the driver looked like.

Finally Olney said something like, "Don't bother me again. Do you hear me?"

Then she thought she heard something from the man in the car like, "We'll see."

Olney came back toward her, his face set in a frown and mumbling. When he looked up and saw her, he managed a small smile. "I'm sorry about those two. I used to keep those two guys for contacts. They think they can come see me every time they need some help. One of these days they'll learn I'm retired and don't want anything more to do with them."

"Are you okay?" Ethel asked. "You looked pretty angry."

"I'm fine and I'm sorry those two clowns arrived and messed up our walk. Let's just try and forget they stopped. Okay?"

"Sure." Ethel followed his lead, and they started to walk in the same direction along Riverside Drive. She took about three steps, then turned and watched the car for a moment. Roger had taught her to always be vigilant. She memorized the license number, but didn't say anything to Chester. Sometimes you never knew what might happen.

15

Staten Island Ferry, Thursday, 8:45 a.m.

Laura stood in the middle of the crowd at the tall glass doors, waiting for them to open. The doors opened and people pushed onto the John J. Marhin Ferry.

She glanced around, hoping to see Kinsey but no luck. What could have happened to her? There's plenty of room on the ferry, Laura thought, why does the crowd have to push so hard? Then she figured, this is Manhattan. People are always in a hurry.

She looked again for Kinsey, but didn't see her. She did see a young man and woman running across the terminal toward the ferry. Both ducked around the police officer with the dog, and made it through the glass doors just before they closed.

The man wore sunglasses and a hat as did the woman, and both carried a backpack. They ended up near Laura. "Wow, too damn close," he said. "I thought sure we'd miss the ferry."

His partner, a woman who looked slightly familiar to Laura, also carried her purse. "Yep, we need to get to Manhattan by ten o'clock for an important meeting."

Laura smiled at them. "And you know they never hold the ferry for anyone."

"That's true," the woman called and smiled back at her.

Laura decided to stand on the outside ring so she could enjoy the warm morning and the view of the Statue of Liberty. The view made her feel good.

After a couple of minutes, she felt the tremor of the engines and the ferry inched forward. The outside ring was two deep with people in most places.

She leaned on the railing and glanced around once more, checking for Kinsey. It would be fun to have someone to talk with. She had enjoyed playing soccer with Kinsey and talking to her. She'd like to pick her brain about the coach and some of the other players. Also about the course load. She had chosen five tough courses so she'd be studying her butt off and playing soccer too. Oh, man, when the team was on the road, it'd be tough.

As the ferry moved forward, Laura stretched, catching a little of the breeze on her face and enjoying the smell of the salt air. It'd be about another five minutes before the statue came into view. The sunlight seemed to dance on the water giving her a feeling of relaxation. What a great way to start the day. Perfect.

***

Zack and Shelia were a little slow getting started. They lay side by side, Zack rubbing her back and Shelia rubbing his stomach.

Zack pulled her closer. "You know if you keep that up, I'll never get anything else done."

Shelia put her hand on his arm. "Yesterday was terrible. All that shooting and Mr. Frost on the ground. I needed lots of hugs to get past it. Thanks."

The events of the last three days flooded through Zack's mind. "The first thing I'm trying to figure out is why the muggers picked on Olney, and how they got into his apartment? The building is locked up tight at night. He was definitely the target, not some random action."

"Good point," Shelia replied. "They'd have to know how to get in and where he was. Do you think someone else in the building let them in?"

A picture of Evey flicked into his mind. "Certainly possible. Something worth checking out, but Sergeant Huna said the police looked into all the alternatives. We'll have to ask Olney if there is a building super. He should keep tabs on things."

Shelia put her leg over Zack's thigh and rubbed against him. "See, I'm good for something other than hot sex. Although my body seems to be getting warmed up."

"Oh, man, I love it when you do that." He pulled her closer. "One other thought to consider. Who were the men who shot at us yesterday and why?"

"Do you think they were Angelo's men?"

"I'm not sure. Doesn't seem to be his style. What would he have to gain? Everyone already knows his father was in a battle with the cops. What would be his reason?"

Shelia kept rubbing against Zack. "Maybe it's cops. Cops could get into the building and cops have a motive to cover things up. Maybe they threatened Olney and tried to kill Frost because he knows something that someone doesn't want out."

"Good point. I bet someone is trying to cover up what happened that night and here I am sniffing around. But what?"

Zack leaned back for a moment, then pulled Shelia closer. "Let me touch base with Laura before I forget all of my responsibilities."

"All right, buddy, but my motor is on overdrive. I'll try to shift into neutral for a few minutes. But don't wait too long."

Zack dialed Laura's cell number. In a moment he heard "Hi, Dad, I thought you'd never call." She laughed. "I bet you've been busy."

"You could say that. Where are you?"

"On the ferry. Should be in Manhattan in …, wait a minute." The cell went dead.

***

Laura had just started talking to her dad when a voice came over the ferry loudspeaker. "Ladies and gentlemen, this is the captain speaking. We've had a minor incident and will need to stop the ferry for a few moments. Please pay attention to our crew and follow their directions. We will be coming through in a moment to collect all cell phones and cameras. Please don't make a mistake by attempting to hang onto your electronics. We don't want to see anyone get hurt."

Laura glanced around. *Collecting cell phones? Why? A chorus of shouts and groans rose around her. Worries about being late to work or late to school. Why?*

The voice continued. "We are representatives of The Forgotten Warriors. Rest assured no harm will come to any of you if you follow our simple instructions."

Warriors? Laura thought about her dad and his three tours in the Middle East. How those deployments had torn their family apart and caused the divorce. Then the PTSD. Fortunately, her dad's case seemed mild enough so he could function as if everything was okay. He did sneak off to see a doctor at times, but didn't want her to know. *What should she do? Tell them about her dad?* Maybe that would allow her to be part of their group so she could help other people.

Members of the crew walked along the deck, holding large bags. They wore plastic masks over their head and were dressed in camouflage fatigues with boots. Some carried pistols. As they moved around, they directed passengers to put their phones and cameras in the bag, then told them to go inside and take seats.

"You must get out your cell phone and any cameras," a crew member called. "No one talks on their phones. Don't even try and take pictures."

Laura's eyes widened when a female member of the crew stepped out onto the deck and spoke to one of the passengers. The woman moved like Kinsey. When she spoke, it sounded like Kinsey even though her voice was muted by the mask. *Were they being hijacked? Yes. Hijacked.*

A tall man in a suit approached one of the hijackers and yelled, "What the hell is going on? I have an important meeting in downtown Manhattan in one hour. I'm not going to sit here twiddling my thumbs while you screw around. I demand to see the captain."

"Sir," one of the hijackers replied, "you'll have to step inside while we check things. I don't believe this will take long. Now, give me your cell phone."

The suit pushed the smaller hijacker who almost fell over. A second pulled a gun out of his pocket. "Now, just stop there.

No pushing. Just go inside like we told you and no one will get hurt."

The man laughed. "I'm not afraid of you, and I'm not afraid of your pop gun." He reached for the pistol. A shot sounded from the doorway. Laura turned to see another hijacker pointing his weapon into the air. "Do not interfere with us. If you do, you will be shot."

People screamed and those still outside ran into the cabin. A woman collapsed.

Laura hurried over and dropped to her knees to check the woman's neck for a pulse. "She's fainted. Is there a doctor on board?"

A hijacker stopped next to her. "I'll check."

Laura placed her backpack under the woman's head. "Well, put out a page over the loud speaker. This woman needs medical attention right now."

A female who Laura thought might be Kinsey, whirled and moved inside. In a moment, a call for a doctor came over the loudspeaker.

Soon a short woman with trimmed white hair and dressed in a suit ran over. She knelt next to Laura and felt for the woman's pulse. "I'll need water and towels."

Laura ran into the bathroom and found some towels in the adjoining janitor's closet along with a glass. She filled it with water and hurried back to the woman. The doctor sponged the woman's forehead. Soon she let out a groan and opened her eyes.

"Where am I? What happened?"

"You're on board the Staten Island Ferry," the doctor replied. "A group of people seem to be taking over the boat. One of them fired a shot. You fainted. How are you feeling now?"

The woman raised her hand to her forehead, then brushed her eyes. "Better."

The doctor turned to Laura. "Help me get her on her feet so we can move her inside."

The two lifted the woman, then balanced her as she staggered inside.

The cabin was a frantic explosion of talking, screaming. Hijackers blocked the exits, pistols in their hands. One had what looked like an AR-47. Laura's dad had taken her to a range one day, and she'd watched one of the soldiers fire it.

People milled around, pointing, some crying. *Her dad?* She'd forgotten his call.

A voice sounded over the loud speaker. "Ladies and gentlemen, we sincerely regret any inconvenience. We are members of the Forgotten Warriors Coalition and a part of a larger group that is protesting around the country today. Again, we regret any inconvenience, but the future of our world is on the line. The first thing we ask is that you make sure we have your cell phones, computers, and cameras. Do not attempt to hide them. We do not want to hurt anyone, but you must do what we ask."

Laura didn't like the sound of that. She leaned over to the doctor. "I guess we know more now than we did a little while ago."

The doctor smiled. "Guess so. Let's hope it works out okay."

Laura planned to text her dad. Tell him what had happened. He certainly knew by now something was wrong and would be scared for her.

16

On the Highway to San Antonio, Thursday, 8:30 a.m.

Lieutenant Colonel Rene Garcia sped south on Route 35, about halfway to San Antonio from her parents' house in Austin. She'd received a call about seven o'clock that morning from her boss, Admiral Steele, the president's national security advisor. He told her a group of veterans had taken over the Alamo. The admiral wanted her to hustle to San Antonio and find out what was happening and provide him a status report.

After a quick shower and two cups of coffee, she hit the road. She loved riding her motorcycle, so free and clear. She debated checking in with her partner on Steele's task force, Zack Kelly, but since he was on leave with his daughter, she decided to leave him alone.

It surprised her a group of vets had taken over the Alamo. She'd heard through the grapevine a number of vets were frustrated about not being able to get timely care at the VA hospitals. Long waiting lines were the norm and no one seemed to care. Well, it would be interesting to find out what the complaints of these particular vets were. Maybe their protest would help.

It took about an hour for her to reach downtown San Antonio. The admiral said the FBI command post would be at the junction of Alamo and Crockett. She had taken friends to see the Alamo several times so she knew exactly where it was.

Traffic in San Antonio was always heavy, but today it was nuts. She wove her way through the mobs of cars, but a uniformed police officer stopped her about about three blocks from the site. She flashed her credentials and told the officer she

93

worked for the president's national security advisor and planned to meet with FBI Special Agent Frank Ryan.

"Just a minute, I'll need to check." After a quick call on his radio, he motioned her through the barricades. "You'll need to park your bike in the designated area and walk about half a block to the crime scene tape. Agent Ryan will meet you there. By the way, great bike."

"Thanks." She waited until he moved the barricade, then she pulled through and found the parking area. Sirens sounded in the background and a helicopter hovered overhead. People pushed around her, running here and there.

When she reached the entrance to the site marked by the crime scene tape, she flashed her credentials again and asked for Ryan. A number of police officers with rifles guarded the site. One of them pointed her toward a group of men in suits.

Suits, she thought. Must be the Feds.

When she asked again for Ryan, one of the agents pointed at a small, beige trailer. "He's inside the command post."

She pushed through the crowd until she reached a tall, stocky agent, with light brown hair and what looked like frown lines around his eyes. Ryan was surrounded by people, pointing, yelling. She tapped him on the shoulder.

He turned and shouted at her, "What?"

She flashed her military police badge. "Lieutenant Colonel Rene Garcia. Admiral Steele told me to get down here and see if I can help out."

"Look, Garcia, I've got my hands full with a group of pissed-off vets who claim they aren't getting the help they need. I don't need any more bureaucrats sniffing around."

"Look yourself, Ryan. We can do this the easy way. You and I work together, or I can call my boss and he'll have your boss tell you to quit being such a shit head."

Ryan's face broke into a grin. "Well now, you do have a way with words."

"I've been on your side before. I know more help can be a pain in the ass. Since I've been to Iraq twice, had myself knocked silly by a couple of IED's and wounded once, Admiral Steele thought I'd be able to talk with these guys better than anyone else. Also, I represent the president's national security advisor, a navy admiral which should carry weight with them."

Ryan motioned her toward the map board displaying a square around the Alamo with all of the interior buildings highlighted. "Point taken."

"What's the deal?"

"At six o'clock this morning, a group of about fifteen vets, at least we believe most of them are vets, arrived and hunkered down in the Alamo." His hand spread around the corners of the chart. "It appears they're about equally divided between the Long Barracks, the church, and the gift shop."

"What about security?" Garcia asked. "How the hell did they take over?"

"There's a night watchman to make sure goof balls don't steal stuff or deface the buildings. The vets flashed their weapons and told security guy to hit the road. He did. A prudent course of action. Security called the police who notified us. Homeland Security put me in charge."

"Lucky you. Who's the leader?"

"He goes by the name of Lion Six. They're wearing masks so we haven't been able to determine identities. There may be a few women in the crew."

"Have you talked to this Lion Six?"

"Our negotiator's been talking with him. His right hand, goes by Lion One."

"Definitely sounds military. In the army, we call the commander 'Six' and the personnel officer 'One'. Makes sense. At least in the way any of this mess makes sense."

"Be careful what you say. There's press all over the fucking place. We have a chopper in the air, but there are least two press choppers up photographing everything. Gonna be a goat rope."

Garcia laughed. "Love the way you say that. Let me give it a try. See what I can find out."

"What do you suggest?" Ryan asked.

"Let me first talk to the negotiator. Like I said, been there, done that, so I may be able to get through to them. But, I sure don't want to screw up anything he's been doing."

Ryan pointed to his right. "Okay. He's over there."

***

Zack tried several times to contact Laura, but kept getting dropped into her voice mail. "What the hell happened? She just got cut off."

Shelia jumped out of bed. "Is Laura in trouble? What should we do?"

Zack rolled out and reached for his pants. "I don't know. All I know is that she got cut off, then I couldn't get her back. Something happened."

"Oh, Zack, I'm scared."

"I'm going to call Tomlinson. He'll know if something is going on. I wanted to get that Internal Affairs report from him anyway."

Zack dialed Tomlinson's number. A harried voice answered, "Commissioner Tomlinson's office."

"This is Colonel Zack Kelly, I met with the commissioner three days ago. I need to talk to him again. He told me to call if I have something important and this is important."

"I'm sorry but he's in an emergency session."

"What's the problem?"

"I'm sorry, but I'm not at liberty to say anything."

"Look, my daughter is on the Staten Island Ferry. I was talking to her when she got cut off. I need to know what's happening."

"I'm sorry but I'm ..."

Zack cut her off and threw the phone on the bed. "I need to get dressed and catch a cab over to police headquarters. Tomlinson's secretary said there is some problem and he was in an emergency meeting. Laura wouldn't cut me off like that unless she had no choice. Now I can't get through to her."

His cell phone rang and he grabbed it. A voice said, "Hold one for Admiral Steele, please."

In a moment, "Zack, this is Steele. I just received a message from the Joint Operations Center at the Pentagon. Apparently there is some problem with the Staten Island Ferry. I want you to go over to the Emergency Operations Center at NYPD police headquarters and see what you can find out."

"Sir, could you call and clear the way for me. Otherwise they may not let me in."

"Okay. Let me know what you find out. There may also be a problem in San Antonio. Garcia is checking it out. Gotta go."

Zack clicked the phone off. "Admiral Steele. There is some problem on the ferry. I gotta get over to police headquarters."

Shelia stared at him. "You didn't mention Laura."

"He's got enough on his mind now. I'll tell him when I know more."

Zack tripped over his pants leg and in his rush had trouble tying his shoes. All he could think of was Laura. *Laura in trouble? Was she hurt?*

Shelia began getting dressed.

"I think I'd better go alone. The admiral is clearing the way for me at the operations center. I suspect they won't let you in."

"Oh, that's probably right. I'll head over to work. Let me know what's happening."

"Will do." He gave her a hug, then hurried out the door and pushed the button for the elevator to the lobby. As he ran through the lobby, he spotted a coffee pot and stopped long enough to pull a cup. Definitely needed some coffee this morning.

Zack ran outside to hail a cab, He jumped in and called, "Police headquarters. Hurry."

At police headquarters, Zack pushed his way through the crowd and jabbed the button for the elevator.

"What's going on?" Zack called to an officer.

"I don't know, but I think the Staten Island Ferry has been hijacked."

"What? Why?" Zack squeaked out "Ah, when?"

"That's all I know," he replied.

The elevator arrived and he got on. Zack tapped his foot and drummed his fingers on the walls as the elevator crawled its way to the seventh floor, stopping at two floors on the way.

When the doors opened, Zack dashed out. The commissioner's office was blocked by two officers with AK-47s. "I'm sorry sir, but you can't go any further."

Zack flashed his ID. "Look, I'm representing Admiral Steele, the President's national security advisor. I should be on the authorized roster."

The officer ran his finger down the roster. "Okay, here you are." He looked at Zack's ID, then checked his face and pointed toward the door. "They're meeting in the commissioner's office."

When he pushed open the door, mayhem reigned. Phones ringing, people calling to one another. He rushed up to the secretary. "Colonel Kelly."

She glanced up at him "Colonel Kelly, I'm sorry, but this isn't a good time."

"Admiral Steele should have called. I'll be representing him. What do we know?"

"Oh, okay. I think some fools have hijacked the Staten Island Ferry. The group is meeting in the commissioner's office."

Laura. He headed for Tomlinson's office.

Zack pushed the door open. Tomlinson looked up from his meeting. "Kelly, not now."

"I'm representing the president's national security advisor and am on the access roster. My daughter is on the hijacked ferry."

Tomlinson's eyes widened. "Oh, man, I'm sorry. You, of course, are welcome to stay. I can tell you we don't know much yet. We believe there are around 300 people on the ferry. It was about a third of the way across when the hijacking occurred."

Zack nodded, stepped back and leaned against the wall.

In a moment, the door slammed open and a tall black woman in a dark blue suit with a white shirt and a red scarf hurried into the room. "What the hell is going on?"

Tomlinson stood. "Madam Mayor, it appears some group, name yet to be determined, hijacked the 8:45 Staten Island Ferry."

The mayor's eyes widened, "The what ...?"

Tomlinson nodded. "We just received the report. I haven't had a chance to find out much yet. I do know the Coast Guard has dispatched two of their cutters to check on the ferry."

"Who's involved?"

"Initial reports indicate about 300 passengers on the ferry. Course we don't have any names since there are no tickets or reservations required to travel on the ferry."

"Well, find out what's going on and get back to me. I'm going to notify the Governor. Gather our emergency action group. I'd like a full briefing of what you find out in an hour."

"Yes ma'am. Tomlinson slumped in his chair, then stood again. "I'm headed to the terminal."

Zack tapped his arm. "I'd like to go with you. I'll need to report the status to Admiral Steele in the president's office."

"Okay, I can use your pipeline to the White House. This is going to get hairy before it's over."

17

On board the Staten Island Ferry, Thursday, 10:15 am

Kinsey hurried on to the bridge and called to Eagle, "That damn Horse, his ass is out of control. I told you he would be a problem and he is. He's overreacted. You shouldn't have given him one of the real guns."

Eagle turned from standing next to the man at the wheel of the ferry. "Can't you see I'm busy? What are you talking about?"

"Some jerk didn't want to give our staff member his cell phone and started making a fuss. I guess he pushed our guy. That fool, Horse, was standing outside and shot his pistol into the air to scare the jerk. Scared the hell out of everyone else. Some woman even fainted."

Eagle's eyes widened. "So that's what I heard."

"Some people are trying to help her. We weren't supposed to hurt anyone. Only get the country's attention about problems vets are facing. Now what are going to do?"

Eagle looked out the porthole for a moment. "We'll just have to move forward with the plan. Maybe we were too optimistic about what we wanted to do. What is important is that we all maintain our cover. If no one knows who we are, then we can still get away after it's over."

Kinsey squinted up her face. "That may not work for me any longer. One of my soccer teammates saw me at the terminal. Recognized me even through my disguise. She knows who I am. If she doesn't see me during the hijacking, she'll figure I'm one of forgotten vets. I'm not Kitten anymore, I'm Kinsey."

Eagle stared at her. "That's not good. We may need to do something about her. We can't have anyone find out who we are now. We could all end up going to jail."

Kinsey grabbed Eagle's arm. "This is nuts. I can't do something to a member of my soccer team. I know her, for god's sakes."

Eagle moved her hand from his arm. "You have to make a choice. We are on a path now. A path we all agreed to. There is no turning back. Don't you understand? There is no turning back. You'll have to do what needs to be done. This is not a time to worry about teammates. This is a time for decisive action."

Kinsey stormed off. This was not what she had signed up for. She simply wanted to make a statement, a statement of what had happened to her and her twin brother, a lowly sergeant who had worked in the executive offices for the Secretary of State. She'd even ridden in Marine One, the president's helicopter, on the way to Camp David to help set up a meeting for the Israeli ambassador.

Kinsey stopped and looked over the water, stifling a tear. God damn Eagle. She'd only been here because she'd been crapped on by the VA. They were supposed to take good care of her after the helicopter accident, but then they put her on some waiting list. A long waiting list while her back hurt like hell. Couldn't play soccer. Took six months to get it fixed and it never got fixed quite right.

Now she was supposed to kill one of her teammates. Teammates didn't do that to one another. God damn Eagle.

***

When Zack reached the White Hall terminal, chaos reigned. The front entrance was blocked with yellow barriers and crime-scene tape encircled the area. A crush of blue stood in front of the entrance and checked each vehicle as it arrived. No pedestrians were authorized into the terminal or anywhere around the entire area.

He jumped out of the police cars in Tomlinson's caravan, sirens wailing and lights flashing. They all hurried through the front door of the terminal and followed Tomlinson up the escalator to the main waiting area. They were met by a heavy-set police officer with two stars on his uniform. He moved over to Tomlinson and saluted.

Tomlinson returned his salute. "What's going on, Peterson?"

"We've got a pretty crazy scene on our hands, Commissioner. It looks as if some group has hijacked the 8:45 ferry. As yet, we don't know much about the group or what their motives are. We do know one of them fired a gun shot. Don't know if they hurt anyone."

"Any communications with those on board?" Zack asked.

Peterson looked at Zack as if he had just arrived from outer space.

Tomlinson stepped in. "This is Colonel Zack Kelly. He works for the President's national security advisor and happens to be here on vacation. His daughter is on the ferry."

Peterson shook hands with Zack. "Hey, I'm really sorry about your daughter. We keep trying to call the bridge, but so far no one answers. It must be nuts on the ferry."

Zack cleared his throat. "I started talking to my daughter on my cell about an hour ago when all of a sudden she got disconnected. I haven't been able to get her back. Nothing but voice mail."

A tall man in a blue pin-striped suit walked over to the group. Zack would bet a million bucks, FBI. And he was right. *Shoulda bet.*

"Commissioner, I'm Senior Special Agent Matt Holiday. Since there are a number of agencies involved in addition to the NYPD, such as Homeland Security, the Port Authority, and the Coast Guard, Homeland Security has directed the FBI to head up the investigation."

Tomlinson's red face looked as if he were ready to explode. "That's a bunch of crap. You have no right to come into the middle of an NYPD investigation and flap your gums about taking over."

"Normally you might have a point, Commissioner," Holiday replied. "But you see this may only be one part of the problem.

It appears this is part of a larger operation. There could be a number of groups who have taken over sites in the country, and we're trying to sort it all out right now."

Tomlinson jerked back. "What the hell are you talking about? I'm not even sure what's going on here yet and this is in my damn city."

Zack's frustration built. "While you two are pissing on each other's shoes about turf, my daughter is on the ferry. I need to brief Admiral Steele on what we're going to do."

"Zack, I'm really sorry to hear about Laura," a female voice said.

All eyes swiveled to a slender, blond-haired woman, her hair worn short on top and swept back on the sides to a short block cut in back. Her square shoulders looked as if she pushed weights.

Zack smiled in surprise. "Fairchild, what are you doing here?"

"Who the hell are you?" Tomlinson exclaimed.

"Special Agent Tara Fairchild," she replied. "I was the Deputy Chief of the FBI's Computer Crimes Division in D.C., until I recently transferred to the Office of the President's National Security Advisor Special Task Force. That's how I met Zack."

She paused for a moment, adjusting the crease on her tailored navy-blue pants suit.

Zack remembered she'd left the Secret Service because she'd made a complaint about sexual abuse, but no one listened. Then she joined the FBI. A top agent, she helped stop an attack against the President, and that's how Admiral Steele selected her to join his task force.

One of the NYPD officers gave her the eye. Be careful, Zack thought, men always gave her the second look and those looks really pissed her off. Poor devil doesn't want to be on her shit list.

"Now to Zack's question," Holiday said. "Fairchild, why don't you go over the background as we know it.

"It appears the first attack began this morning about six o'clock. A group broke through security and took over the

Alamo in San Antonio. From the little we know, the hijacking of the Staten Island Ferry may be coordinated with the effort in San Antonio. My boss, Admiral Steele, dispatched me here to coordinate with the other services and agencies. I'll be working this issue with my partner on the task force, Zack Kelly."

"Do you have any idea who's doing this?" Tomlinson asked.

"We're not exactly sure," Fairchild replied. "It's got something to do with military veterans. The name 'Forgotten Warriors' is being used. I believe the name is self-explanatory."

"Forgotten Warriors?" Tomlinson exclaimed. "I've never heard of them."

"You may not have," Fairchild replied. "This is a fairly new group, and it appears there are branches of the group around the country. I believe many of them have recently returned from the Middle East with a number of medical and emotional problems."

"Are they all veterans?" Zack asked.

Fairchild pulled a notepad out of her jacket pocket. "We're not sure, but a number may be college students who came back from the war in the Middle East and used the GI Bill to go back to school. It looks like that's how the group formed. The little bit we have is they are pissed off because we sent them off to fight in the Middle East. When they return home, they can't get jobs and have troubles with college because of the medical and emotional problems."

Zack nodded. "Well, they certainly have a point. I've heard roughly twenty percent of returning vets have serious challenges with PTSD to say nothing of all the physical problems they face. But the question is, what do we do now?"

"First," Holiday said, "we need to sort out exactly what's happening on the ferry. The Coast Guard has dispatched boats to surround the ferry. They have been directed to not get too close, but just keep an eye out to determine what's happening on board the ferry."

"How about a helicopter?" Zack asked.

Fairchild gave Zack a thumbs up. "Good point. The Coast Guard has dispatched a chopper to fly low over the ferry and report what they see. On their first pass it was hard to see much of anything because whoever is in charge has pulled everyone off the outside deck. Everyone is under cover."

"What about the possibility of using navy SEALS?" Tomlinson asked. "Maybe we could use them to sneak on board and rescue the passengers."

"That's a good idea," Holiday replied, "but we need to wait and use the cover of darkness. If we try something now, they'll see the SEALS and might even shoot at them."

"Dammit," Zack said, "we can't do anything to risk the lives of those passengers."

"You're right, Zack," Fairchild replied. "Passenger safety will be our first priority."

"Do we know what they have for weapons?" Zack asked.

"Not exactly," Holiday replied, "but we must assume they have an extensive collection of weapons and explosives."

Zack leaned forward. "If they're ex-military, they'll have weapons and will sure as hell know how to use them."

There was silence for a moment, then Zack asked, "How the hell did these forgotten warriors get weapons and explosives past the police at the terminal? They've got bomb sniffing dogs just to stop stuff like this. Who beat the system and how?"

Holiday shook his head. "I don't know, but I sure as hell plan to find out."

Zack looked at him. "Doesn't help us now."

***

Governor Mason Harbaugh was chairing his weekly staff meeting at the state capital's office complex in Albany when his administrative assistant hurried into the room and handed him a note. The note read, *The Staten Island Ferry was hijacked at 8:45 this morning. It appears no one has been hurt and we are trying to determine who the hijackers are and their demands. Details to follow as we learn more. Mayor Summer.*

Tall and slender with a full head of white hair, Harbaugh had been the police commissioner in New York City, then mayor of New York City before he was elected to the governor's chair five years ago. Now he was being considered for vice president by his party's presidential candidate. He sure as hell didn't need something like this to make him look bad.

Harbaugh stared at the note, then whispered to his chief of staff, "Find out what the hell is going on and let me know right away."

He banged his gavel to silence the dull presentation from the Secretary of Transportation. "I've just received a note some group of nuts have hijacked the Staten Island Ferry. I have no idea what this means, or who's involved, but I expect you all to get involved and let me know immediately what's going on. Now get moving."

The room cleared in a matter of minutes, leaving Harbaugh by himself.

He couldn't believe it. All his planning. All of his hard work. Now some fruitcake might mess it up. Well, he couldn't let it happen and he wouldn't.

18

Outside the Alamo, San Antonio, Thursday, 10:15 a.m.

Rene Garcia followed Agent Ryan as the two elbowed their way through the maze of agents hunched over computers and talking on cell phones. They reached a smallish man who looked to be Hispanic. He glanced up when the two arrived.

"Santos," Ryan said, "this is Colonel Garcia. She works for the president's national security advisor. Admiral Steele asked her to come here to see if she could help out. Fortunately Garcia happened to be on leave in Austin. As a military officer who's been to the Middle East on two tours, she might be able to get through to these guys and find out what they're thinking."

Santos held out his hand. "Hey, Colonel, I want you to know I appreciate all the help I can get. So far I haven't been able to establish a solid contact with these guys. I've been talking to a guy named Lion Six, but he hasn't been very forthcoming. Maybe you'll have more luck."

"I've had experience with these sorts of problems," Garcia said. "And I think my military experience and time overseas should be helpful. I'd certainly be willing to give it a try. What have you been able to find out so far?"

"Not much. Lion Six was in the military, maybe as a line officer. He obviously has served in the Middle East, although I'm not sure exactly where. I know he spent some time in a military hospital, probably overseas before returning to the states. Must have been wounded because I think he's currently being seen somewhere in the VA system."

"That may be a big part of the problem," Garcia said. "I know there are huge waiting lines at some VA hospitals and a great deal of frustration waiting to see docs. Want me to give it a try?"

Santos nodded and handed her the phone.

Garcia put it up to her ear. Heard ringing then a voice, "Yeah."

"My name is Rene Garcia. I'm an army lieutenant colonel and a military police officer, plus I work for the president's national security advisor. My boss, Admiral Steele, sent me here to see if I can find out how we can solve this thing peacefully."

"You're lying, you lousy sack of shit. How did you get here all the way from Washington to San Antonio in such a short time? I'm no fool."

"You may not be a fool, but you're kind of an asshole. My home is in Austin, Texas, and I was on leave when you started this protest. The admiral called and asked me to see if I could help. So I hopped on my motorcycle and here I am. Actually it's a beautiful day for a ride so I thank you for the opportunity."

"Okay, I believe you. So?"

"I understand you're pissed about the way you've been treated by the VA."

"Not totally. The VA is so underfunded by the political dingbats in Washington they can't help us like they want to. Have you ever been in the Middle East?"

"One tour in Iraq and one tour in Afghanistan."

"Ever been shot at?"

"I had my bell rung by an IED in Iraq twice, and got evacuated out of Afghanistan after being wounded. Fortunately it was in the shoulder and with the help of some great docs, I'm doing pretty well. So I've been able to return to duty."

"How were you treated in a military hospital?"

"Very well. They evacuated me to a military hospital in Germany. Kept me there after surgery for about a week, then I was evacuated again this time to Brook Army Medical Center here in San Antonio. It was nice to be near my family."

"Being near family helps vets heal."

"The gang at Brooke helped me through the rehab for my arm and shoulder, then I was able to return to duty. I was scared I wouldn't be classified fit for duty."

"I understand. The bastards got me in the belly, and I couldn't get classified fit for duty. A real bitch. I lost everything, including my earning potential. And no one cares."

"Understood. I'm lucky. That was a couple of years ago and other than the damn thing aching when it's cold, I'm not doing too bad. How about you?"

"Why don't you come in and I'll tell you about it."

"Okay, don't shoot me. I'll be on my way in after my conference call with the admiral; short, dark hair wearing a military uniform."

"As long as you're not lying to me, you'll be fine. But if you're lying..."

A click and he was gone.

***

Laura walked around the cabin of the ferry talking to people and trying to calm them, then she returned to check on the woman who collapsed. Kneeling beside the doctor she asked, "How's she doing?"

"Better," the doctor replied. "But, I'd like to get her to a hospital. I don't know if she has problems with her heart. Without some way to check, all I can do is keep an eye on her."

Laura stood and looked around. "Unfortunately, I don't think we'll be able to get any passengers off the ferry for a while. But these guys don't seem like terrorists, so maybe we can talk them into letting some of the passengers who are sick or have other problems be evacuated off the ferry."

The doctor was shorter than Laura with gray hair. She glanced at Laura through her dark-rimmed glasses, a puzzled look on her face. "I'm Jane Cincotta, a retired family practice doctor."

"Hi, Jane. Laura Kelly. My dad and I are visiting New York on vacation. Some vacation."

"Well, you'll have to admit, New York can be an exciting place to visit."

"Yeah, guess so. It's been really crazy. My dad was born here, but his father, a New York City police officer, was shot and killed in action. After that, his family moved to Minneapolis where he grew up."

"Oh, my, I'm really sorry. The police lead such dangerous lives."

Laura nodded. "It happened a long time ago, and my dad is still trying to uncover why."

"Well, good luck. The NYPD bureaucracy is huge and difficult to fight through the red tape. I know, because my husband died, and I've been trying to determine exactly how it happened so I can file for compensation. It's really a mess." She looked up and whispered, "Oh, oh, watch out."

Two of the warriors, a man and a woman, entered the room. "For those of you who haven't done so yet, please put your cell phones, computers, and cameras in this basket. We ask that you not try and keep any mode of communication as it will be a major problem. We trust you to do the few things we ask so no one will get hurt."

While the two started at the other end of the sitting area, Laura ducked into the ladies room and slipped into a stall. She stood on the toilet seat and ducked down so she couldn't be seen over the top of the stall.

Taking out her phone, she texted her dad: *Ferry hijacked. All OK so far. More later.*

Getting down from her perch, she tucked her phone down the back of her jeans and pulled her sweater down over it. Not exactly what she had in mind for her new phone, but she hoped it worked and no one had the guts to check her there. Flushing the toilet, she pushed the door open and stepped back into the room.

Maybe, just maybe, she could stay in contact with her dad.

***

Zack stood next to Tara Fairchild waiting for Mayor Olivia Summer to convene a meeting in the temporary emergency operations center set up at the terminal. He mind kept switching to Laura. *How was she doing?*

Once everyone was seated, the mayor opened the discussion. "Now, Commissioner Tomlinson, please give us a status report."

Tomlinson stood, scanning a dossier in front of him. "Here is the latest information I have. A group calling themselves the Forgotten Warriors hijacked the 8:45 Staten Island Ferry enroute from Staten Island to Whitehall Terminal. It appears the hijacking occurred about eight minutes into the trip."

"What do we know about the group?" Summer asked.

"Not much. From the title we are assuming they have ties to veteran groups. Apparently this is the second incident of the morning."

"What is their motivation?" Summer asked.

Tara Fairchild stood. "Let me insert a few points. My name is Special Agent Fairchild. Zack Kelly and I are members of the president's national security staff. At approximately six o'clock central time, this morning, a group, we believe to have ties to the group here on the ferry, took over the Alamo in San Antonio. Because of who they are, we don't believe they are of any special danger to themselves or to any hostages they may have, but of course we can't be sure."

"What do you base that on Agent Fairchild?" the mayor asked.

"The name of the group and their actions so far. It appears from their title, they believe they are not getting the attention they deserve. The title implies they believe their country has forgotten them. But, I repeat, we can't be sure."

Zack tried to concentrate on Fairchild's briefing, but his thoughts kept slipping away to Laura and what might be happening to her. His hands shook as he stood there so he jammed them in his pockets. What a shitty vacation.

The fucking PTSD was creeping up on him like it always did. He could feel the anger building, his nerves on edge. He needed to fight it.

Should he call his mother and let her know? No, she'd hit the panic button. She'd want to come down here. Nothing she could do, so why worry her until he knew more.

His phone dinged. He forced himself to hold his hands steady so he could press the buttons of his phone. He read the text and exclaimed, "Thank god."

Fairchild stopped talking and turned to him. "What, Zack? What did you find out?"

Zack stepped forward, the other agents moving aside. "I just received a text message from my daughter. She happened to be on the ferry." He read it to them.

Fairchild put her hand on his arm. "She's okay. That's great."

Zack nodded. "Yeah, so far. I keep wondering why we don't get more messages and phone calls from the other passengers."

"I thought about it," Fairchild said. "If these people are smart, they've gathered all the phones, computers, and cameras. Laura must have been able to hide hers."

"What now?" Zack asked. "We've got to do something."

"Not yet," Fairchild replied. "It's too dangerous to attempt a rescue mission until we know more. Admiral Steele is convening a conference call in fifteen minutes. We'll see what information we have after the call. I'll be interested to find out how Garcia is doing with the group in San Antonio."

"All right," Mayor Summer called, "is there anyone else with information that will be helpful?"

A young man with sandy brown hair raised his hand. "I'm Lieutenant Black with the Coast Guard. We have dispatched two cutters to observe the ferry and provide security. Also, we have a helicopter circling overhead taking film footage. So far these efforts haven't been particularly helpful because the hijackers have moved all of the passengers inside."

"What is your recommendation?" Summer asked.

"I question the advisability of doing anything now," Black said. "If we're going to try and take back the ferry, I believe it would be best to do that under cover of darkness. Our recommendation is to gather all the information about the group we can and who is on board the ferry, then prepare an action plan for this evening.

Summer nodded. "Your recommendation sounds like the best alternative, at least for now. If they start taking more aggressive actions, our options might change." She motioned for a young woman in a beige suit to stand. "Let me introduce my public relations chief, Margaret Barrett. I'm asking for all contacts with the media to go through her.

Barrett stood. "The only way to keep this under control is to make sure all media requests are funneled through me. We have received a number so far and I'm sure more are on the way. I'll be putting out hourly updates on what we know, more frequently if something happens. If you want to be on the list for updates, please sign the form on the table."

Summer cleared her throat. "Thank you, Margaret. "Let's plan on getting together in two hours. That would be one thirty. Thank you for your time. Please send any important updates or changes in the situation to me immediately. Thank you."

The mayor stood and left the room.

Fairchild stepped over to Zack. "What brings you to New York? Did I hear it has something to do with your dad?"

"Yeah, unfortunately it does." Zack told her about his father and what he'd done so far.

"Are you getting anywhere?"

He shared his suspicions about Tomlinson. "Once I get a chance to review the Internal Affairs report, maybe I'll find out more."

"I know at one time the FBI actively tried to bust up the Mafia in New York City," Fairchild said. "If I remember right, a question arose as to the involvement of senior officials in the city government. When this settles down, let me check with the chief of the FBI files section. See what I can find out."

"Thanks. I appreciate anything you can do. This damn thing is driving me crazy. Has been for years."

"We'll get it sorted out."

"I'm headed outside to get something to eat and a cup of coffee. I definitely need some coffee. Can I interest you in a cup."

"Sounds great," Fairchild said. "But first I need to talk to the commissioner. Give me a few minutes, then I'll join you."

_
Long Walk Home_

"Okay. I'll do a recon and see what I can find."

Fairchild gave him a thumbs up. "Black, no damn cream."

Zack laughed. "Never doubted it."

19

The Alamo, San Antonio, noon

Garcia followed Ryan through the crowd of agents, police officers, and suits back to the FBI command post located in the trailer. They climbed into the trailer. Ryan pulled the door shut, muffling the clatter of noises from the outside. Three agents sat at a table arguing about something. Another agent posted information to a map while talking on a phone.

Garcia walked over to the coffee pot and poured herself a cup. "I definitely need one of these. Pour you one?"

Ryan picked up a cup. "Please." He added cream to his coffee.

Garcia took a sip. "I thought you FBI guys were tough. You know, drink your coffee black and your scotch straight. Now, what can you tell me about the layout?"

"Hey, just to let you know, Garcia, guy's gotta have a little cream in his life." He pointed toward the agent posting the map and motioned with his hand. "We've got a map of the area. Let's go over and I'll give you a breakdown."

The walked to the map board. The agent stepped back.

Ryan took a pointer out of his pocket. "There are three buildings of interest. First one is the church. That's here."

Garcia took another sip. "I've been in the Alamo a number of times, so I have a general idea of the layout."

To the right of the church is the gift shop." He pointed. "Here. It's about thirty by thirty square feet. Walled in."

"Yeah, I've been inside the gift shop. Can't bring anyone here to sightsee unless you buy some things to take home to the family."

Ryan pointed at another building. "Here is the Long Barracks. We believe there are about six or seven warriors inside the Long Barracks and a like number in the gift shop."

"What about the church?" Garcia asked.

"As far as I know there aren't any in the church. That's why it's important you get in there. We need to know for sure how many there are, what sort of weapons and ammo they have. If you can get a feeling for their mental status. You know, do you think they'll explode and start shooting, or are they pretty cool. Also, it would help to know how well trained and organized they are."

"Do you have a plan?" Garcia asked. "Any idea when and how you're going to move in? How much time you're going to give them?"

Ryan stepped back so the agent could keep posting materials. "Nothing definite as yet. I know we can't let them stay in there forever. We'd then have to watch for copy cats. Maybe today, but if we can't figure a way out of this, we'll probably have to bust in there tonight."

Garcia nodded. "Makes sense."

Ryan took a sip of coffee and stared at the map. "I hate like hell to have to bust in, but we can't let any group take over downtown San Antonio and stay as long as they like. There's going to be a lot of sympathy in the public for these vets who have served their country yet can't get the medical help they need."

"They have a point. I know there are problems with vets getting jobs. I've even had friends who have come to me for help. I'm sure in many cases it's justified as some of these guys have serious PTSD and mental problems."

"What about a wire?" Ryan asked. "That way we'd know for sure how you're doing."

"I don't like it," Garcia said. "Not much of a way to develop trust."

"Ah, shit, you're probably right. If you get in trouble and need help, try to get a message out, use the code word Davy Crockett. That way we'll know you're in trouble."

"And what exactly will you do?"

Ryan smiled again, a small grin. "Damned if I know."

Garcia enjoyed Ryan. She liked his smile. Hell, she liked him. "That's what I figured. We'll just have to play it by ear. But first I have to take a conference call."

***

Tara led Zack into an adjoining room with several police officers and people in civilian clothes sitting at makeshift desks, talking on phones and working at computers.

She pointed him toward another room. "Let's head in there. We can shut the door and get on the conference call with Admiral Steele." She pushed in a number on her cell. She set it on a small table and put the phone on speaker.

In a moment, the admiral's administrative assistant came on the line. "Agent Fairchild, the admiral is waiting for your call. Colonel Garcia is already on the line."

Zack and Tara sat on the two gunmetal gray folding chairs and waited a moment, then Admiral Steele's voice sounded on the phone. "Zack, Tara, welcome to our call."

"I wish we had better news, Admiral," Tara said. "I just found out a little while ago that Zack's daughter, Laura, is on the ferry that's been hijacked."

There was a gasp. "Oh, no, Zack," the admiral said, "I'm sorry to hear it. And here the two of you were all set for a fun vacation in the Big Apple. What a crappy break.

"I'm really worried about her, sir, because we don't know much of anything about the hijackers. What kind of people they are, what their goals are, and how desperate they are. But she's got a good head on her shoulders and hopefully, should come out of this okay." He prayed that was the case. "What do we know about the group so far?"

"Let me take a piece of this," Garcia said. "First though, I'm sorry to hear about Laura, Zack. That's a pisser."

"Yeah, bout sums it up," Zack replied.

"From what my FBI contact said, the warriors moved in at 0600 with guns and told the security guys to get out of there. The security guys, not being stupid, hit the road like pronto."

"I don't imagine those security guys are armed to the teeth," Fairchild said. "Do you know how many warriors there are?"

"Ryan thinks there are around a dozen. We're not sure what they are armed with and what sort of mental conditions we're dealing with. Definitely military. The FBI negotiator is dealing with a Lion Six. And his ace right hand is Lion One."

"Is that Special Agent Frank Ryan?" Tara asked.

"That's him. Do you know him?"

"I do," Tara said. "Good guy and knows what he's doing."

"Yep," Garcia replied. "I'm impressed so far. The FBI crew seems well organized."

"Good to hear," Admiral Steele said. "Because this is going to be really tricky. We can't let them take over downtown San Antonio, but on the other hand we have to be careful. These are our vets. People will not want to see any of them killed."

"Zack and Tara, you may not be aware I'm here in San Antonio myself," Garcia said. "I was in Austin on vacation when this hit."

Admiral Steele had to chuckle. "Guess in the future, I'd better be careful when I sign vacation requests for you two."

"Oh, well, vacations can be overrated." Garcia chuckled. "Now, don't say too many nice things about Ryan because he's sitting next to me."

Tara laughed. "I'd have to think more about what I said. Don't want him to get a swelled head. Hi, Frank."

"Hey, Tara," Ryan said, "good to hear your voice. It seems like we've got a real mess. I'm glad Garcia is here to work with us."

"What's your strategy?" Steele asked.

"Let me take that one," Ryan said. "We've had a negotiator working with this Lion Six for the last couple of hours, but not making much progress. When Colonel Garcia arrived, she volunteered to give it a try."

"It worked," Garcia said. "I figured as another military person, I might be able to get through to him and I think I may have. He wants me to come in and talk ."

"I don't know," Admiral Steele said. "We're not sure if they are on a death wish or simply trying to make a point."

"I don't think I'm in any real danger, Admiral. The guy I talked to seemed like he's okay. Not a nut case. I'd like to head in and see what's going on."

"I agree with Garcia," Ryan said. "We need to find out for sure how many are in there, what they have in the way of weapons, and what they really want. If it's only to bring attention to their issue, that's one thing."

"What you say is true," Admiral Steele said. "But if they plan on blowing themselves up, I don't want those guys taking Garcia with them."

"Well, makes two of us, Admiral," Garcia replied. "But maybe I can get an angle on both of these groups. Zack, do you know much about the folks who did the hijacking?"

"Unfortunately, we haven't been able to establish communication with them so we don't know much. Laura texted me and told me she was okay. Hopefully she'll be able to feed me more information."

"If we do something to rescue those hostages," Tara said, "it probably won't be before tonight. We could use Navy SEALS after dark. Right now, we've got two Coast Guard cutters patrolling the area providing security for the ferry, and a helicopter overhead. We don't want any crazy press people or anyone else trying to sneak on the ferry."

"Good point," Garcia said. "There are enough nuts out there to try something stupid."

"The press is having a field day so it's going to get complicated fast," Zack said. "Mayor Summer of New York City, has taken charge of our group. I like her. Her PR person, a Margaret Barrett is coordinating press queries and conferences."

"Send me her information," Steele said. "I'll get our press guy tied in to her."

"Admiral, I'd really like to meet with this Lion Six," Garcia said. "Once I find out about his group, then we can decide on an appropriate course of action."

"Do we have any idea if there are other groups out there preparing to take over some other place?" Fairchild asked.

"Not a clue," Garcia replied. "If I were a betting person, I'd say there may be more to come."

"What are their demands?" Zack asked.

"We have not received a formal list," Garcia said, "but I think it's obvious. They don't think we're doing enough to help our veterans."

"I'm sure that's right," Zack replied, "but we can't fix it in a short period of time. They must realize we won't let them keep these places indefinitely."

"That's true," Fairchild said, "but these vets apparently are carrying weapons and may be threatening people with bombs. To be honest, I'm supportive of their goals, but I don't think they are going at it the right way."

"Yeah," Zack cut in, "but they're going to say without this type of action, no one will pay attention. And in thinking about it, I believe they're right."

"We can't let this go on indefinitely," Admiral Steele said. "I'm convening a meeting of the National Security Council at 1700 hours. I need for all of you to forward information papers on each group not later than 1530, then I'd like to reconvene at 1600. Zack, I'll call the commander of SEAL Team Six and get a group to you in case you need them. We should be prepared to implement a plan after dark. No doubt, better than broad daylight. It should go without saying, I'd like to settle this peacefully. No injuries and certainly no deaths."

An admirable goal, Zack thought, but I'm not sure how practical it is.

20

Staten Island Ferry, Thursday, 1:15 p.m.

Laura slipped out of the bathroom after sending her text, ducking low to use the benches as a screen from the two warriors who were still busy collecting cell phones and computers. She crept back to one of the seats in the center of the group and edged into it.

Looking around, she saw most people were staying calm although a weeping woman sat in the corner holding onto a friend. What should she do next? She couldn't believe they would harm anyone. Seemed to be well-educated, mostly ex-military.

A tremor buzzed her feet. What was it? The motor starting up? Maybe the warriors had made their point and were headed into the terminal.

Looking out the window, Laura observed the boat turning. From what she remembered, they should maintain their current heading to reach Manhattan. Off to the right, she saw the skyline of Manhattan. Wait a minute, the skyline should be ahead of them, not off to their right.

One of the warriors came by carrying a basket of cell phones and computers. She thought it might be Kinsey. Gearing up her nerve she asked, "Excuse me. I notice we started moving. Are we headed into the terminal? The skyline seems to be off to our right."

"Don't ask so many questions. You'll find out what you need to know in due time."

The warrior walked away carrying the basket. Laura patted the cell under her pants to make sure it stayed hidden.

Laura watched off to the right. The skyline seemed to move backward in relation to their forward movement. They weren't headed toward the terminal.

***

Garcia disconnected her phone from the conference call and turned to Agent Ryan. "Well, what do you think? I'm ready to head into the gift shop."

Ryan rubbed his chin before speaking. "Okay, what bothers me is this seems like a big operation. At least two sites we know of. There may be more we haven't heard from yet. These guys are serious. I'm with Admiral Steele. I don't like the idea of you becoming a captive."

How does he think she felt. "I don't either, but right now I don't see a better course of action."

"Unfortunately, neither do I."

Garcia stood, and headed out of the trailer, stepping down the four steps. "Wish me luck."

Ryan snapped a salute. "Remember, 'Crockett'. We'll come running."

Garcia waved back. "Got it." She picked her way through the crowds and arrived at the barrier surrounding the Alamo. She flashed her ID card to one of the police officers.

The officer checked her ID to make sure she matched the photo, then handed it back to her. "You're cleared. Good luck. I hope you can talk some sense into these guys."

"So do I. So do I."

She took a deep breath then walked across Alamo Street. Normally it was bustling with tourists, cars, bikes, and baby carriages. Now congested with emergency vehicles forming a barrier.

After crossing the street, she stepped up on the curb and kept walking around the wall toward the gift shop. When she got within about fifteen feet of the door, a voice called, "Halt."

She could almost feel his eyes glaring at her from behind the door. *How to handle this? Probably just straight on and see what develops.* "Lieutenant Colonel Rene Garcia. I talked to Lion Six on the phone. He told me to walk over here. So here I am. All I want to do is talk."

The door opened part way and the barrel of an M-16 poked out. Behind the rifle was a bulky man with a ski mask over his face. "Put your hands above your head and keep walking forward slowly. No funny stuff. My trigger finger is itchy, and I know how to fire my rifle."

"Just take it easy with your rifle. I know what it can do." Garcia began to walk forward one step at a time as directed. *No sudden movements, Garcia, no sudden movements.* Now she could see his camouflage fatigues.

"All right, keep coming. No rash movements."

"Don't worry," Garcia replied, "I'm not in any hurry to get shot."

"You've got the right attitude, Colonel. If you keep thinking that same way we'll be fine. If not, be aware, I'm not hesitant to shoot you. This is too important to have somebody screw it up."

When Garcia reached the door, a woman, shorter than the man, pulled the door the rest of the way open. She, too, had a ski mask covering her face. "I'm going to pat you down. No fast moves."

Well, that's an improvement. At least it's a woman patting me down. These guys aren't animals.

The woman was thorough in her search and uncovered nothing except Garcia's cell phone. She pulled the cell out of Garcia's pocket and put it on a table by the door.

"I'd like to get that back when I leave. It's got a gazillion contacts in it."

"You'll get it back unless you do something really stupid, and you don't look like someone stupid."

Garcia stepped inside "Thank you. May I ask who you are?"

"Call me Lion One."

Garcia smiled. "You must be the personnel officer."

Lion one nodded. "Very good. We're vets with a military organization. I'm going to put a blindfold on you, then I want you to walk forward slowly. I'll take you to Lion Six."

Lion One blindfolded Garcia, then pushed her forward.

Garcia stumbled a little, but kept walking. Thought she smelled mold. Voices sounded behind her, but she couldn't make out words.

The woman knocked on a door and a deep voice called, "Enter."

Garcia heard the click of a door handle and a creak as the door opened. "Okay," Lion One whispered, "move forward. Remember, slow movements. No jerky moves."

Garcia took a step forward. Heard whispers. Smelled cigar smoke.

After about three more steps, Lion One said, "There is a chair to your left. Sit."

Garcia reached out and felt the back of the chair. Holding on to it, she sat. A wooden chair with arms. She tried to visualize the gift shop from the times she had visited. Couldn't remember.

When she sat, Lion One said, "All right, reach up and remove your blindfold."

Her eyes blinked to adjust to the light. One of the lamps had been moved so the light shone directly in her eyes. "Can you cut off the damn light? It's blinding me."

"No," the deep voice said. "Get used to it."

Garcia blinked a few times and looked off to her right, away from the light. "Look, I came here to talk, not be interrogated. Can't you turn off the damn light. It really hurts my eyes."

"Nice try, Colonel, but you and I both know you came in here to find out about us. Who we are? How many? What do we have for weapons? How the hell do you get us out of here?"

Garcia smiled. "Well score one for Lion Six. You got me figured out."

"I'll tell you some of what you want to know, but since you're on my turf, I expect you to recognize it and play by my rules."

Garcia decided she'd have to play along with him. Maybe build up a little rapport. The cigar smoke burned her eyes. The guy really puffed away. "Okay. Fair enough. Who are you?"

"Colonel, I'll ask the questions. Now what's with you and why the hell are you here?"

"My name is Rene Garcia. As you can tell from my uniform, I'm an army lieutenant colonel. My career branch is military police."

"A fucking cop. I might have known."

"Just you wait a damn minute. I grew up in Austin, Texas. I'm currently assigned to the President's national security advisor's office. I was home on leave this morning when all this crap broke out. My boss, Admiral Steele, called me and asked me to hustle down here to see if I could find out what's going on. So I ask again, who are you and what the hell are you doing?"

"You said on the phone you spent two tours in the Middle East."

"Yes, the first one in Afghanistan and the second in Iraq."

Lion Six laughed. "Beautiful places aren't they?"

"Garden spots," Garcia replied. "Have you been to those fun resort areas?"

"Army ranger. Four tours, three in Afghanistan and one in Iraq."

"Do you know my partner on the task force, Colonel Zack Kelly?"

A gasp. "You work with Colonel Kelly?"

"Hell yes," Garcia replied. "I've worked with him for the past eighteen months. Do you know him?"

"Like I said, Colonel, I'll ask the questions."

"Oops, sorry. Forgot. It's my type-A personality. I like to be in charge.

"You said you were wounded and had a couple of run-ins with IEDs."

"One of my platoons provided security for convoys in Afghanistan, and I went along. We ran into a road block. Got hit with IEDs and small arms fire. I'm told I've lost some hearing."

"I understand. Me too."

"We weren't careful enough with our planning. Our convoy didn't have enough perimeter defenses. My fault. It's haunted me ever since."

"Go on."

"Never should have let those bastards get so close to us. The IED blew me out of my jeep, and I was hit in the shoulder by small arms fire. It would have been one hell of a lot worse if our shadowing choppers didn't arrive in time to drive them off. Not all of the convoys had chopper support. Two of our drivers were killed and four were wounded before the choppers arrived."

"What happened next?"

"Four of us got evacuated to the closest medical facility. Hustled into surgery. I'm told it took the docs about three hours to glue me back together. Then I got sent back to a supporting hospital where I spent a couple of months in rehab. Those guys were really good and helped me a lot to be able to move my arm and shoulder."

Lion Six's voice rose. "You got returned to duty?"

"Hell yes, I wasn't going to let a crappy shoulder wound stop me. My guys needed me, and I wasn't going to leave them. Argued like hell with my boss, but finally won. So I was sent back for another five months before I rotated back to the States. While I was there, I supported the rangers and it's how I met Zack Kelly. He was headed back to a tour with Admiral Steele and gave the Admiral my name. Great assignment."

"What is this task force?" Six asked.

"As I mentioned, Admiral Steele is the President's national security advisor. He's a super guy and a top-flight leader. The admiral has pulled together this small group to help him cut through all the bureaucratic bull shit and get things done."

"Like how?"

"Like now. If it weren't for me, the Admiral would have to go to the Attorney General, then the Director of Homeland Security, then the Director of the FBI, to find out what's happening. And I'm here to tell you, it ain't like the military. Road blocks and defensive behavior wherever he goes. Everyone protecting their fiefdom."

"That's true."

"But, he called me. Asked me if I'm having fun on my leave. If I wouldn't enjoy a quick trip to San Antonio. I told him, 'Admiral. I am at your bidding.' And guess what, here I am. Now, let's figure out what's going on and what we're going to do about it."

Garcia saw the shadow of Lion Six move, then the angle of the light changed.

"Okay, maybe we'll get along okay after all. How would you like to have had your legs blown off by an IED? What happened to my brother."

"Oh, shit," Garcia said, "I'm sorry."

"Ya know what, Colonel, I've heard a lot of that sorry bullshit, but none of it helps him get a job and pay his bills. That's the problem with the Forgotten Warriors. Congress keeps sending guys to the most god-awful places on earth, then getting arms and legs blown off and sinking into fucking PTSD. Then they don't fucking help us. That's why we're here. It's gotta damn stop."

21

New York City Hall, Thursday, 2:00 p.m.

Zack sat in the back of the emergency conference center, waiting for the mayor to enter. Someone called attention. They all stood as Mayor Summer walked in. "Please be seated."

Summer paced around the stage like a caged panther. "All right, we need information. I have no idea what the hell we're dealing with. Who is it? How desperate are they?"

A slender blonde hurried into the room and handed the mayor a note.

She read it quickly. "This is what we've been waiting for. The hijackers have asked for a communications link so they can speak to the country. Their spokesperson is on the line. I'm going to patch him in to the system here in the auditorium."

Soon a voice came over the loud speaker. "Who am I speaking to?"

"I am Mayor Summer, Mayor of New York City. Who are you?"

"You can call me Eagle," the voice said.

"What is it you want?" Summer asked.

"We are veterans. You can call us the Forgotten Warriors. We all joined the military and have done our job as best we could, sometimes in terrible circumstances."

Zack stepped forward and motioned to the mayor. She backed up and invited him up on the stage.

"Eagle, my name is Zack Kelly. I'm an active duty army officer. As an army ranger, I, too, served in terrible places, one tour in Iraq and two in Afghanistan."

"Kelly," Eagle replied. "You know what we're talking about."

"Yes I do. What is it you want and how can I help you?"

"Recognition. Recognition for what we went through and help getting oriented back into the world. There are many of us who need medical help, mentally and physically and aren't getting it. And this country needs to stop pouring its young people into these awful places without much reason."

"Certainly a reasonable request," Zack said. "Were you treated in a VA Hospital? How was that? Did you feel you were treated properly?"

"I was and so were certain of my fellow warriors."

"So was I," Zack replied. "I spent four months in Walter Reed. They helped me through the wounds and the pain. What they had trouble helping me with was the post traumatic stress crap. Damn thing has stayed with me like an elephant sitting on my shoulder."

"That's a good way to put it, Colonel. I know the feeling. But it appears you were able to return to duty, PTSD and all."

"That's true," Zack said. "I was one of the lucky ones. I know several of my friends whose wounds were so severe they weren't able to return to duty."

"That's me," Eagle replied. "You know, we blew into Afghanistan after 911 and sailed through all of the opposition. We had the bastards by the balls, but then the damn politicians entered the picture. Dropped us into that hellhole of Iraq."

"I know what you're saying," Zack said.

"Yeah, but that doesn't help us vets. We allowed the Taliban to have all kinds of safe havens in Pakistan. If we got near them, they'd run across the border and we couldn't touch them. Frustrating. Particularly when they had just shot and killed your best buddy or blown his leg off."

"I know it all too well," Zack said. "Ran into it several times myself."

"You have floated back into active duty and things are going great for you. But there are thousands of us who came out of a VA Hospital and got dropped in the mud. Can't get a job, can't get in to see a doc, and here we sit. Nobody gives a shit."

"I give a shit and want to help you. I'll make sure we get your materials out to the public. Mayor Summer, who should be the contact?"

"Margaret Barrett is our Public Affairs officer," Summer said. "She is coordinating all of our contact with the media. Here she is."

"Eagle, my name is Margaret Barrett." She gave him her contact information. "I'll be waiting for your call, and I will get your information out to all of our media contacts."

"I'll be checking to make sure you do what you say you'll do," Eagle said.

"We want to work with you," Barrett said. "We'll do what we say."

"All right. I'll be back to you."

A click and he was gone.

***

"My uncle was born in Chicago in 1928," Lion Six said. "A first lieutenant, he completed fifty combat missions in Korea with the 17th Bomber Group flying Douglas B-25 bombers, and was honorably discharged in 1955."

"I understand things were pretty rough over there," Garcia said.

"Millions of soldiers died in that police action. We didn't even call it a war. He earned military awards, citations, and even the Distinguished Flying Cross."

"Sounds like a lot of other guys," Garcia said.

"Although he left the Air Force upon completion of his three years, the recurring and troubling memories of Korea never left him. He carried those nightmares with him for almost fifty years. You know the worst part, he had no one to share them with. No one wanted to listen to him. It finally broke him."

"There are so many stories like that," Garcia said. "How about yourself?"

"After 911, entering the military was the way to strike back against the bastards who had hit the towers. A chance to avenge all those who died."

"Where did you end up?"

"Afghanistan," Six replied. "We went after the Taliban and al Qaeda. The Taliban were religious fanatics who'd been at war all their lives. Didn't know any difference. We were just another mark on the wall. And we were spending millions and my buddies were getting killed because of those bunch of assholes. And no one cared. You wanted to know why we're here. That's why."

***

Laura sat on the bench inside the ferry cabin. She tried to figure out what she ought to do. The boat began to move. She jumped up and moved to the doorway. Yes, the boat was moving. What now?

In a moment, the doctor came by and stood next to her. After looking around to check for members of the Forgotten Warriors, she asked. "What do you think is going on?"

"I have no idea," Laura said. "I suspect we'll find out soon."

As if on cue, a male voice came over the loud speaker. "As you may have noticed, the ferry is beginning to move. No one should be alarmed. We do ask for your cooperation. Each of you is requested to take off any outer clothing, coats, any boots. You may keep on your normal clothes, but no coats or briefcases. Please accomplish this task immediately."

The doctor looked around. "What the hell?"

One of the hijackers came through the area where they stood. "You heard the announcement. Please take off any outer clothing and move out to the railing."

Laura slipped closer to the doctor. "They're going to make us jump into the water."

"I can't believe it. Gonna be colder than crap."

"Fortunately it's July and not December. And it is mid-afternoon and the sun is out."

The doctor nodded. "There is that."

Laura looked around. A few of the passengers were beginning to strip off their outer coats. Oh, crap, she thought, here goes.

She unbuttoned her sweater and pulled it over her head. When she finished that, she moved toward the railing.

The same male voice came over the loudspeaker. "I am not going to ask again. Each of you are to take off any heavy outer clothing, then move out to stand by the railing."

More passengers began to comply.

Laura tried to spot Kinsey. Saw her by the railing, still in her camouflage pants, but she'd taken off her jacket and boots. The mask and hat were still in place. She moved over to stand next to Kinsey. "You know, there will be some here who can't swim."

"Don't talk," Kinsey whispered. "Don't talk and you'll be okay."

In a moment another one of the hijackers came outside, holding life jackets. "He began to distribute them. "Please take a life jacket."

A woman yelled, "I can't swim. I'm afraid of the water."

"Take a life jacket," the man said. "This will keep you afloat. You will be rescued immediately by the Coast Guard."

People began crying, shouting.

"It'll be all right," Laura said to the distraught woman. "We'll be all right. We can do this together."

More yelling and crying.

Laura moved to the front railing. The boat was headed toward the Statue of Liberty. Laura began to wonder if they were going to crash into the island. Was that why the hijackers wanted all the passengers to get off the boat? Could they be doing that?

More and more life jackets were passed out. Laura was an excellent swimmer, but she took a life jacket anyway. She was smart enough to realize the water would be cold and trying to swim very long could be a problem. A big problem.

22

New York City, Thursday, 2:30 p.m.

Governor Harbaugh gathered the members of his emergency operations group around the table set up in a conference room of the ferry terminal. Along with Mayor Summer, there were members of the FBI, Homeland Security and the Coast Guard. Zack, as a representative of Admiral Steele, was invited to join the group.

"So far we haven't been able to come up with a viable option to rescue the hostages, which really pisses me off," Harbaugh said. "With all the brain power in this room, we should have developed a workable plan. The concern I have, is even if we are able to rescue the hostages on the ferry, we still have the site in San Antonio. These actions seem to be coordinated, and well coordinated at that. We have all the talent? Why the hell are they constantly ahead of us?"

Mayor Summer raised her hand. "Remember, we are still working on possible options. A few moments ago I met with the hostage families. At least as many of them as we've been able to contact. To their credit, I must say they have remained calm. No screaming and running to the press, at least not yet. I suspect their current attitude won't last much longer."

Harbaugh looked at the mayor. "When will you have a plan?"

"I should be ready to brief you on our plan as soon as the meeting of my emergency group is over. Now I'd like to introduce my PR person to summarize for you what she has received from the hijackers. Margaret has distributed the following statement to all news outlets."

Margaret Barrett stood and walked to the podium. About a half hour ago, I received the packet of materials from the veterans on the ferry and distributed it to all of our media outlets. I'll read the opening paragraph. You can get a complete copy on the back table.

She began to read:

FORGOTTEN WARRIORS MANIFESTO

People will question why we have taken this action today. Our goal is not to interfere with anyone, but to help the many veterans who need our help. There are thousands of veterans who have served their country under extraordinary conditions and have served honorably. Then, when they returned home, they were promised care for their injuries, mental as well as physical, but the promised care has not been forthcoming. People say it is funding, but we believe it is really priorities. Our plea to all of you is to shift priorities and care for those who have given so much whether it's lost limbs, PTSD, scars from sexual abuse, or young men and women descending into hopeless depression, alcoholism, or drug addition.

"The writer goes on to explain each area on the list," Barrett said. "For example in the sexual abuse paragraph, he shares that twenty percent of our female veterans have experienced sexual abuse and up to eighty percent, sexual harassment. Unfortunately many of these veterans have not received proper care or counseling, leading them into homelessness, depression, or worse."

She looked out at the audience, her voice breaking. "These are the concerns we're dealing with. My plea is not to hurt any of these veterans and to be kind to them. An IED exploded near my daughter in Afghanistan and her recovery is very slow. They do have a point and a good one."

"Okay," Harbaugh said. "Now we still need to help our hostages. The President and the members of Congress are all over me which is not fun. Not a good place for me to be, and I'm not going to stay there long. If you all can't fix this thing, I'm going to get someone who can. Do you understand me? Now get out of here and get busy."

As the group stood and moved toward the door, Harbaugh called to Mayor Summer. "Would you stay behind for a moment?"

She came up and sat next to him and whispered, "I'm sorry we haven't gotten more for you. This thing has developed so fast, it almost took my breath away. But, we're amending one of our current emergency plans and I think it should work."

"I know and appreciate your efforts. I wanted to ask you about this Zack Kelly. What is he doing here?"

"His dad, Roger Kelly ...."

"I know all about Roger Kelly," Harbaugh said. "I was Police Commissioner when his father was killed. It was a bad deal. Drug bust gone bad. What I asked is what is he doing here now?"

"He apparently is trying to find out what happened. Doesn't believe his dad was a dirty cop. He's been poking around with Tomlinson and looking at old files."

"I want you to personally keep an eye on this for me. I hate to wash up old news. Could embarrass both of us. I'm on the short list for a vice presidential position. If I go up, you go with me. If I sit still, so do you. Do you get my point?"

"Yes, sir. One thing you need to know is he interviewed one of the cops in on the operation, Curly Frost. What you may not know is after the interview, someone took a shot at Frost and he's in the ICU."

Harbaugh launched back. "Shit, I thought he was dead."

Summer shook her head. "Wounded, but he's in bad shape."

"Where is he? Which hospital?"

"I don't know, but I'll find out for you."

"Right away and get back to me. I don't want a bunch of old news getting sprayed all over the papers. Not now."

Summer stood. "I'll do it right away and let you know."

As she walked out, Harbaugh sat at the table. Why the hell did Kelly come back now? Could he really dig up anything? Nothing should stop his vice presidential bid. Certainly not some thirty-year-old shooting bullshit.

***

Immediately after the governor's meeting, Commissioner Tomlinson and his staff gathered to finalize a military option, with the assumption a rescue plan might be needed. They had cordoned off a corner of one of the conference rooms and posted guards outside the door for security.

The tension inside Zack continued to grow. They needed to get Laura off that boat safely, and they needed to do it right away.

"Now," Tomlinson said, "we need to keep this plan top secret. No one outside of this room should realize we are even developing a military option until the Mayor approves it and takes it to the Governor. Do you all understand what I'm saying?"

There were nods around the room. "All right, to this point, we haven't been able to receive much intelligence. The text from Zack Kelly's daughter was helpful. She said she thought there were seven hijackers, plus someone piloting the ferry who appeared to know what he or she is doing." He turned to Zack. "Have you heard anything further?"

Zack shook his head. "Nothing more from her. I thought the phone call was helpful. The man seemed willing to work with us if we helped publicize their concerns. We need to make sure we follow up with whatever he sends us. I'm sure he'll be able to track whatever we do. His trust will be critical."

"I absolutely agree," Tomlinson said. "Whatever actions we plan here will be with the assumption our negotiations have not been effective and action must be taken to protect all of the hostages. Whatever we do here must be considered the last straw."

Zack nodded. "We need to get those folks off peacefully if at all possible."

Tomlinson opened the discussion. "The Coast Guard currently has two ships near the ferry, watching and gathering whatever information they can. What we're thinking is the Coast Guard would add two more ships later in the afternoon, then at dusk if all else fails, a group of navy SEALS will swim up to the ferry, hook up lines to the deck and board."

"My concern," Zack said, "is this plan has the potential to become a blood bath if the SEALS are discovered before they can get on board. I think you must wait until it's completely dark."

"There are many problems with a military option," Fairchild said. "As Zack mentioned, we don't want the hostages to get caught in a shootout. Something else to remember is these guys are our vets. They are military vets who have served their country and now have real problems. They are frustrated and rightfully so about their level of care. This is a very different case from a group of ISIL terrorists bent on killing as many as they can. These are our guys."

"That's true," Tomlinson said, "but they have broken the law, may have hurt a number of people. We can't let this go on indefinitely. No way do we want any group with some bitch to hijack the Staten Island Ferry. They have gone beyond simply protesting in front of a building."

"Is there any chance of using a helicopter to drop in paratroopers while the SEALs are boarding from the water tonight?" Fairchild asked.

"I've been involved in a number of these operations in Afghanistan," Zack said. "They are very dangerous and normally require a number of practice runs. If something goes south and the helicopter crashes onto the ferry we're going to have a lot of injuries and some deaths. Besides, these are vets. They'll know when the helicopter gets close something is going on. Most of them have probably been involved in these types of operations."

"How about if we regularly do flyovers with choppers?" the Coast Guard rep, a Captain Newberry asked. You know, taking pictures, checking things out. They may think it's just another flyover."

"What are the chances of successfully landing a chopper on the deck?" Fairchild asked.

The engineer representing the Port Authority stood and shook his head. "I don't think there is enough room. I'll take another look at the schematic, but don't think it'll work."

"Plus, if the water is rough at all, the ferry will be moving back and forth," Zack replied. "Frankly, I don't like the idea. Too dangerous and will be a real mess if something goes wrong."

"How will they get close enough without alerting the hostage takers?" Fairchild asked.

A navy lieutenant commander named Johnson stood. "I represent SEAL Team Six. Admiral Steele sent me here to help with this operation. We do this sort of operation a lot. We'll paddle up to the ferry in small rubber rafts or swim in, depending on the circumstances. It's got to be completely dark, hopefully with no moon."

"What do you think of a combined helicopter drop and ground operation?" Tomlinson asked. "Can we coordinate it. The timing would need to be perfect."

Johnson stood again. "The danger is more for the paratroopers than for the SEALS. Once the choppers are above the ferry and the paratroopers are shimming down ropes, they're sitting ducks for anyone with a machine gun."

"Do you think our own vets would shoot our own paratroopers?" Fairchild asked.

"I don't know, but I hate like hell to chance it," Johnson replied. "Now what might work is if the SEAL team arrives first. Then the paratroopers could come down from above after they have secured the deck. The hostage takers might still be inside the cabins. But at least they wouldn't be shooting at the troopers. Maybe a ten minute lead time. The extra force might encourage the hostage takers to give up."

"What about medics?" Zack asked.

Johnson gave a thumbs up to Zack. "I can tell you've been in a number of these operations. We've got to be ready to take care of hostages who have been hurt or who are hurt in the rescue, not to mention our own soldiers. We'll bring in our cross-trained medics for the initial triage of casualties."

Newberry stood. "We'll have a doctor with a medical team on board our cruiser which could pull in close to the ferry. I'd suggest the SEAL team and the paratroopers bring at least two medics each with aid bags for initial care. We can move the doctor over to the ferry quickly once it's secure."

"All right. I need to brief the Mayor as soon as she finishes talking to the Governor," Tomlinson said. "I wish our plan was better, but it's what we have. Keep working on our plan and trying to improve it. We will probably have to move tonight. We can't let this go on too long, and I'm not sure how things will develop."

Zack leaned over to Johnson. "I think using your men has a chance, but the helicopter idea is fraught with danger. Here is an ideal situation for 'Murphy's Law.'"

Johnson smiled for the first time. "Right. If anything can go wrong, it will."

23

Whitehall Ferry Terminal, Thursday, 4:45 p.m.

Tension permeated the room as the assembled staff awaited the arrival of the Governor. Zack and Fairchild sat quietly in the back. Zack leaned over and whispered, "I wish I'd get another text from Laura. This waiting is killing me. Something has got to give and soon."

"Your raised a squared-away young woman," Fairchild said. "She'll be fine. Got a good head on her shoulders. Don't worry about her. We need to focus on what the Governor is about to say."

"I know, and I appreciate the pep talk. It's just the damn waiting, particularly when it's Laura in danger."

"I can't pretend to know all you're going through," Fairchild whispered, "but I do know Laura will handle herself well and come through this okay."

"Thanks. I needed that."

The door opened and Governor Harbaugh strolled into the room followed by his executive officer and Mayor Summer. Everyone stood.

The Governor stood at the lectern. "Please be seated. What I'm about to say must be considered to be classified information. I've just been briefed on a military option to rescue the hostages if it comes to that."

The group leaned forward, some with their mouth hanging open. Most just stared at him.

"Mayor Summer's people have taken a hard look at it," Harbaugh said, "and this is the course I propose to take if we can't resolve the incident through negotiations in the next few hours. We cannot negotiate with these hostage takers forever. Something has to give, and I propose we do it tonight. I've asked Mayor Summer's PR person to coordinate the release of all information to the media about the operation once it's underway. No one but Ms. Barrett should release any information." He stopped and looked around the room, his gaze sweeping past everyone. "Do I make myself clear?"

All attendees stared back at him silently.

"Can you give us an idea of possible casualties?" his PR person asked.

Harbaugh looked at the wall for a moment. "To be honest, I have no idea of possible casualties. I'm sure there will be injuries to the rescuers as well as to the hostages. But even considering the possibility of injuries or perhaps deaths, I believe this is what we must do."

Zack stood up. "Colonel Zack Kelly, sir. I think I speak for the families of passengers on the ferry. Easy for you to say, Governor. Your daughter isn't on that ferry."

Harbaugh grimaced. "I understand. I have three daughters who are dear to me. But sometimes we have to take chances. I've got to consider the 300 plus passengers on that ferry. We can't let this go on forever. We have complied with the hijackers' request to release their statement to the public. Is that right?"

"Yes," Ms Barrett said. "I have forwarded their statement to all of our media outlets. Hopefully they will see it on the news and release the passengers."

"We will do all in our power to resolve this peacefully," Mayor Summer said. "What we are discussing is what happens if we can't. I, too, am concerned about injuries, but I agree with the Governor. I believe we must do something to break the log jam and probably tonight."

"How about if I go onboard the ferry?" Zack asked. "With my military background, maybe a face-to-face discussion can break things open."

Harbaugh thought about that. "That is an idea we can propose. But I'm going to keep moving ahead with the rescue scheduled for later tonight. This can't go on forever. I have said in the absence of anything else, we must negotiate. Now we have a feasible plan, so I believe we must be prepared to take it."

Mayor Summer stood. "If we do nothing, then this hijacking wins and we run the risk of a number of copycat actions."

"Thank you, Mayor Summer," Harbaugh said. "You have hit the key point. Now, I'm going to ask Commissioner Tomlinson to outline in detail the proposed plan."

Tomlinson stood and took them through the plan. "The key is stealth and subterfuge that lies at the base of our plan. We'll rehearse it several times and hopefully improve it each time."

"What about weather?" the Coast Guard representative asked. "Who makes the call on weather. Rough seas could be a real problem and wind could raise hell with the helicopters."

"You're right," Harbaugh said. "We can't go in bad weather with a helicopter option. I'll depend on the SEAL team commander and the helicopter pilots to make the call. They are the experts. Any other questions?"

There was silence in the room.

"All right, we are set for tonight. Thank you for your time and I remind you, no one talks about this plan. No one."

Harbaugh watched the group file out of the conference room. He leaned back in his chair. This is going to be perfect. His PR man had set up a briefing for the press. He'll get publicity as the Governor who had things in hand. When the rescue operation was over, Harbaugh could step forward as the savior of the hostages. Somehow he'd been blessed by divine intervention. This was coming at just the right time as he planned to announce his interest in being considered for Vice President in two weeks. Yes, this was going to work out perfectly.

***

Laura and the doctor moved between the other hostages, trying to calm the nervous ones and help those who needed help getting ready.

One woman sat on the floor, head in her hands, sobbing.

Laura dropped down next to her. "It's going to be all right.

Just remove some of your outer clothing, and I'll help you with a life jacket."

"I am scared to death of the water. I almost drowned once. I can't face going into the bay. It's going to be dark soon and the water will be cold."

"Oh, I'm so sorry," Laura replied. "Let me get you a life jacket and we'll stay together. I expect we'll be forced to leave the boat so we won't have much of a choice."

The woman stared at her. "Thank you. Maybe I can do this." She started to remove her jacket.

More of the passengers had removed extra garments to comply with the demands of the hijackers and were working to strap on life jackets.

Laura wished she still had her cell, but when she took off her sweater she was afraid they'd see it. On impulse, she moved back to where she had left her sweater and reached under it to retrieve the cell. She put it behind her back and moved to get a life vest. Stuffing the cell in between the folds of the vest, she moved into a corner.

Glancing around, she saw the hijackers were watching the passengers get ready. She walked toward the bathroom, vest in her hand.

"Wait a minute," one of the hijackers called. "Where are you going?"

"I gotta hit the john," she called. "You know, it sounds like it'll be a while before I'll get another chance. And I can't wait. You gotta understand that."

"Okay, but hurry. You don't have much time."

Laura looked around once more then slipped into the woman's restroom. She went into a stall and shut the door. Quickly, she pulled out her cell, then texted her dad, *"Stripping outerwear. Issuing life vests. Leaving ship."*

She dropped her cell into the toilet and flushed it, knowing she wouldn't have a chance to use the cell again. Hopefully her dad got the message. Please dad, do something to help us.

***

As the meeting broke up, the sound of an inbound text caused Zack to pull his cell out of his pocket. He read the message, and shouted, "They are getting ready to abandon the ferry and make the passengers jump into the water."

The Governor turned away from the group he talked with and glanced back toward Zack. "Wait a minute, what are you saying?"

"My daughter was able to sneak her phone," Zack said. "She texted me, they are issuing life jackets. Looks like they're getting ready to make them all jump from the ferry."

"The boat is moving toward the Statue of Liberty," Tomlinson said. "Do you suppose they're going to abandon the ferry, then crash it into Liberty Island? We gotta get our group together. Call them all back. Now."

One of Tomlinson's officers ran out into the lobby and yelled, "Hey everyone, back here."

In a few minutes the emergency action group had formed again.

"Zack," Tomlinson said, "why don't you go over what you just received from your daughter?"

"Right. Apparently Laura hid her phone somewhere. She just texted me the hijackers had made the passengers strip off their outer coats and sweaters and are issuing life vests. We need to adjust our plan for this contingency. And quick."

"Let me ask the Coast Guard," Mayor Summer said. "They practice emergency measures for this all the time."

"We'll immediately launch three more of our ships and be prepared to pick up the passengers in the water," Captain Newberry said. "We'll have emergency teams on board each ship to help with any who have been injured in any way. Hypothermia is bound to be a problem."

"Okay," Tomlinson said, "get busy on that. Where will you bring the passengers?"

"It makes the most sense to bring them here to the terminal," Mayor Summer said. "We have sealed off an area and set up an emergency treatment center. The Red Cross is bringing in food and clothing. Okay everybody, let's get busy."

Zack sat silently. "Laura, be safe."

Fairchild put her hand on Zack's shoulder. "She's tough, Zack. She'll be fine."

He reached into his pocket and pulled out his cell. Dialing in Shelia's number he soon heard her voice. "Zack, I've been waiting for your call. Is Laura safe?"

Zack had trouble talking. He finally blurted out, "So far she's okay. Can you come over here. I need you now."

"Oh, Zack, I'll be there as soon as I can."

"I'll get your name on the contact list."

"I'm on my way."

24

Staten Island Ferry, Thursday, 6:00 p.m.

Kinsey stood next to Eagle in the pilot house of the ferry, watching as they drew closer to the Statue of Liberty.

"Are the charges set to go off as we near Liberty Island?" Eagle asked.

"I already told you they are." Eagle's constant worrying really pissed her off. So nervous, he was making her nervous. In the military, they just moved forward. If adjustments were needed, then they made them. Not all this second guessing.

"Fifteen more minutes and we'll make the announcement to abandon the ferry." He smiled, Kitten figured for the first time in four days she'd seen him smile. "What about the girl, your friend from school? Are you prepared to take care of her?"

The comment caught Kinsey off guard. She'd been dreading what to do about Kelly. Made no sense to kill her, but what else could she do? She had to do something. "I keep trying to think of another way to deal with her. She's a pretty good egg. I don't want to kill her. Maybe I can figure something else out."

Eagle whirled on her, his eyes blazing. "We've talked about this. There is no other way. If she survives, she knows who you are. That means she'll give your name to the police. Once the police know who you are, they'll be able to find the rest of us."

"I'll talk to Kelly. Tell her to keep her mouth shut."

Eagle banged his hand on the counter. "Are you serious? I mean really serious. Do you think for one moment she won't say anything? You can't be that stupid."

Kinsey slugged him in the arm. "Don't you dare call me stupid. I'm the one who put this entire plan together. After all I've done, don't you dare call me stupid."

Eagle reached over to hug her. "I'm sorry. I know you're not stupid. It's just you've got a weak spot for the woman. You must be strong. You must take care of her."

Kitten sagged against the wall of the ferry. "I don't know I can. It's murder. I've never killed anyone in cold blood before. Looked them in the eye and shot them. If I do it on the ferry, then all the other passengers might see. We'd start a panic."

Eagle glared at her. "If you're not going to be able to do it, then I'll have to. She can't be allowed to leave the ferry alive. If she does, she holds the key to putting all of us in jail."

Kitten took a deep breath. Eagle was right. Dammit, he was right. This had to be done. Otherwise they'd all be facing long jail terms. If it hadn't been for Kelly, they would get away with it. With Kelly alive, they were all in trouble.

"All right." Kinsey turned to walk off. "No other choice. It must be done."

She opened the door and walked out onto the deck. Pulling the door shut behind her, she glanced out at the Manhattan skyline. What a beautiful sight. Then she spotted the Coast Guard cutter shadowing them. Reality sunk in. She had to take care of Kelly.

Pushing back her shoulders, she hurried toward the deck and her upcoming date with Laura Kelly. Sorry, Kelly. A tear formed in her eye. "So sorry," she murmured.

Pushing in the code and opening the door to the lower deck, she felt the tears coming. No one else could see the tears. Women had to be tough. No damn tears.

***

"When did you arrive in Afghanistan?" Garcia asked Lion Six.

"Summer of 2005. What a hell hole. Six of my best friends died trying to make something out of nothing. I sat in that sorry ass country with about 21,000 other Americans and maybe

18,000 NATO troops. Not much of anything to do except allow the Taliban to run all over us. And guess what, the Taliban ate our fucking lunch."

Garcia needed to keep Lion Six talking. Figure a way to convince him to give up before his people got hurt. The FBI and the local cops weren't going to wait forever. These guys were a pain-in-the-butt, but they didn't deserve to die. *Come on, Garcia, use your brain.* Think.

"What's the matter?" Lion Six asked.

"Just thinking. It was a terrible time. In early 2008, I ran the MP operation in one part of the Green Zone. I watched the huge resources we poured into that country wasted. Absolutely wasted trying to shape things. The hatred I saw between the two religious factions had been there for centuries and wasn't about to change because ..."

The door opened and Lion One hurried into the room. She whispered to Lion Six.

He turned to Garcia. "I'm sorry, but we need to end our discussions now."

"Sit still." Lion One picked up the blindfold. "I'm going to place this back over your eyes."

The knot on the blindfold tightened. Garcia stayed silent.

"Please stand and turn around," Lion One said. "We'll be walking toward the door."

"Wait a minute," Garcia said, "we need to finish our talks."

"I enjoyed our talk, Colonel Garcia, and am sorry we must end it. But now you have some idea of what we've been through and why we're doing this. No one helps us. That has to change."

Garcia stood. "Wait, don't do this. We can work something out. No one has to get hurt."

Lion One pushed Garcia on the back. "Get moving. No more talking. We must hurry."

"Why the rush?" Garcia asked. "You've got other plans?"

"None of your damn business," One replied. "Start walking and don't ask so many questions."

Garcia heard a door open, and a hand pushed her harder. She stumbled forward.

***

In the darkening skies, Laura Kelly stood at the side railing and watched the bubbles mark the course of the ferry as it drifted closer and closer to the Statue of Liberty.

"Put on your vests," the voice from the loudspeaker called. "There are two Coast Guard ships following us. They will pick you up. Don't worry. We don't want anyone to get hurt. But you will be hurt if you stay on the ferry. Please be prepared to jump."

Laura heard a noise behind her, then felt something blunt poke her in the back. Shit, a pistol?

"Turn to the right," a female voice said, "and walk to the rear of the ferry. Don't say anything or yell out."

Kinsey. Could Kinsey really shoot her. Laura started dragging her feet in the direction indicated by Kinsey. Her heart pounded and her hands began to shake. "What are you going to do?"

"You'll find out."

"Look, Kinsey, I want to help you. My dad works for the President's national security advisor. Whatever is going on, I can help you. I can't pretend to know all the things that have happened to you in the military, but I do know we need to bring a peaceful end to all this. Neither of us wants anyone to die. We've got to figure out how to pull it off. Let me help you."

"Shut up, Kelly, I don't need your help. No one can help me now. So just do what I'm telling you to do. Keep moving and shut up."

Laura tensed, her heart racing so hard she could hear the blood pulsing in her ears. Would Kinsey actually shoot her? She trembled.

"All right, Kelly, just keep moving. No stalling. It won't help you to stall."

Laura sensed a hitch in Kinsey's voice. Was she crying? Could she use that to her advantage? *Think Kelly, think. You could die.*

"Look Kinsey, we're teammates. Partners. Let me help you. It's not too late to turn things around. Find a peaceful ending to this thing."

"Shut up and keep moving."

They continued to walk toward the stern of the ferry. Laura searched her mind. *Jump from here? Try to take the pistol?*

When they reached the stairs, Kinsey pushed her. "Down the stairs. Hurry up."

At bottom of the stairs, Laura opened the door. The rush of air and the sound of waves hit her. *Could she jump now? Before Kinsey was ready? Off the left side?*

She stood at the railing, looking down at the water. Her trembling increased. *Was Kinsey really going to shoot? In cold blood? She couldn't do it.*

"All right, Kelly, fasten your vest, then climb over the railing and jump in."

Laura turned to Kinsey, "What?"

"Just do as I say and do it now before I change my mind."

"Please Kinsey, I don't want to die. For Gods sake don't do this."

Kinsey pushed her. "Hurry. Time is running out."

Laura lifted her foot over the railing. She pushed up, then balanced for a moment looking down at the swirling waters. She had to jump. Had to do it now before Kinsey could shoot.

As she dove, two shots sounded. She flexed, expecting to feel the sharp pain of a bullet. Her dad had told her about the feeling when he was shot. She closed her eyes, tensed. But she felt nothing other than the shock of the cold water. She went deep, then bobbed up again to the surface.

Laura leaned back and swept her hair back to get it out of her eyes.

Kinsey stood at the stern some distance away as the ferry moved forward.

Alive, Laura thought. *Damn. She was alive.*

***

Zack hurried from the meeting room out to the lobby of Whitehall Terminal and saw Shelia running up the stairs from the entrance way. The families of people on the ferry milled around, talking, yelling at one another, crying, pleading for more information.

She ran over and hugged him. "What's going on? Is Laura all right?"

Zack held up his hand and pointed. The Governor moved to a podium which had been set up with a microphone. "May I have your attention, please."

The noise dropped and people pushed in closer to where the Governor stood.

The various television reporters moved in, pads of paper in one hand, phones in the other. A number of TV cameras stood set up in the back.

"I'm Governor Harbaugh," he began. "First of all I want you to know we are doing everything possible to keep your loved ones safe and help them through this terrible situation. For those of you who are not aware of details, a group that calls itself the Forgotten Warriors, hijacked the Staten Island Ferry at 8:45 this morning."

"What are you doing to get our people off that ferry?" someone shouted. "Why has this gone on so long?"

"Our goal," the Governor said, "is to bring this event to a successful ending with no one getting hurt. So far as we know, there have been no injuries to any of the passengers. Now it appears the ferry is moving toward the Statue of Liberty and not here toward the terminal."

"Why?" a reporter yelled. "What's going on? Tell us."

"We don't know why. We have received indications the hijackers are planning on abandoning the ferry and have issued life vests to all of the passengers."

"What?" someone yelled. "Are they going to be transferred to another ship? What's going to happen? Tell us for Gods sake."

"We don't know anymore than what I've shared with you. As the situation changes, we will keep you advised as soon as we know anymore. The Coast Guard is shadowing the ferry to be prepared to assist all of the passengers when it becomes possible. We hope to resolve this soon."

"When do you expect to know more?"

"Rest assured, you will know when we know. In the meantime, please join us and get something to eat or drink in the area we have set up."

25

Alamo, San Antonio, Thursday, 5:45 p.m.

Garcia felt Lion One take her arm and spin her around. She nudged Garcia and they moved back toward the main door through which Garcia had originally entered.

"Okay," One said, "here is your cell phone. You're at the front door. I'll open it for you. Walk forward at least twenty steps, then remove the blindfold. Do not look back. I'll be watching you. I repeat, do not look back. Just be happy you're returning to your fellow agents."

"But, what's going to happen here?" Garcia asked. "What are you planning?"

"That's none of your business. Quit asking so many questions before I change my mind. Otherwise I'll tie you up and drop you in the corner like a sack of potatoes."

Garcia had to smile. "That doesn't sound great so here I go." She stepped forward. It was cooler than when she entered the Alamo earlier. *Must be late afternoon. Gentle breeze blowing.* She'd lost track of time.

As she walked, putting one foot in front of the other and feeling her way, she heard shouting. After about another fifteen steps, she reached back and removed the blindfold. Spotlights blinded her. She covered her eyes with her hands, then opened them slowly. As her eyes adjusted to the light, she could see dusk was coming.

She walked about ten more steps toward the outer ring.

"Garcia, over here," Agent Ryan called.

She looked to her right and spotted him waving at her from near the command post.

He hurried out to meet her. Taking her arm, he asked, "Are you all right?"

"I'm fine, just a little tired of the blindfold. I was treated well by the crew."

"Come on, let's get you to our command post."

As they walked, he asked, "Did they give you any indication of what they have planned?"

Garcia took a minute to organize her thoughts. "Not really, although I don't think this will last much longer."

"Let's go inside and get you coffee and something to eat."

Garcia took a deep breath. "Sounds great."

Once inside, Ryan called to one of the other agents. "We need coffee and a couple of sandwiches."

One of the agents handed her a cup and they moved toward the map board. A number of others gathered around behind her.

Garcia sipped her coffee. "Hot. Oh, man, that's good." She pointed at the map. "Now, I entered the visitor's center here and was immediately blindfolded by someone who called herself Lion One. I assume she is the assistant to this Lion Six."

Ryan made a note. "So 'One' is a female?"

Garcia nodded. "I didn't see her because of the blindfold, but from the way she bumped me, I'd estimate she was a little taller than I am. Slender, maybe a hundred or so pounds.

"Anything else?" Ryan asked.

"She wore a ring on her left hand. Might be married. And she wore perfume, but I'm not sure what kind. Scent was kinda strong, From the way she moved me around, she had to be in good condition."

"Okay. That's good."

"After she left, 'Six' regaled me with stories about how veterans have gotten lost in the shuffle. They're disgusted so many young people keep getting sent over to god-awful places, then don't get the help they need when they return. This shouldn't come as a surprise. It's been all over the press."

"What do you suggest we do?" Ryan asked.

"All of a sudden, they were in a rush to get rid of me." Garcia replied. "I sensed things are about to come to a climax."

"I'd hate to storm the place," Ryan said. "People on both sides are going to get hurt."

Garcia found a chair and sat. "Agreed. They do have weapons and I'm sure they know how to use them. We should be able to close this out peacefully. These guys are fellow vets. I don't want to see a bunch of them hurt, or any of our agents for that matter."

Ryan started to pace. "But this can't go on forever. People can't take over the Alamo whenever they feel like it or have a bitch about something."

An explosion shook the command post, causing two cups to fall off the table.

Garcia snapped her head around, jumped up and looked outside. Flames poured from the visitors center. "What the hell?"

***

Laura bobbed up and down in the water, watching the ferry cruise slowly toward Liberty Island and the Statue of Liberty. *You're alive. Get moving.*

Treading water, she tried to sort out which direction to swim. It appeared to be about 200 yards to Liberty Island. Her body ached, but she had to get moving. Where are those coast guard ships? Find those ships. Head toward them. Too far to reach the White Hall Terminal. So damn cold.

Swimming helped her warm up, but she could feel herself fading from the cold. Keep moving, she thought, don't quit. Your dad wouldn't quit and you won't, either.

The ferry floated on, churning up water as it moved farther and farther away from her. As it neared Liberty Island, it appeared to stop. Then she saw the spotlights.

Two Coast Guard cutters shadowed the ferry, loud motors sounded in her ears. A voice called to her from the deck of one of the boats. "Ahoy. Can you hear me?"

"Help me." Laura's teeth chattered as she cried, "Help. Cold."

"I'm going to throw you a life preserver. Are you able to grab hold of it? I'll pull you in."

"Hurry. Please," Laura yelled. "Cold."

A rope flew out from the side of the boat and landed about five feet away. "Can you reach it?" the voice called.

"I'll do my best," She stuttered. *So damn cold. Tough to talk.* She paddled hard. Reached out. *Grab it. Gotta hang on.* Gotta.

"Hold tight. We'll pull you in."

Exhausted, she held on to the life preserver as if it were gold. Slowly the two sailors on the cutter pulled her in. When she reached the side of the cutter, they lowered a hoist.

Laura shivered. *Hard to hold on. Had to do it.*

"Climb on and we'll hoist you up."

"Almost on." She made a massive effort and grabbed it, her fingers slipped. She grabbed it again. "Okay pull me up. I can hold on."

Laura felt herself being pulled upwards and was soon level with the deck.

"Easy now." The sailors reached over and swung the hoist onto the boat.

"Take it easy now." Strong hands took hold of her and helped her off. One of them wrapped her in a blanket, then a second one.

She shook and her teeth chattered.

The younger of the two gave her a warm feeling. Really cute when he smiled at her. "Are you okay?"

He made it feel better. Laura shivered. "Cold, but okay. Thanks."

"You must be freezing."

She had to plant her feet as the boat rocked. "I..., I am. Water so damn cold."

The cute one wrapped his arms around her and began to lead her toward the door. "Can you walk okay?"

Laura nodded.

"Then, let's get you inside so you can have something hot to drink."

As she moved toward the door, the other sailor exclaimed, "Holy crap."

She turned in time to see people jumping from the ferry. Lots of people.

The cutter began moving again, headed toward the group of swimmers, bright lights reflecting in the water. Laura watched in helpless fascination as people jumped into the water. It seemed like hundreds of people jumping in. All shapes, all sizes, all stages of dress.

The young man next to her murmured, "Well I'll be damned. Look at them."

More cruisers moved in, slowly, trying not to hit anyone.

"They held us all hostage. No cell phones, cameras. Scared the crap out of me and probably everyone else."

Bright light flashed from the cutter as they slowed and began to drop life boats into the water.

Laura shook her head. "I hope everyone is going to be okay. The water is freaking freezing."

***

Zack Kelly paced up and back the Whitehall Terminal lobby, the helpless feeling grating on him. All he could think of was Laura. He had to do something. Otherwise he'd go crazy.

Shelia took his arm. "It's okay, Zack, It'll be okay. She'll be fine. I can feel it."

"I know you're trying to help, but I'm going nuts waiting. I fucking hate waiting anyway."

Agent Tara Fairchild hurried through the crowd toward Zack, waving her arms. She took Zack by the hand. "Come with me. Now."

Zack hurried after her asking Shelia to wait for him.

"What is it?" Zack called.

Tara called as she pushed through the crowd, "Just follow me and hurry."

They arrived at a door. Tara threw it open. They rushed inside.

Tomlinson and a group of the emergency responders gathered inside. "It appears the ferry has stopped and the passengers are jumping off both sides."

"What?" Zack called. "Must be what Laura texted to him."

"We don't know yet," Tomlinson said. "Events are coming to a head. Coast Guard cutters are moving to pick up passengers from the ferry. Five so far. Life boats in the water. We'll be adding more cutters, but we don't want them to get in each other's way. We sure as hell don't want them to start running over passengers."

"Do you have any names yet?" Zack asked, praying Laura would be okay.

"Not yet, but it won't be long," Tomlinson said. "I've asked our Coast Guard rep to begin collecting names so we can notify those waiting in the terminal. People are going to start going nuts as we began to release names."

Zack turned away to hide the tears blurring his eyes.

***

Eagle ran from the bridge and stood next to Kinsey. "Keep the people moving," he yelled. "We need to get everyone off the ship. You, too."

He watched Kinsey hurrying along the railing, imploring people to jump.

"The Coast Guard will rescue you," she called. "It will be all right. Just hurry." She ran up to one of the passengers who was hesitant to jump. "Jump now. You must jump."

Eagle trotted back into the cabin and double-checked the explosives, then glanced forward once more to gauge the distance to Liberty Island. He took a deep breath then started the timer. Checking once more, he ran back toward the stern of the ferry. Only five minutes before the damn thing blew.

He spotted two elderly women huddled in the corner. "You must leave," he yelled again. "It's not safe. Leave. Now."

Stupid women, they were going to die. "You have life vests," Eagle screamed at them. "They'll keep you safe until the Coast Guard rescues you."

Kinsey headed his way. "We've got to jump," Eagle whispered to her. "I've set the fuse and the bomb will explode in four minutes. These two won't leave."

One of the women started sobbing. "I almost drowned once. I'd rather die on the boat than in the water. I've seen the Coast Guard boats nearby. They won't let us get hurt if we stay on the ferry."

Kinsey hurried over to the two women. "I understand you're afraid. We can do this together."

She took both women by their arms and began to walk toward the stern of the boat. "Hold on to me." She called to Eagle, "Help me get them off the boat. They're coming with me."

Eagle said, "Go. Go. You can't stay on board. Gonna explode."

The woman stood there crying and managed to stutter, "I'm, I'm afraid."

Kinsey helped one to the edge, placed her arms around the woman, and together they jumped.

Eagle pushed the other woman into the water, jumping in right behind her. He surfaced. Looked back toward the ferry. Checked in a circle. Fuck, no woman.

Kinsey bobbed up with the other woman a short distance away. "Where's the other lady?"

"I don't know. Start swimming. We need to get away from the boat."

Two minutes later, a loud explosion sounded. Fire flew from the cabin of the ferry, shaking Eagle and churning the waters.

He glanced around again. Smoke and flames. Spotted the woman. Floundering. Shit. He swam to her, then pulled her away from the boat. He had to keep swimming.

26

Alamo, San Antonio, Thursday, 6:15 p.m.

Garcia ran across Alamo street to what used to be one wing of the visitors' center. Flames shot up from the building. People ran in all directions. She called back to Agent Ryan, "Watch out. There may be other bombs. Don't know if these guys would set more or not."

Three fire trucks arrived. Firemen jumped off and connected hoses to the hydrants. Two firemen hurried to the front door to check if there were people still trapped inside.

Garcia stopped and stared. No sense going any farther. She watched for any vets running from the building. No way could she get inside until the firemen brought the blaze under control.

Agent Ryan puffed up behind her. "Damn, that baby is blazing. But why? Why set a fire?"

"The vets are using this as cover to sneak away," Garcia said. "Bet they had a change of clothes. Pretty damn smart."

She and Ryan stood there for a few minutes. Ryan kept receiving reports. So far none of the Forgotten Warriors had been found and arrested. The light from the blaze lit up the night sky.

It took about fifteen minutes before one of the firemen came up to them. "You Ryan?"

"Yeah. How you doing with the fire?"

"Won't take much longer. We've got it contained. Looks worse than it is."

Garcia kept running things through in her mind. What else could she be doing? They had a ring around the Alamo so those inside shouldn't get out unless they had friends on the outside. Was it possible? Hard to believe but maybe...

She glanced at Ryan. "Do you think they had outside help?"

A voice sounded behind her. She knew it. Whirling around, she stood face to face with a tall, state police officer, dark glasses and a mustache. "I know you. You're Lion Six. Goddammit, Ryan arrest this man."

Ryan glanced at her. Shook his head. "What the hell are you talking about? This is Sergeant Gerry Strong from the Texas Highway Patrol."

Strong looked at her, grinning. "Who the hell are you? Who is this Lion Six? You should be careful of accusing a guy of something when you have no idea what you're talking about."

Garcia started to pull her pistol from her holster. Stopped. Couldn't do that.

"Garcia," Ryan yelled. "Put the damn thing away."

She kept her hand on her pistol. "Don't give me any shit. I know who you are." She pointed at him. "You're under arrest."

Strong held up his hands. "Whoa, what the hell are you saying? I'm on your side. I don't know who you are, but you'd better take your hand off that gun before one of my buddies blows you away."

"It's okay, Garcia," Ryan said. "Sergeant Strong is helping with the state police. You must be mistaken. His people have been helping us coordinate security for the Alamo."

Garcia moved her hand from the pistol. "Okay, okay."

She stared at Strong. Sure as hell he was Lion Six. She knew his voice. She knew it. Something seemed to be very wrong.

"Look, I'm sorry," Garcia said. "I just finished meeting with the head of the Forgotten Warriors who took over the Alamo. I was blindfolded, but I heard his voice plenty. Do you have a brother in the military. Maybe someone who was in a VA hospital or had been seen by the docs at a VA Hospital."

That smile again. "Sorry, I can 't help you. I was in the military, but I joined the Highway Patrol six years ago."

Garcia watched him. Damn smile. Was he laughing at her? The guy was Lion Six. She knew it. How to prove it?

Strong smiled again. "You have me confused with someone else. I've never heard of this Lion Six. I certainly didn't take over the Alamo. I've been working security and trying to get this mess under control like the rest of these cops."

Garcia had to back off. She knew she was right. But Ryan seemed to know this Strong guy. "Can you tell me where you've been for the last few hours? That's the time I was with this Lion Six."

"Sure. Been here all the time. My deputy can vouch for me. Hey, Manson, come over here."

A young woman, her blond hair tucked under her cap, dark glasses, walked over. "Yeah, boss, what's up with this woman. I saw her start to pull a gun on you. I was about to blast her."

"She's some Colonel who's working with Agent Ryan. Would you believe she accused me of being involved with the group that took over the Alamo?"

The officer started to laugh. "Good one. I've been with you all the time. So unless you have a split personality, I don't know what she's talking about."

Goddamn, Lion One, Garcia thought. The woman is Lion One. Now she knew how they were able to get away so fast. They must have gone through the police lines during the confusion from the fire. Probably had someone on the outside helping them with the security. If she lashed out at this woman, she'd be the laughing stock of the group.

Garcia shrugged. "I guess it was a case of mistaken identity. Sorry for the confusion." She needed to change the subject. "Have you been able to round up any of the soldiers who were in there?"

Strong shook his head. "Not yet. Lots of confusion with the fire, but we will. We'll catch them. No one will get away with this."

Garcia shrugged. Yes they will. They already have. She turned and walked off.

***

Zack waited for any word about Laura. He felt in his heart she'd be safe, but doubt nagged at him. *When would he hear?*

Shelia leaned against him. "We'll hear something soon. Laura is too sharp. She's not going to let any two-bit hijackers mess her up."

The comment made Zack smile. "You sure do have a way with words."

As he turned to start pacing again, they were rocked by a loud blast, then another. Zack hurried to a window and looked out to see a fire raging high into the sky.

Shelia turned to him. "What the hell was that?"

"Sounded like some sort of explosion to me. I wonder if they blew up the ferry after everyone got off it. Does it make any sense?"

"None of this makes any sense?"

Tomlinson burst into the room, eyes wide. "The Forgotten Warriors blew up the ferry after it hit Liberty Island. It appears the hijackers got all of the passengers off the ferry, then blew it up. Would you believe it?"

Zack pulled on his arm. "Do you know for sure about passengers?"

"I'm waiting to hear more from the Coast Guard."

Oh, man, why blow up the Staten Island Ferry? Are these guys nuts?

Shelia hugged him. "Oh, Zack. It's going to be okay."

***

Garcia pushed in the numbers, then heard the phone ringing. "Agent Fairchild."

"Hey, Fairchild, it's Garcia. I need your help."

"What's up?" Fairchild asked. "Things are pretty crazy here. Damn ferry just exploded. Kidnappers must have set a bomb to go off just as the ferry hit the Liberty island."

"Oh, no," Garcia cried. "What about Laura?"

"We don't know. We don't know."

"Oh, man, tell Zack I'm praying for her. Now, I need your help. It's really important."

Garcia summarized what had happened with the Alamo. "They set a fire which is almost under control. While I was blindfolded, I spent a couple of hours with the leader of the team that took over the Alamo. I got to know his voice. It turns out the guy who sounds just like him is a member of the Texas Highway Patrol. But, I know it's him. I know his voice."

"What?" Fairchild said. "Gotta be impossible."

"Ya know what, exactly what I would have said if it hadn't happened to me."

"All right, give me the name, and I'll see what I can do."

"Sergeant Gerry Strong, Texas Highway Patrol. At first I thought he belonged to the Texas Rangers, but I'm pretty sure it's the Highway Patrol. I don't know much more than that. I'd do it myself, but I figured with all of your hot-shit contacts, you could do it faster and with lots more stealth."

"Give me a few minutes. I'll check both the Highway Patrol and the Texas Rangers just to be sure. This ferry thing has us all jumping. And now with the explosion ..."

"Thanks. Do what you can."

Garcia disconnected and stood for a few minutes staring at the map board. *This shit doesn't make any sense.* But she knew deep down Strong was really Lion Six. Had to be him.

Agent Ryan walked up behind her. "What the hell are you trying to do? Start a war with the state cops?"

"Hell no, but I know what I heard. It was him. I don't know how it happened, but the guy is Lion Six. I'm pretty sure Lion One was the other cop." She stopped. Snapped her fingers. "Wait a minute. Wait just a damn minute. Didn't you record our conversation with Lion Six. We spent time talking to him. You can check it for yourself."

"Damn, you're right. We did record his voice. Let's go talk to the negotiator."

Garcia followed Ryan over to where the negotiator had been set up, but he was gone. "Where the hell did our negotiator go?"

One of the other agents looked up from his laptop. "He took off a little while ago since the hostage situation had ended. We figured we wouldn't need him anymore. What's up?"

Ryan's face turned red and he started to yell, "Goddammit, I didn't release him. Where does he get off just taking off like that? We need him."

"I think the guy from the Texas Highway Patrol offered him a ride back to the office."

Garcia and Ryan stared at each other.

Garcia had to smile. "Maybe you're beginning to get it now."

About that time, her cell rang. "Garcia."

"Hey, Garcia, it's Fairchild."

Garcia had a pretty good feeling what she was about to hear. "Okay, let me put it on speaker so Agent Ryan can hear what you have to say."

"Hey, Ryan, how you doing? I hear you've got a pretty crazy thing going on down there. For your information, we're busier than shit here."

"Good to hear from you," Ryan said. "What did you find out?"

"First of all," Fairchild began, "are you sure you've got the name right."

"Yeah, I do," Garcia said. "I believe you're going to confirm we've been had."

"I can't find a Texas Highway Patrol officer or a Texas Ranger by the name of Gerry Strong."

Garcia and Ryan stared at one another. They'd been had.

Garcia's face brightened. "Wait a minute. He bragged about his motorcycle. I have one too and he rattled on and on about his. Let me see if I can remember the model. Supposed to be a super fancy one. Maybe we can run him down that way."

Ryan ran his fingers through his hair. "Oh, man, I hope so. Otherwise we're gonna look like real chumps."

It was Garcia's turn to smile. "What do you mean we, partner? Got a frog in your pocket? Ryan stormed off.

27

Upper New York Bay, Thursday, 8:00 p.m.

The waves from the explosion rolled Eagle and Kinsey up and down in the water.

Kinsey shook water out of her eyes. "Did you know the bomb would do all that?"

Eagle nodded. "We had to make a big blast to cover our escape, plus do some damage to Liberty Island. We have to make the public notice. They're screwing their veterans and nobody gives a shit. Well, they will now. And no one can link us to any of this. The only one was the Kelly woman and you took care of her."

Eagle glared at Kinsey, spitting water out of his mouth. "You did take care of her, didn't you? She's the only one who can send us to jail. If she's out of the way we're in the clear. Now answer me, you did take care of her."

Kitten floated with her arms out stretched. She was afraid to tell Eagle the truth. But if he was right and Kelly was the only one who could put them in jail, then she had made one hell of a mistake.

Eagle grabbed her arm. "You did take care of her. You did."

"She jumped as I was getting ready to shoot. I'm not sure if I hit her or not. She may have only gotten wounded and not killed."

"Dammit, Kinsey, you were supposed to take care of her. I know you are soft-hearted, but I didn't think you were soft-headed."

"Don't you dare talk to me like that."

"I'll talk to you any way I want if you've fucked this thing up. I don't want to go to jail and I know you don't either. You don't know this Kelly other than as a passing acquaintance. Then you may have let her get away. Do you know what this means?" He grabbed her arm again. "Do you?"

Kitten started to cry. She'd let Kelly get away, and she could finger all of them. Probably would. Had to fix it. And fast.

***

Zack's mother's frustration boiled through the phone line. "I can't believe you didn't let me know Laura was on that ferry. Why didn't you call me? Why?'"

Zack knew he was in hot water with his mother. "I didn't want to worry you when there wasn't anything you could do. Laura just texted me to tell me she was okay."

"I'm coming down there and right now. Chester will be all right by himself. Anyway, he'd just slow me down. You'd better be right, Zack. You'd better."

Zack noticed the hitch in her voice which matched his feelings exactly. "I'm sorry Mom . . . " He found himself talking to an empty phone.

Shelia leaned into him. "Everything okay with your mom?"

"She's pissed I didn't call her."

"Do you blame her? It's her granddaughter. I suspect her only granddaughter. Suppose she didn't call you in the same circumstances?"

"All right, all right. You made your point. Can't go back. Now I've got to figure out a way to get her in here when she arrives."

***

The call Zack had been waiting for finally came.

Tomlinson came hurrying over. "The Coast Guard just called with the list of passengers they have rescued so far. They confirmed your daughter is on the cutter. She's safe."

Zack's shoulders sagged. He didn't realize how much tension had pounded on him. He turned away and started to weep. He'd been so tight. Didn't realize how tight. "You're sure?"

Tomlinson nodded.

"When will she get to the terminal?"

Tomlinson wore a huge smile on his face. "Probably in about thirty minutes."

Shelia had been over at the windows, watching through the gathering dusk. She ran over to him. "Zack, what is it? Is it Laura? Tell me."

He couldn't talk for a moment. Emotions bubbled up inside him. Finally he squeaked out, "They've confirmed she's safe. On board one of the Coast Guard ships."

Shelia hugged him. Reached back to give him a kiss. "Oh the relief. I've been so worried. Maybe you should call your mother right away. Let her know the good news. Might even get you back in her good graces again."

Of course, he should call her. She'd be frantic, racing to get here. Racing to see what had happened to Laura. Should have thought of it right away.

Zack pushed her number in on his cell. She answered on the first ring, a frantic sound to her voice. "Zack is it you? Is Laura all right?"

"Commissioner Tomlinson received confirmation from the Coast Guard Laura was rescued a little while ago. I called you right away."

"Thank heavens for the Coast Guard. I'm at the ferry exit. A short walk and I'll be at the terminal. Oh, I'm so relieved."

"Commissioner Tomlinson has your name on the approved list. When you reach the terminal, show them your ID. You should get in right away. If there is any problem, call me. And again, I'm sorry I didn't think to call you sooner. It's been an awful time."

"I know, son. I know. Thanks for your call. See you in a few minutes. Love you." She disconnected.

Zack and Shelia moved closer to the gate where the hijacked passengers were scheduled to arrive. A few had already come through the turnstiles. They looked like drowned rats, wrapped in blankets and wearing slippers.

"Oh, man," Zack said. "I can hardly wait."

"You can relax. You know she's all right. She'll be here soon."

"Yeah, yeah, I'll believe it when I see it." He started to pace. Came back around. Then paced some more.

"All right," Shelia said with a laugh, "why don't you come over here. You'll wear out the floor."

Finally, after what seemed like forever, the door opened. Two Coast Guard officers came through the door, escorting a number of passengers. There were four men, then two women.

Zack broke into a huge smile. "There." He yelled and pointed, jumping a little so she could see him. Laura saw him and waved back. She blew him a kiss.

"Dad." Laura ran toward him, holding the blanket around her. Hair still wet, hanging down, scratches on her face, but she looked terrific to Zack. She threw herself into her dad's waiting arms. He hugged her like he never wanted to let her go.

Zack leaned back, studied his daughter. "Are you all right? I mean anything serious we need to get checked out right away?"

"Scratched up, exhausted, still scared, but yep, I'm cool."

He glanced down. "Where are your clothes?"

"They had us strip off outer clothing before forcing us to jump into the water."

Shelia reached over to hug Laura. "I'm so glad you're safe. We were so scared. Aren't you really cold?"

"Better now. These blankets help a lot. Before they wrapped me up on the Coast Guard cutter, I shook like mad. Man, the water's cold."

"Don't worry, the Red Cross has dry clothes and food in the other room for you."

"Yeah. The Coast Guard told us they would be taking us into a debriefing room with the FBI. I'm told it should probably take about an hour."

"Laura, Laura," a voice called.

Zack turned to see his mother running across the hall. He didn't realized she could run that fast.

Ethel swept Laura into a hug. "Oh, Laura, you're safe." Tears moistened her cheeks. "I was so worried about you. Couldn't believe what was happening. Are you all right?"

Laura smiled at her grandmother. "Like I told my dad, I'm all right. Not too worse for the wear. But, I've got to follow those officers to some big debriefing with the FBI."

Ethel had a bag hanging from her left arm. "I've brought a change of clothes for you. You must be freezing."

"Grandma, that's wonderful. Thanks so much."

Zack had to smile. Leave it to his mother to think of everything.

"There's a ladies room right over there. Come on, it won't take a minute and we can get you all fixed up." Ethel smiled. "I even thought to bring a hair dryer."

One of the Coast Guard officers called, "Wait, she must come with us. We're already late for a debriefing."

Grandma Ethel whirled on him. "If you think for one moment, I'm going to allow my granddaughter go into any debriefing in a blanket over soaking clothes, you're out of your mind." Her tone mellowed. "We'll hurry, we really will."

Zack put his hands up in the air. "I learned a long time ago it's really tough to argue with her when her granddaughter is involved."

The officer turned away, hiding a smile.

Laura and her grandmother disappeared into the ladies room.

Zack laughed and turned to Shelia. "Never underestimate the power of a momma bear taking care of one of her babies."

The officer turned back toward them with a smile on his face. "Please hurry them along."

Zack nodded. "No problem. Will do. Thanks."

At that moment, the Governor hurried up the stairs followed by the Mayor and Commissioner Tomlinson, the press madly snapping pictures behind him. "I understand some of the passengers are beginning to return."

"That's right, sir," a Coast Guard officer said. "The first couple of groups just arrived. We're taking them into a room for a debriefing about what happened on the ferry. We want to establish a time line for all the events."

The Governor stared at a couple of the returnees. "Are they still wet? For God sakes, get them dry clothes. We can't have them running around soaking wet."

Tomlinson turned to one of his inspectors. "Don't worry sir, we've got warm dry clothes and food next door. They need food and something to drink."

"I understand the Red Cross is taking care of that in the next room, but I'll double check." The inspector hurried off toward the door into the room.

Zack turned to see Laura and his mother hurrying out of the bathroom. Laura's hair had been blown dry. She wore a blouse and slacks with a sweater over her shoulders and sandals on her feet. She hugged her dad. "Ah, that's much better. Grandma took care of everything."

Ethel crossed her arms and laughed. "I'm not going to have my granddaughter running around soaking wet. I don't care who wants it."

The Governor walked by, stopped and started at Ethel. "Wait a minute. Aren't you Ethel Kelly?"

"Why yes I am. You've got a good memory."

He looked like he was at a loss for words. "Ah, what brings you here?"

"My son and granddaughter were in New York on vacation. I came out to help a long-time friend recover from an assault. Then I learned my granddaughter was a passenger on the ferry." She turned toward Zack. "You've probably met my son, Zack Kelly."

"I met Colonel Kelly, but didn't realize he's Roger's boy."

"Yes," Ethel said. "It's been a long time since Roger had been branded a criminal."

Zack figured this would be a good time to chase down some information from the Governor. "Sir, I wanted to look into the death of my father. I never believed he was a dirty cop and I plan to prove it."

Zack's comment obviously caught the Governor short. "That was a long time ago, Kelly. I understand the case was thoroughly investigated."

"I'm not sure of that," Zack said. "Anyway, I am checking all of the details to see if the inspectors missed something of merit. Zack turned to Laura. "You'd better go get debriefed.

As Laura hurried off, Shelia turned to Zack. "I believe it's time for a cup of coffee."

Zack laughed. "Maybe two or three. Come on, Mom, let's go get some coffee."

***

He watched the action on his television, not believing anyone would hijack the Staten Island Ferry. All those poor people arriving, soaking wet. He supported the military but this seemed a little much.

Then he stopped and stared. The man looked like Zack Kelly. Was he talking to his mother What the hell was she doing there?

He continued to watch. Soon the Governor came up the stairs, stopped and looked at Zack's mother. She turned and started to talk with him. Shaking hands, Smiling. Why the hell was she so animated with that asshole?

Oh, and there was Laura Kelly. What a frightening experience. He couldn't stay here. Had to go and wait outside the terminal. Who knew what might happen?

He'd made up his mind. Getting up and turning off the TV, he stepped to the mirror. His beard had gotten longer, but didn't need trimming. He put on his blue jacket and pulled his favorite Yankees cap down over his forehead. Then he put on the sunglasses.

Patting his back pocket to make sure he had his wallet and his ID, he stepped toward the door. He'd had so many identities, sometimes it was difficult to keep them all straight.

He walked out and closed the door, locking the two dead bolts and replacing the string.

Being careful is how Casey Matheson stayed alive.

28

San Antonio, Thursday, 7:45 p.m.

Garcia sat on her bike across the street from the condo and waited. She had checked the three motorcycle dealers who sold motorcycles like the one Lion Six talked about. She found a store who'd sold a bike to a man in San Antonio named Paul Cartwright. Only man living in San Antonio with that type bike. Had to be. She rode over to the condo and waited a couple of houses down the street.

Time passed. She grabbed a sandwich at a near by sub shop. This was probably a wild goose chase, but something nibbled at her. Lion Six was so proud of his bike, obviously his weakness. Could she exploit the weakness and use it to find him? Maybe.

A man and a woman walked out of the building. He had dyed his hair and was wearing glasses but it was Lion Six. No doubt about it. So Cartwright was Lion Six.

The blond behind him fit what Garcia remembered about Lion One. Garcia sank down on her bike and looked at the ground. Her heart beat rapidly. What should she do? Didn't make sense to challenge the two of them. Wait until they left, then see where they went. No need to call Ryan yet.

The two split up, Cartwright getting on his bike and heading in the direction of downtown San Antonio. Garcia had to make a choice. Which one to follow? It would be tougher to follow Cartwright on his bike, but Lion One got into an old model Ford. Probably much easier to follow. She also headed in the direction of San Antonio.

Garcia followed her as she got onto Route 281 and headed southeast. She traveled until she almost reached highway 410 when she turned off a side ramp close to the airport. Garcia followed. After about six blocks, she pulled up in front of a two-story office building. Lion One got out of the car, locked it, then walked inside the building.

After a few minutes, Garcia dismounted her bike, then walked inside the building. The lobby looked clean and contained two elevators and a set of stairs. The locater indicated two agencies on the first floor, three on the second. The one that seemed to make the most sense had to be a private detective agency on the second floor, named, "Three C's Detective Agency." Now, who were the three C's? Obviously it could be Cartwright. Would he use his own name? Probably because he wouldn't realize Garcia could trace him here.

She waited a few minutes in the corner. Then when Lion One didn't return to the lobby, Garcia walked up the stairs, moving carefully. The door read Cartwright, Cartwright, and Connor. Now who the hell could be Connor? Probably Lion One.

The ding of a elevator reaching the second floor sounded. Garcia ducked back into the shadows and looked down at her phone as if checking something. A slender, blond-haired man in a wheelchair rolled out of the elevator and headed toward the door. He looked back and saw Garcia. "Can I help you?"

Garcia had to think fast. "Maybe. My mother told me there is a real estate agency in this building, but I didn't see anything on the locater. She may have been mistaken. Must have gotten it wrong."

"What was the name of the agency?" the man asked.

"Red Hill Realty," rolled out of Garcia's mouth. She wasn't sure where it came from but sounded good. At least she hoped it did.

"I'm afraid you've got the wrong building," the man said. "I'm Frank Cartwright, and have been here for five years and never heard of any Red Hill Realty in this building or in the entire neighborhood. I'm afraid your mother gave you a bum steer."

Garcia had to laugh. "My mother has the tendency to get confused so I'm not surprised, but thank you anyway. By the way, what do you do here?"

"My brother and I have the private detective agency here along with a friend who just left."

Garcia glanced out the window. She didn't want either of the other two coming back while she was talking to this guy. "Ah, what sort of cases do you handle?"

Cartwright smiled up at her. "You're probably wondering how a guy in a wheelchair can be a private dick."

Garcia smiled back. "Busted. Sorry, guess it's a cliché. Guy in a wheelchair always sits behind a desk?"

"Yeah, at least you admit it. Most people think it but don't say anything."

Garcia took a couple of steps forward. "I've had a lot of friends in the military who got all screwed up from an IED and other treats in the Middle East and had to make a new path. I happened to be guarding a convoy when one blew. Lucky as hell. They picked all kinds of crap out of my ass and my legs. My right arm didn't work right, but my legs kept working. Just lucky as hell."

"The Medevac system was super after I got hit," Cartwright said. "Flew me to Europe, then back to Walter Reed. Did it in warp speed. Reed was great. But then the VA really screwed me over. Made me wait for surgery, then fucked it up. That's why I ended up in this chair. And I still have to fight them for benefits. Would you believe it?"

Footsteps on the stairs, then the same voice again. "Now you know, Garcia. What are you going to do about it?"

Garcia didn't need to turn around to know who said those words. She turned, and as she suspected, he stood there with a Glock in his right hand pointed directly at her.

"What the hell are you doing?" Frank Cartwright called up from his chair. "This woman is just looking for a real estate agency."

"Oh, so that's what you're looking for."

"Not actually, Paul. It is Paul Cartwright isn't it?"

"Guilty as charged. You're smarter than I gave you credit for."

"I'm not sure I was so smart, because right now you seem to be holding all the aces."

"Well, why don't we head into our offices and talk this over. That's what you wanted to do anyway isn't it. Get into our offices."

"What the hell is going on?" Frank asked.

"It seems that Colonel Garcia has seen through my little charade today, which is certainly not good for us. Course I don't believe it's good for her either."

***

Eagle followed Kinsey through the door into the terminal. Each of them were soaked to the skin and wrapped in a blanket like all of the other hostages. His heart beat fast and he was sweating in spite of the cold.

He glanced around the terminal, then whispered, "All we have to do is to get through the FBI briefing and their questions. Then we'll be free to go." He paused for a moment. "Now you do have your cover story straight, don't you?"

Kinsey whispered through clenched teeth. "Quit treating me like a little kid. I'm not your kid, I'm a full grown adult with brains so knock it off. I don't ask you if you're ready. I trust you will be ready for whatever falls on us, so quit. You're making me nervous. Maybe I should be worried about you. Should I?"

"Okay, I'm sorry. You're right. I'm nervous myself. So much is riding on the next few minutes. If we can get through the debriefing without any problems, and all of the others do the same, we're home free. Once we're out of here, no one can catch us. No one."

She put her hand on his arm. "Now, this will go smoothly. No reason they should suspect us of anything more than choosing a really bad time to ride the Staten Island Ferry."

That comment made Eagle smile. "Okay, here we go. It's almost over."

The two followed a group of about 25 passengers into a large room. They were divided into male and female, then led into a dressing room where teams of people stood ready with tape measures and clothing.

They fit Eagle with a tan shirt, underwear, pants, a light jacket, and even a pair of dock siders which almost fit him perfectly. When he returned to the main terminal area, he spotted Kinsey standing in a far corner. She was wearing a pair of jeans, white shirt and sandals. Wet hair hanging straight to her shoulders.

She stood at a table nibbling on a sandwich and drinking a soft drink. He remembered now he hadn't eaten in almost 24 hours. The food looked good.

When Eagle reached the table, a woman in a white and blue outfit with the words Red Cross stenciled across the chest smiled up at him. "What an experience. You must be really hungry."

"I am," Eagle replied. "All of this food looks wonderful. Thank you so much for putting it together for us."

"It's the least we can do after all that you've been through." She pointed at a large pot. "I suggest you start with a bowl of soup. We have chicken noodle or tomato. It'll warm you from the inside, and I'm sure will hit the spot after all that cold water. Also we have coffee, tea, or hot chocolate."

"Sounds wonderful." Eagle took the tray she offered and joined Kinsey at a table in the corner. Famished, he wolfed down the soup, crackers, and bread, then sat back and sipped from his cup of coffee.

A short, slender man in a blue suit stepped to a microphone. Eagle whispered to Kinsey, "We need to get out of here and we need to do it quickly before they start asking too many questions."

"Good evening," the man said. "My name is Frank Tomlinson. I'm the New York City Police Commissioner. We are all so glad you all made it out safely. You've just gone through a terrible experience and you need to know we were all worried about you. What we'd like to do is talk to you briefly, then ask each of you individually a few questions before you join your families in the waiting room. They are waiting excitedly for you, so this won't take long."

Tomlinson reviewed what they knew so far about the incident. "We have a number of agents who will come to each of your tables. Please tell them anything you remember about the incident. This will help us put together a time line of what happened. So please give us as much information about the individuals who did this as you can remember. No detail is too small. It will help us fit together the big picture. I know you are exhausted so we will be quick."

A tall, blond-haired woman stepped over to their table. "Good evening. Welcome back. I'm FBI Agent Tara Fairchild. As Commissioner Tomlinson said, we know you've just had a very traumatic time."

"Thank you," Eagle said. "I'll have to say I for one am exhausted."

"I only have a few questions for you, then we'd like each of you to talk individually to one of our counselors before you're released to meet with your families. We appreciate your time and focus. I will be taping this discussion so we can use it to piece together exactly what happened."

Heads nodded around the table. Eagle tried to think of a way to get the hell out of there without raising any interest. He had to be careful. Very careful.

"When did you first know there was a problem?" Fairchild asked.

Kinsey raised her hand.

"What is your name?" Fairchild asked.

"Ann. Ann Stewart."

Eagle could have brained her for volunteering anything, but he couldn't risk saying anything without raising the suspicion of the agent. At least Kinsey remembered to provide a false name. This would lead the agents in the wrong direction.

"First, an announcement came over the loudspeaker the ferry had to stop for a few minutes," Kinsey said. "The announcement didn't raise any concerns among the passengers, but when they said they were going to come around and collect all of the cellphones, it raised red flags in my mind."

Eagle decided to get involved. Could be the best course of action. "As soon as they said they were collecting cell phones, we all became worried. You could hear murmured comments and concerns."

"I can understand your worry," Fairchild said. "Now what is your name?"

Eagle gave a false name. He didn't have any ID so the agent couldn't confirm what he said. "We really got worried when one of the crew fired a shot in the air after one of the passengers refused to give up his cell phone. This seemed to confirm a possible hijacking attempt. I was scared and so were many of the passengers around me. One of the passengers even fainted."

"Do you know who she was?" Fairchild asked.

Eagle shook his head. "Sorry, I was busy trying to figure out what was happening."

"Did you see any of their faces?" Fairchild asked.

"I didn't." Eagle looked at Kinsey. "Did you?"

She shook her head.

"Could you describe them?" Fairchild said.

"Sure," Kinsey replied. "I never did figure out how many there were. I think I saw about four different ones. From what I could tell, two men and two women. They all seemed pretty big to me, and they wore hats and masks which covered their faces."

"How about voice?"

Eagle got an idea. "The one man I heard spoke in heavily accented English. I couldn't tell where he was from. Sorry. I'm not very good with language."

"I understand," Fairchild replied. "You experienced a traumatic time."

"That man definitely spoke English," Kinsey said. "Even though accented, I could understand him. Also, they wore military uniforms. No name tags or identification."

"Could you tell if they wore US field uniforms?"

"Sorry, but I couldn't."

Agent Fairchild asked a few more questions When she finished, Fairchild stood and pointed toward the door. "After you reach the other room, your family, if they are here, will be waiting for you. Otherwise we have representatives who can arrange transportation to wherever you want to go."

Eagle took a deep breath and forced himself to remain calm. "Thank you very much for all your kindness. As you can imagine, we want to get out of here, go home, and take a long hot shower, then go out and get something to eat and drink."

Leading Kinsey to the door, he waited for another agent to open it. People were yelling, flash bulbs popping. They found themselves with microphones stuck in their faces. Eagle raised his hands over his face and kept moving. One of the police officers yelled at the reporters, "Please move back. All of these passengers have had enough trauma. Please leave them alone for now."

Eagle took another deep breath. They were almost through this maze. If only their luck could hold for another few minutes, they'd be out of the madness and free. His heart beat rapidly. Yes, they had made it. Soon they would be gone so no one would ever find them.

Eagle turned toward one of the escalators and stopped dead in his tracks, the smile dying on his face. There stood the bitch friend of Kinsey's. The one Kinsey supposedly had taken care of. What the hell was her name. Kelly, yes, Kelly. She was supposed to be dead. He never should have trusted her. Never. They were in big trouble. He had to get rid of the bitch and do it right away. Before she gave up Kinsey. Maybe she already had.

He turned back to Kinsey and nodded his head.

Her eyes opened wide when she saw Laura, her mouth falling open.

"You bitch," Eagle hissed. "We're all fucked."

He stormed off, pulling her past the reporters all trying to get photos of each of them and shouting questions.

29

San Antonio, Thursday, 8:00 p.m.

Paul Cartwright led Garcia into an adjoining office and pushed the door shut with his foot. "Sit the fuck down."

"And if I decide to stay standing."

Cartwright pushed her toward a chair. "Sit the fuck down. And I mean it."

Garcia lurched back and fell into the chair, banging her elbow against the arm. She looked up at him, biting her lip to stop from telling him to go fuck himself. *Keep it a little light.* "I didn't take you for the cave man approach with women. You looked like you had more maturity than that."

"You don't know anything about me. And I planned to keep it that way."

"Yeah, I do know a lot about you. When we were in the Alamo, I took you for basically a good guy who was on a mission to help his fellow veterans screwed by the system. I respected the guy. What the hell happened to him?"

"Goddamn it, you couldn't leave it alone. Had to keep pushing. Couldn't just back off and head back to all the big comfortable chairs in Washington. What the hell am I supposed to do with you now since you've found me and my brother?"

She smiled up at him. "Kinda pushed you in a corner didn't I. Can't let me go, can you. You know me well enough to know I won't let it drop. No harm, no foul. Not in me. So tough shit, Paul. You can't let me go and you won't kill me."

"What the hell makes you think I won't kill you? You're going to blow the whistle on me. Send me to jail. Maybe my brother to jail also. And I can't let it happen. A bunch of real motivation."

"Paul, you're not that kind of guy. I know it. Otherwise I wouldn't have let you trap me in here. I'd have called the Feds and brought a ton of backup. But I didn't want to do it. I thought maybe between the two of us we could figure something out."

"I need some time to think about this. Get up. You're going in the closet. Make a bunch of noise, and I'll have to bang you over the head, something I wouldn't like to do."

"Really," Garcia replied. "Really?"

"Yeah, really. Now get up and start moving."

As she stood, she heard another voice. Frank Cartwright rolled into the room.

He sat in his chair as before, but he had a gun pointed right at her. "You thought you were so goddamn smart. Didn't you. Figured the cripple would never figure it out. You're no better than the rest of the pricks around here. Well, that ends now."

"Wait a minute, Frank," Cartwright said. "Put the gun down. We need to figure out what to do with her."

"I know exactly what to do with her. She blows through Iraq, comes out without a scratch and thinks she can push everybody else around. Just another damn bitch who stayed in the background and let the rest of us take the hits. Never thought about all those guys stuck in wheelchairs for the rest of their lives. Well, no more. I want justice."

"Stop it, Frank. Let me take care of this."

"Bull shit. You were going to take care of everything. Figured I couldn't handle it. Well, I'm going to handle it right now. Get away from her. I'm going to blow her goddamn head off, then we'll take her out and bury her on the farm."

Cartwright took a step toward his brother. "Don't do it, Frank. We've got to think this thing through. So far we haven't hurt anyone. Murder isn't in the room yet."

Garcia glanced around, trying to figure out what she should do. *Could dive toward the left, behind the desk. Damn, no weapon. Locked in the bike. Not smart at all.*

"This is for all those miserable bastards out there."

Cartwright yelled, "No, Frank," and dove in front of Garcia as the gun barked, the noise deafening. The force of the bullet pushed him into Garcia.

Garcia caught him, then pushed Cartwright over toward his brother. She ducked down and crawled toward the brother, sure he was going to shoot her too. But he just stared at his brother's body on the floor, dumb stuck.

Garcia reached over and grabbed the pistol.

Frank Cartwright started to scream. "Paul, what the hell did you do? Paul, I love you."

Garcia turned back to Cartwright. Blood flowed from his chest.

She laid him on the floor and tore open his shirt, his chest a pool of blood. Reaching in her pocket, she pushed in 911. Gave the operator the address, then called Agent Ryan as she ripped off part of her shirt and stuffed it over the wound. It looked bad.

***

Eagle reached back and grabbed Kinsey's hand, then pulled her through the doorway before some reporter could take her picture and start asking questions. One thing they didn't need was fucking publicity. Kinsey had already screwed it up for all of them. Just wait until Cartwright heard what she had done. He'd be crazy.

She glanced up at him. "Stop. What are you doing? You're hurting me."

"Just keep moving," he hissed through clenched teeth. "Your friend, the one you told me you took care of is right there. You've got to duck down or she may see you."

"You're nuts to make a scene. I saw her, but doing what you're doing is not going to help. All you're going to do is draw attention to us. Last thing we need."

They reached the outside. Eagle took a deep breath. He figured once they made it here, they'd be safe. Now things were all screwed up, and it was Kinsey's fault.

"Eagle, over here."

Eagle turned to see their friend who was waiting for them as planned. They should have been able to make a run for it. Now they had to take care of the woman first. Damn Kinsey, he could just beat the shit out of her. But no time for that.

He whispered to Robin. "We need to get out of here right now."

Robin turned. "Follow me."

They wove their way down the stairs and out to the street, crammed with people. "I had to park the car two blocks away. The mob scene here is crazy. Cardinal is waiting with the car."

Eagle nodded. "Do you have a weapon with you?"

"What do you need a weapon for? We've got to get out of here before anymore press takes your fucking picture."

"Dammit," Eagle said, "do you have a weapon with you?"

"No way," Robin answered. "I had to pass through security to get to where I did. If I'd brought a weapon with me, I'd be in the lockup. What the hell are you talking about?"

"Call Cardinal and have him bring a weapon here. Right now. I'll explain later."

Robin took her phone out of her pocket and pushed a number. She whispered into the phone, then put it away. "He's on the way. What's wrong?"

Kinsey motioned for Robin to lean toward her. "I fucked up. One of the members of my college soccer team traveled on the ferry. I think she knows who I am. Eagle told me I had to kill her, but I couldn't do it." She started to tear up. "How can I shoot someone in cold blood?"

Robin stared at Kinsey. "Oh, shit, we do have a problem."

"Yeah," Kinsey said, "and her dad works for some big shit in the government. We're cooked."

Eagle wanted to slug Kinsey. "No, we're not. You're going to go back and finish the job. We can't let her live."

Kinsey started to cry. "I can't do it. I can't."

"Stop it. You can and you will."

"No."

He slapped her across the face so hard she fell to the ground. People stopped and stared.

"Stop it, you two," Robin said. "We need to get out of here." She helped Kinsey up. "Sorry folks, a disagreement. I'll straighten it out."

Robin led both of them down the street, walking quickly.

***

Garcia knelt next to Cartwright, waiting for the cops and EMTs. She prayed they'd hurry. Her shirt material kept getting redder and redder, even though she continued to push on it.

Frank Cartwright sat in his chair, head bowed, sobbing.

She heard the sirens. Stood and looked out the window. Two police cars and an ambulance roared down the street and squealed to a stop. Two police officers jumped out of the first car.

She waved and yelled at them. "We're up here. A man's been shot. Hurry with those EMTs." She called again. "For God sakes, up here. Hurry. A man's been shot and he's bleeding really bad."

She turned back to Frank Cartwright, who still had his head down in the chair, sobbing. Her head ached and her ears echoed from the gunshot. In a way, she felt sorry for Frank. He would never forgive himself for what he'd done. Course if Paul hadn't jumped in the way, she'd be on the floor, bleeding and the brother probably wouldn't give a damn. *Well, fuck him.*

She heard footsteps on the stairs, then two police officers hurried into the room, guns drawn, Agent Ryan right behind them. Garcia raised her hands, waving her military ID.

"Rene Garcia. I've been working with Agent Ryan." She pointed toward Paul Cartwright. "The man on the floor has been shot. The guy in the wheelchair shot him. I've taken his gun."

One officer swung his gun toward the brother.

Garcia pointed at Frank Cartwright. "He's the brother. Take him into custody."

Ryan pulled her aside. "You okay?"

Garcia shook her head. "Not worth a shit. Paul Cartwright is a good guy. Got screwed up in the head and pulled that caper at the Alamo. Trying to help his brother and all the other wounded vets who he feels aren't getting good care."

Two EMTs hurried into the room.

The female EMT knelt on the floor next to Cartwright. She removed Garcia's shirt and looked at the wound. "Shit, this is bad. Looks like the bullet might have punctured a lung."

She took a wad of cloth and covered the wound. "Call the hospital, tell them we need a chopper. The chopper can land across the street in a lot. Try and get a surgeon on the chopper. This man needs help right away."

Garcia started blankly at Cartwright. *Goddamn Paul, why. Why did it go this way.* If she hadn't been a smart-ass and come down here, this wouldn't have happened.

"Come on," Ryan said, "let's go downstairs. Let the locals handle the scene. They'll want a statement from you."

"Okay." She let herself be led by Ryan down the stairs and out to one of the squad cars.

A man in a black suit and tie sat in the car. I'm Sergeant Lopez from the San Antonio Police Department. I understand you've been working with Agent Ryan. How did you get here?"

Garcia steeled herself to tell the story. She told about how she caught up with Paul Cartwright. How his brother shot Paul, meaning the bullet for her.

Lopez took notes.

"Look, I'm an army MP," Garcia said. "I understand all you need to have for a murder investigation. But for now, I'd like to follow Paul to the hospital. He saved my life."

Lopez put his pad away. "Go ahead. We'll catch up with you at the hospital."

30

Whitehall Ferry Terminal, Thursday, 9:45 p.m.

Zack escorted Shelia, Laura, and his mother through the crowds and out of the Ferry Terminal toward the subway entrance. It took time to get through the mobs of people yelling and pushing. He planned to take all of them to Chester's apartment. They should be safe there.

As they crossed the street, Laura leaned up and whispered to her dad, "We need to talk. I don't know what to do."

Zack leaned down to hear her. "What's up, honey?"

"You've got to promise me you won't tell anyone what I'm about to say."

"Sure, you know you can trust me."

"Promise?"

Zack began to wonder what he was promising. "Promise."

"Okay, here goes. I know one of the hijackers."

Zack couldn't believe what he was hearing. "Say that again."

Shelia and his mother turned around.

"What's the matter?" Shelia called.

"Every thing's okay," Laura said. "I want to talk to dad for a moment. You two go ahead."

"Okay," Ethel said. "We'll walk slowly."

Laura turned back to her dad after the others had moved out of earshot. "When I was waiting to board on Staten Island, I saw one of my soccer teammates."

Zack kept quiet. He had an uneasy feeling where this might be headed and wasn't sure what to do about it.

"I talked to Kinsey briefly. She's a leader on the team, and I think it would help me get in with the team if I knew Kinsey better."

"You can pick her out in a crowd?" Zack asked.

"Oh, sure. After I got on the boat and the hijackers took over, she changed outfits."

Zack noticed that Shelia and his mother had stopped and were talking, obviously waiting for them. "What are you planning to do?"

Laura started to cry. "I don't know, Dad. I don't know. I don't want to rat her out, but what she did was really bad. I don't know if anyone died. It's a mess."

"Does she know you know?"

Laura nodded. "She knows, and I suspect she's told some of the others."

"We need to get you into some kind of protective custody now. They may come after you."

"That's what I'm worried about. She made me jump off the boat and fired a couple of rounds in the air."

"We need to move. You may be all that stands between them and freedom. This entire operation was well organized. I don't think the police have any clue as to who's behind it other than the name Forgotten Warriors . Not going to help much."

"I know. I know."

Zack took her arm. "Listen Laura, I know you don't want me to do anything without your okay, but we're dealing with your safety and maybe the safety of the rest of us. We can't wait. They are probably planning to come after you. May even be on the way."

"I guess you're right."

"Laura, think about it. We're dealing with long prison sentences, not just for her but the whole group. These people will be desperate. They won't want you to be able to testify against them."

They walked about half a block, neither one saying anything. Zack tried to figure out how to best protect Laura. About to turn around and head back to the terminal to find Tomlinson, he looked up to see a man and a woman walking toward them, both of them in ball caps, sunglasses, and masks. The woman held a pistol in her hand.

"Kinsey," Laura whispered.

Kinsey pointed the pistol at Laura. "You shouldn't have been there."

It all happened in a flash. Zack dove to tackle her, but she was too far away. Two bystanders turned to see what was happening. Screamed. A young man hit the ground.

A man in a blue jacket and New York Yankee baseball cap had shoved into the shooter and pushed her arm up, making the shot go harmlessly into the air. The pistol fell to the ground.

Zack pushed himself up off the sidewalk and moved toward the two of them.

Kinsey and her partner turned and started to run, pushing their way through the crowd. A tall man tried to grab them, but the woman named Kinsey hit him in the face.

Zack started to go after the two, then looked around to thank the man in the blue jacket, but he was gone.

He ran after Kinsey and her partner.

***

He stepped inside the first shop he saw, luckily a men's clothing store. Once inside, he stopped and looked through the front window, then asked a sales clerk, "What's going on outside?"

"I don't know," a clerk answered. "Someone fired a pistol. So many guns on the street."

He glanced around, counted three clerks, two men and one woman. All stood in the front of the store, watching the excitement in the the street. He took that opportunity to wander down the aisle toward the back. Looking at various sport coats as he walked, he kept glancing toward the front of the store.

When he reached the rear, he stopped for a few minutes watching the clerks at the front door. None of them were looking his way. He slipped through a curtain and made his way past boxes of merchandise and rows of hanging suits to the back door.

He unlocked the door which opened onto an alley. Looking toward the front once more, he stepped out and shut the door behind him. He heard the wail of sirens and screams of people. A helicopter circled overhead.

Stripping off the jacket, he checked the pockets to make sure there was nothing in them to identify him, then lifted a garbage can cover and placed the jacket inside the can. Hurt to do that because it was his favorite jacket, but it would identify him and he couldn't have that. He took off the Yankees cap and held it in his hand, then dumped it. Moved the Glock under his shirt.

He sauntered about thirty feet down the alley until he reached the street, then turned left and headed away from all the activity. Being careful was how Casey Matheson stayed alive. He wasn't careful today, but he did what he had to do.

***

Zack glanced up to see Kinsey and her partner round a corner. Laura and his mother were both screaming. He called to Shelia, "Take care of them. I'm going after the shooter."

As he ran, he remembered the man in the blue jacket and the Yankee baseball hat. Who was he? Did he just happen by and see the gun or had he been there for some reason? Did Tomlinson have one of his officers shadowing them in case of a threat? Couldn't be, he would have stayed and helped.

Whoever he was or why he was there didn't matter. If he hadn't been there and acted as quickly as he did, Laura would have been shot. Injured. Perhaps even killed.

The thought sent a chill through Zack. *Killed? His Laura? Erase the thought. Focus.*

Checking again, he saw the scarf on the back of the woman's head bobbing about half a block ahead of him. "Stop her," he called, "she shot someone."

Where the hell were all of the cops? Always on every corner in New York City. Now he needed one and no cop around.

He spotted a cop. Yelled, "The woman tried to shoot my daughter. Get on the phone and call the commissioner. A man in a ball cap and sunglasses is with her.

The cop looked at him.

"Woman, name's Kinsey," he yelled again. "Tan coat. Reddish scarf. Half block ahead."

The cop leaned down and spoke into his microphone, then turned and ran behind Zack.

Zack lost the bobbing scarf in the crowd. Shit. Where the hell was she? She had disappeared.

The police officer came up puffing behind him. "What did you say?"

Zack flashed his ID to the officer. "I'm working with Chief Tomlinson on the ferry hijacking. A woman tried to shoot my daughter. One of the hijackers thinks my daughter can identify her. Tomlinson will vouch for me. She ran that way."

"Description."

"Young woman , probably early-twenties. Reddish scarf, tan trench coat. Male, slightly taller. Dropped the gun at the scene. They're running. I've lost them."

"Okay."

"Got to go back. Find my daughter. She needs me."

***

Agent Ryan dropped Garcia off at the front door of the hospital. "I need to get back to the site," Ryan said, "and see what the hell's going on. Let me know when you're done here. I'll send a car to pick you up. The locals still have a load of questions for you. They didn't want to let you go, but I convinced them you needed to get to the hospital."

Garcia tried to smile. "I know. Thanks for everything."

She hustled inside. The information desk stood right in front of her. A slender woman in a blue Red Cross uniform sat behind it. The woman looked up and said, "Good evening, can I help you?"

"My friend was shot a little while ago. The helicopter brought him here. Can you tell me where he'd be?"

"What is his name?"

"Paul Cartwright."

"Oh, my goodness, I'm so sorry to hear that. You know there are so many guns on the street, it's a miracle more people aren't shot."

"Yes. Now can you please tell me where he would be?"

The woman pushed a button on her computer and ran her fingers down the page "Of course, you need to hurry. Here he is. Paul Cartwright. They took him directly to surgery. That's on the fifth floor." She pointed. "The elevators are over there. I certainly hope your friend will be all right."

"I do too." Garcia hurried toward the elevators, calling back over her shoulder, "Thanks."

Garcia stepped off the elevator on the fifth floor and followed the signs to the surgical waiting room. When she reached the double doors, she pushed one open and rushed inside.

A woman in a white dress sat behind the desk. "May I help you?"

"Yes, my friend, Paul Cartwright, was shot about an hour ago, I understand the helicopter delivered him here for surgery."

The woman looked down at a sheet. "Yes, that's right. He arrived about thirty minutes ago and was whisked right into surgery."

"Do you have any idea of his condition?"

"No, I'm sorry I don't." The woman glanced up at her. "Are you family?"

"No," Garcia replied. "Just a friend."

"Your name?"

"Rene Garcia. I'm an army lieutenant colonel investigating the shooting of Paul Cartwright." Garcia figured a little white lie wouldn't hurt. Not at this point.

"I certainly will let the doctor know you're here, Colonel Garcia." She pointed toward a bank of chairs. "You can wait over there. I assume the surgery will take at least a couple of hours."

31

Whitehall Ferry Terminal, Thursday, 10:15 p.m.

Zack hurried back to where Shelia, Ethel and Laura waited. An army of blue uniforms surrounded them, along with ribbons of yellow crime scene tape. When Zack arrived, he gave Laura a hug. "How are you doing?"

"Shaking like mad. Oh, Dad, I was so scared."

"I know, I was scared for you."

One of the officers came up to him. "What's your name?"

Zack dumped a short burst on what had happened. Then he called Fairchild and gave her an update.

"Don't move," she said. "I'll be right there."

Zack had to yell over the crowd. "Bring Tomlinson if you can."

"Will do. Hang tough."

It took Fairchild and Tomlinson about ten minutes to fight their way though the crowd, siren screaming. When they arrived, Zack pulled the two of them aside. "Look, we need to find a quiet place for all of us to talk. Laura is a nervous wreck and so is my mother."

Tomlinson pointed toward his car. "Let's go back to the terminal. We can talk there while the crime scene guys do their thing here. We need statements from any folks who saw something to help us."

With the siren, it only took a few minutes to get back to the terminal building. They hurried up the escalator and into one of the conference rooms. Once they were seated, Tomlinson told one of his staff to set up a guard outside the door, then get coffee and sandwiches.

Zack sat next to Laura and took her hand. He glanced toward Tomlinson. "You need to take it easy on her because she's been through a lot."

Fairchild sat on the other side of the table facing Laura. She took out her note pad. "How are you doing? I'm sorry for all that has happened to you."

Laura wiped away a tear. "I can't believe it. I can't ..."

"I know," Fairchild said, "I know. Can you tell me what happened after you left this building?"

"I told my dad I was so sorry for not saying anything sooner, but I didn't know what to do. Kinsey was a friend, at least I thought she was."

"That's okay, we can't go back," Fairchild said. "Now, take your time and tell me everything."

Laura shared what had happened on the ferry and everything she knew about Kinsey.

Then Zack told Tomlinson and Fairchild about the shooting. "The police on the scene have been scouring the neighborhood looking for Kinsey and her partner." He looked at Laura. "Do you know her last name?"

Laura thought for a moment. "I think it's Cartwright."

When she finished, Fairchild asked, "Why didn't you tell us earlier when we were talking?"

Tears flowed down Laura's face. "I ..., I didn't know what to do. Kinsey wasn't a close friend, but we were teammates on the soccer team. I guess I didn't want to rat her out, but I knew I had to. I wanted to talk with my dad first. Get his advice on how to handle it."

Zack kept his hand on her shoulder. "You're doing great. Keep it up."

"I told my dad about Kinsey, and we started to walk. I could tell he was thinking about what to do next. When I looked up, there she stood, pointing a gun at me. Then she shot at me." Laura started to shake again. "My God, I thought I was dead. Do you know what it feels like? I mean, dead?" She put her head down and began to sob. "And from someone I thought I knew."

Zack patted her back. "It's all right, honey, it's all right. You're safe now. Can you hear me? I'm with you and you're safe."

Zack told them about the man in the blue jacket. He looked at Fairchild and whispered, "If it hadn't been for him, Kinsey would have shot Laura."

Fairchild's eyes went wide. "What man in the blue jacket?"

"Sorry. A man in a blue jacket and Yankees ball cap must have been standing next to the woman, this Kinsey. He knocked her arm up in the air and the shot went wild. If he hadn't been there ..."

Zack had to stop talking. "I couldn't get to this Kinsey in time. We owe her life to him. I couldn't find him to thank him. Couldn't find him."

Fairchild stood. "I'm so sorry Zack, and you too, Laura. You've both been through so much. Zack what else can you tell me about the man in the blue jacket? Description? Height, weight, you know the drill?"

Zack thought for a moment. "He was tall, maybe six foot, two inches, probably around 200 pounds. He had on the blue jacket, dark jeans, dark shoes, and a Yankee ball cap pulled down over his face. I couldn't see much about his face. He may have had a beard."

"Do you think he just happened to be there?" Fairchild asked. "You know, maybe a good Samaritan?"

"I don't know," Zack replied. "How else could it be. Do you suppose he knew this was going to happen. Waited there to stop it?"

"I have no idea," Fairchild said, "but if he just happened to be there, it's one hell of a coincidence and as you know I don't believe in those."

"But if not, then who? Who the hell is he? Anyway, I think it's time to get Laura back to Olney's apartment so she can recover."

"I'll get a squad car to take you there," Tomlinson said. "We need to place a twenty-four hour guard on Laura until we find this Kinsey."

Zack turned to his mother. "Why don't you go with Laura. I'd like to stay here and check in with Admiral Steele. See how Garcia is doing and what else is going on."

"That's fine," Ethel replied. "As long as we're well guarded. I'm sure Chester will help also. I need to let him know everything that has happened."

"I'll get out there when I can. Any problems, call me right away."

Tomlinson stood. "Okay, let me get you a car, then I'll arrange for a guard. Then we'll see what New York's finest has found out about this shooter."

***

Governor Mason Harbaugh glanced out the front window of his office as he listened to Arnold Hale rant on his phone. "Have you got all this ferry stuff under control? It's going to look like crap if my future vice president can't get his shit together in his own state. It's only a few weeks to the convention, and I don't want any of damn surprises."

"Don't worry about it," Harbaugh said. "We couldn't crack down too hard because as I understand it, these are veterans protesting their lousy care from the VA. We'll hang the noose around the neck of our incumbent president. Make him responsible for what's happening and why these poor vets are protesting."

Hale chuckled. "That's what I like about you. You're always a step ahead of anyone trying to go after you."

"Don't worry, Mr. President, we'll whip his ass." Harbaugh knew how much the senior senator from the great state of South Carolina loved to be called Mr. President. A little bit of a windbag, but he looked sure to be the nominee and had a good shot to be elected. Harbaurgh needed to ride along.

"Thanks Mason. Be sure and keep me in the loop."

"Will do, Mr. President."

He heard a chuckle on the line as he disconnected the call.

Harbaugh sat there for a moment, then picked up the intercom and called for his chief of staff.

Jensen hurried into the office. "What did Old Iron Sides have to say?"

Harbaugh couldn't help but smile. He loved the nickname Jensen had come up with for Hale. "He's nervous about the ferry hijacking. Worried we'll look weak on terrorism if we can't keep our own ferry lines safe."

"Absolutely. I've already started the PR machine turning out fliers describing how these poor vets are being pushed to desperate measures to try and gain the care they deserve. Hell, the care they've earned by their service and sacrifice."

Harbaugh started to laugh. "Perfect. You sound like you're writing my speech. Now what am I going to do about this pain-in-the-ass Kelly. He's trying to cough up the crap that happened thirty-some years ago. I want you to get with Tomlinson and see where this is going. Is there any risk Kelly may uncover something we don't want him to?"

Jensen stood. "Don't worry, Mister Vice President, I'll take care of it."

Harbaugh nodded. "Good. And keep up the flattery. It'll get you everywhere."

Jensen waved as he hurried out the door.

He's a good man, Harbaugh thought. But if he doesn't jam the Kelly problem in a jar and drop a lid on it, he'll be looking for another job.

***

Garcia heard three rings, then the familiar voice of Admiral Steele's receptionist. "Admiral Steele's office. May I help you?"

"Colonel Garcia. I wonder if I might talk to the boss. We have a new development here."

"He'll be glad you called. He's on a call with Colonel Kelly. Let me tell him you're on the phone. Please wait."

Garcia hear a click, then the sound of Zack Kelly's voice. "If the guy in the blue jacket hadn't been there ..."

"Do we have any idea who he is?" Steele asked.

"None at all."

"Hi, sir, Garcia here. I slipped in on your call."

"Great. I need to find out what you're up to. Go ahead."

"Okay, here goes. As you probably remember, I spent time with the group of vets who took over the Alamo." Garcia went on to summarize what had happened and the near miss she had when Frank Cartwright tried to shoot her.

"Well," Steele said, "you two have had quite a day. What's the current status?"

"Let me take that one from the New York side," Agent Fairchild said. "The hijackers blew up the ferry as it was approaching Liberty Island. Unfortunately, they made a mess of the dock, but as far as I understand, didn't hurt Lady Liberty herself. So far we've had no reports of serious injuries from those who were on the ferry. The problem is we don't know the names and addresses of the people who were on the ferry. No way to track everyone."

"How many have you recovered so far?" Steele asked.

"Two hundred and ninety-seven, apparently a normal number for the morning trip. It may be a while before we know more. Many of the people we rescued had mild cases of hypothermia and were taken to the hospital. As far as we know, none of these people are serious."

"What about the hijackers?" Garcia asked.

Fairchild explained what had happened to Laura. "We have a dragnet out for the woman and her partner. I'm told her name is Kinsey Cartwright, but so far we haven't found anyone matching her description. We don't yet know the name of her partner. Nor have we been able to find the man in the blue jacket. This Kinsey is the key. If we find her, we should be able to use her to lead us to the rest. No doubt why she shot at Laura."

All of a sudden, it hit Garcia. "Did you say the woman's name was Kinsey Cartwright?"

"What Laura told me," Zack replied.

"The man in surgery is Paul Cartwright."

"Interesting," Zack replied. "We found the link between these two incidents. Now what do we do about it?"

"Stay tuned. Paul Cartwright's brother shot him and is in jail. Actually, Paul Cartwright saved my life by jumping in front of a bullet. I'm at the hospital waiting to hear from the doc."

32

Brooklyn, Thursday, 11:00 p.m.

Kinsey hurried up the stairs of the dilapidated apartment building, Eagle and Dog right behind her. Her hands shook so hard she couldn't unlock the door to their room. Tears rolled down her cheeks. How the hell had she gotten herself into this? All she and Paul wanted to do was help Frank and the other vets who'd been screwed by the system. It all went so wrong.

Eagle reached over her shoulder. "Here, give the damn thing to me." He pushed the key into the lock and shoved the door open.

The three stepped inside and Eagle kicked the door shut with his foot. He whirled toward Kinsey. "See what you've done, you fool. We were in the clear until you screwed it up. Now we're going to be on the run and it's all your fucking fault."

Kinsey started to cry all over again.

Dog slapped her face. "Stop it. Being a baby isn't going to help anything. We've got a problem, and we've got to do something about it."

Kinsey placed her hand against her cheek and glared at Dog. "You bitch. Who do you think you are, slapping me?" She stepped forward and punched Dog in the face.

Eagle stepped between them. "Stop it. Both of you. This isn't going to get us anywhere." He switched on the television. They saw Kinsey's picture with a caption over it. *Have you seen this woman? She is armed and should be considered dangerous. Do not approach her. Call the police. She is wanted for attempted murder.*

Dog turned to Kinsey. "Are you satisfied now? We were in the clear. Now you're going to bring all of us down."

"Stop it," Eagle said. "Arguing isn't going to help. It's too late for that. The only way we can get out of this is to get rid of the woman. Even now, if she isn't able to testify, the cops can't prove it was you. You kept your hat down over your face. No one else saw you. No one else knows who you are. You can claim the woman was mistaken. We just need an airtight alibi for where you've been."

"You might have something," Dog said. "How are we going to pull it off?"

"Kinsey can't be the one. She's radioactive and can't be seen anywhere near Kelly."

"I'll do it," Dog said. "They don't know me. Where is this woman?"

Kinsey looked up, brushing tears from her cheeks. "Her name is Laura Kelly. She's staying with a detective in Manhattan. Let me think. She told me his name. Chester something. Chester Olney. Yes, Chester Olney."

"You've got at least one thing going for you," Eagle said. "Your memory."

Dog picked up her computer. "I'll find his address."

Eagle started to pace. "Now what are we going to do? We can't stay here. We've got to figure someone in this building has seen you."

"I don't think so," Kinsey replied. "I spent all my time in the motel on Staten Island. No one saw me enough to remember me." She glanced at Eagle. "You registered us and we paid cash in both places. The best thing for me to do is lay low."

"I agree," Dog said. "The others will be here soon. You've got to stay out of sight until I can get rid of the bitch." She turned to Eagle. "You've got to come with me. I'll probably need some help checking the place out and figuring how to get to her. You know the cops are going to ring the place. It won't be easy but I agree, it's our only chance."

Kinsey stopped and stared at the television. A picture of her brother came on the screen. The reporter's voice filled the room.

"The individual the FBI believes coordinated the incident at the Alamo was shot this afternoon, apparently in an accident by his brother during a face-off with an army Lieutenant Colonel." Garcia's picture came on the screen. "Colonel Garcia was at the office of the Cartwright brothers when there was gunfire and his brother shot Paul Cartwright.

Kinsey cried out. "Paul, my god, Paul."

"Cartwright is currently in surgery," the reporter continued, "but we can't get a report on his status."

"On, no, not Paul. Frank shot Paul? I'm going to San Antonio. Get a flight out. Kill the Colonel who caused Paul to get shot."

"You're in no condition to go to San Antonio," Eagle said. "You need to lay low."

"What are you talking about?" Kinsey snapped. "You just said I need to get out of here. Let Dog go after Laura Kelly, and I'll take one of those boats across the water, and get out of here through Newark. I'll wear a hat and sunglasses, and I've got a fake passport. I'll be out of your hair. After I kill the bitch who screwed up Paul, I'll get lost in the hills of central Texas. I know the area. Spent my life there. Won't be a problem."

"I think she's right," Dog said. "Let her go and let me do my thing. Maybe we'll get out of this mess once and forever."

Eagle thought for a moment. "Okay, maybe this will work."

***

Zack Kelly paced around the command post at the ferry terminal, exhausted but unable to relax.

Shelia reached over and pulled his arm. "Stop it. You're making me nervous. Why don't you decide what you're going to do and do it? Quit with all the pacing."

"Good point," Zack walked over to where Tomlinson sat at a desk, a cell phone at his ear.

Tomlinson put his hand over the speaker part and said, "Sorry. I'm on a conference call with the Governor, then his chief of staff wants to talk with me."

"Understand. What I'd like to do is head back to your office. Get everything in the case file about my dad out and see if we've missed something. Nothing more I can do here."

"Makes sense," Tomlinson replied. "After I get off this damn call, I'll phone over and tell my receptionist to gather everything for you. We went over it a dozen times and found nothing. But you may come up with something."

Zack wondered what Tomlinson might be hiding. He'd kept back some of the files. Hadn't told Zack about the Internal Affairs file. Why? "Sounds good. I'll go nuts if I sit here any longer."

"I can see that." Tomlinson held up his finger. "Just a minute. Here's the chief. Let me put it on speaker."

Zack stood near the table and recognized the voice of Harbaugh's chief of staff.

"Tomlinson," the man said, "are we on speaker?"

"Yes, sir."

"Who else is there?"

"Colonel Kelly."

"Take me off speaker."

From his side of the conversation which was not more than a bunch of yes sirs, it sounded as if Tomlinson was getting his butt reamed.

Finally Tomlinson put down his cell and shrugged his shoulders. "I will never understand politicians."

***

He hurried down Third Avenue, unlocked the front door, and took the steps two at a time. Unlocking the two dead bolts, he made sure the string had not been disturbed.

He hated to rush, but he had to get inside and see what the television was showing. As he listened, he walked over and reached under the bed, pulling out the police scanner and turned it on low. What the hell was going on? Why the shooter?

He watched the television and saw a picture of the woman who had tried to shoot Laura Kelly. He blazed her picture in his brain, then told himself to settle down. Develop a plan. That's how he stayed alive.

He stood and began pacing around the room. Apparently Laura Kelly was the one person who knew this woman. Seemed to be the only person who could identify the shooter. A dangerous position to be in. He knew how dangerous. His life.

A chill blew through him. If Laura couldn't identify the woman, the state would have no case. All she'd need would be an alibi. The cops would give Laura protection, but they couldn't protect her like he would.

He'd heard they were staying at Chester Olney's apartment. He could take the red line out to Olney's. He'd have to take the yellow line and transfer. Double check to see if anyone followed him.

He could hide in the woods across from Olney's place. No one would see him there and he could be ready for any developments.

Hurrying over to the bed, he picked up his Glock. Maybe he'd better take the stun gun just in case. Putting on another jacket and ball cap, he stepped out into the hall. He stopped, fixed the locks, tightened the string, and took a deep breath. Slow and steady. That's how Casey Matheson stayed alive. *Take deep breaths. Slow and steady.*

***

Rene Garcia sat next to Paul Cartwright's bed in the surgical intensive care ward. An oxygen mask covered his face and tubes seemed to come out of every conceivable place on his body. Brief moans seemed to interrupt his sleep.

Once in a while he thrashed around on the bed. When he did, Garcia reached over to pat his arm and talk softly, trying to encourage him. Poor bastard must be in real pain. Probably best for him to sleep.

She chuckled thinking she might sing to him, but sadly her voice sounded like shit. Always out of tune. Forget any singing.

The nurse hurried in every twenty minutes or so to check all of his tubes and vital signs. She always smiled at Garcia as she zipped back out again.

Garcia stepped out into the hall to call Agent Ryan. She nodded to the guard on duty as she walked down to the main hallway by the elevator so her cell wouldn't mess with any the medical equipment.

Pushing in his number, she heard, "Ryan."

"It's Garcia. What's going on?"

"The locals have booked Paul Cartwright's brother. What a sad case. Frank Cartwright is a basket case. He can't believe he shot his own brother. They have him on a suicide watch. Not much else of importance."

"I almost feel sorry for him," Garcia said. "But then I remember who he wanted to kill."

"True. We've rounded up a number of vets who were friends of Cartwright's. I suspect some of them were in the Alamo with him. We have to break one of them, but it shouldn't take too long. Once we do that, it should be pretty easy to round up the rest."

"How much damage to the Alamo?" Garcia asked.

"One of the pieces of good news. They must have set the explosion for maximum smoke and noise with minimal damage. Some reps from the Alamo committee are checking things out, but I don't think it will take much to repair it. I don't believe the vets intended to damage the Alamo. They just wanted to make a point."

"That's the way I see it too," Garcia said. "I sat in on a conference call and found out the woman who shot at Laura Kelly was named Kinsey Cartwright. Agent Fairchild from my team is checking it out, but I suspect there is a link between Paul and Kinsey Cartwright."

"She is his sister and Frank's too," Ryan said. "Fairchild called me about forty-five minutes ago and gave me the news."

"Have they caught her yet?" Garcia asked.

"Not that I've heard. I'll check in with Fairchild in a little while. How is Paul Cartwright doing?"

"The docs moved him down to the surgical intensive care from the recovery room about three hours ago. The police have a guard outside the door of the room, but the nurses are letting me stay in his room until he wakes up. Ah, I kinda threw your name around to get some priority."

Ryan laughed. "Probably one of the few times my name has ever done anyone much good."

"It rang the bell here. I'll let you know as soon as he comes out of all the pain medication and can talk."

"Do you need me to send a car over? You've been there quite a while."

"Nah, I don't think so. This is probably the best place for me now. Admiral Steele asked me to keep him apprised of the status here, and Zack is doing the same thing from New York. Besides, I owe the guy. He took a bullet meant for me. I'm sure Frank Cartwright would have gotten me." Garcia shivered. "He definitely meant business."

"Okay. You've got my number. Give me a call if you need anything."

"Will do. And thanks."

Garcia walked back into Cartwright's room. Paul slept soundly and appeared to be thrashing around less. She wandered over to the window and looked out. Man, what a close call. Makes a believer out of how a person's life can change in a minute.

She turned back to the bed and walked over to sit. Now, Paul, wake the hell up and let's talk.

33

Upper Manhattan, Wednesday, 11:45 p.m.

Dog watched as Eagle drove slowly by Chester Olney's building. Things were quiet. Not many people on the street.

"Shit," Eagle said, "look at the cop. Right there at the front door."

"What did you expect? Someone tried to kill their little princess. They sure as hell are going to try hard to protect her. We just have to get by him."

He pulled away from the curb. "What are you going to do?"

"An old trick I used once before. Let's circle the building and pull up the next block over. I think I saw a pizza place in the middle of the block."

"So now you're hungry? Now, for God's sake? This late? With all the crap going on?"

"Just shut up and drive the fucking car. Let me do the thinking."

They drove around the block until Dog spotted the pizza parlor. She checked out the name. "Okay, just what I need. Let's go."

"Where?"

"About two blocks south and one block over."

"What the hell?"

"Just do what I tell you." Dog pulled out her phone. "Come on, for God sakes, let's go. We've got stuff we have to do and don't have all night."

As they pulled around the corner, Dog pushed in a number on her phone. "Hi, this is Cynthia at 8419 Riverside Drive. I'd like to order three pizzas, two pepperoni and one sausage."

She listened. "Yes, that's right. 8419. My phone is 246-3174. How long will it take? We're really hungry and I heard you guys were super fast. Twenty minutes. Sounds good. I'll be waiting."

Eagle stopped two houses up from 8419. "What now?"

"We wait."

About twenty minutes later, a Honda with a pizza sign on top pulled up in front of the building two blocks north of Olney's. The driver jumped out and reached into the back seat, extracting a red bag. He slammed the door and headed around the car, then started up toward the building. As he came around the car, Dog slipped out and walked down the sidewalk. Looking both ways, she ran up behind him.

He must have heard her and as he started to turn around, she hit him over the head with her pistol. He dropped to the ground like a rock. She reached down and picked up the red bag. She had what she needed.

She ran back to their car and reached in the window. "Okay, you follow the Honda to Olney's condo building. Stay a couple of houses back and watch for me. When I come out of Olney's building, pick me up and we'll get the hell out of town."

Dog jumped in the idling Honda. She pulled out around Eagle's car and started down the street. When she reached Olney's building, she stopped the car and jumped out. Hurrying toward the front door of the building, she reached up and pulled the ball cap over her eyes.

As she expected, the police officer stopped her. "I'm sorry, but you can't go inside here without authorization."

"Hey, someone in number 804 called in an order for three pizzas. I need to hurry up and get them upstairs so they don't get cold. It's my ass if the pizzas are delivered cold, and as you can see," she raised her jacket, "I ain't got enough ass to spare."

The officer laughed. "Well if you say so, but your ass looks mighty fine to me."

Dog laughed. "I just need to hustle up there, then get back to the shop and pick up another order. That's the way I make my money."

The officer opened the door for her. "Okay, but keep working on that cute ass."

Dog laughed again, then hurried inside. Men were so easy to manipulate. She stopped a minute to check the building locater then hurried to the stairwell.

***

A police officer dropped Zack at One Police Plaza. He hurried up the front stairs of the building, opened the door and stepped inside. Walking over to the police officer on duty, he pulled out his military ID and showed it to him. "Chief Tomlinson sent me over to check out some files."

"Yes, sir," the duty officer replied. "His receptionist called down and said you would be coming in. Must have been quite a time at the ferry terminal earlier this evening."

"You bet." Zack put his ID back in his billfold. "One I hope to never live through again."

"I understand your daughter rode on the ferry. One of the kidnappers tried to kill her. God, damn awful."

Zack turned toward the elevator. "A close call, but she's at a safe place now and under guard."

When he reached the right floor, he headed over to Tomlinson's office. He couldn't get over the view of the river. Looked so peaceful late at night.

He opened the door to Tomlinson's office, and the receptionist waved and pointed toward a desk. "Hi, Colonel Kelly. You're still at it. I retrieved all of the files and put them on the desk over there. Most of these papers are old so some of them are in pretty rough shape."

"I understand," Zack said. "Thanks for your help."

"You'll have to be careful as you pick them up and move them around. Most of the papers are legible. Let me know if you need anything else. You may remember the coffee pot is over there. Go help yourself. You'll probably need a fresh cup after the time you've had. How is your daughter?"

"Probably sound asleep by now. I want to thank you for getting all of these papers together. It helps a lot to not have to run around and gather everything myself."

"It's the least we can do. Let me know if there is anything else."

"I'm sure it will be fine," Zack replied. "And thanks again."

"You're welcome." She chuckled. "Happy hunting."

Zack drew a cup of coffee, rubbed his eyes, took a big swig, and sat down at the desk. He shuffled through the stack, reading each page carefully, then either setting it aside or placing it in a separate pile he would review again. He wasn't exactly sure what he was looking for, but thought he'd know it once he found it.

Time passed. He checked his watch and realized he'd been at it over an hour. Stood, stretched, and walked over for a refill of coffee. He stopped and looked out at the river.

"Isn't that a beautiful sight?" the receptionist said.

"Nice and so peaceful early in the morning."

"I love the view. Makes the night shift more enjoyable."

Zack stretched again, then sat down and pored through the rest of the papers. He had set one stack aside and began to work his way through the same stack again. Something tickled at him. What the hell was it?

He studied the forensics one more time, then he saw it. What had been bothering him was the angle the bullet had entered.

He picked up the phone and called Agent Fairchild.

"Fairchild."

"Zack Kelly. I'm over at police headquarters going through the file about the night my dad was shot and killed. Something in the forensics looks suspicious me. Could you have your lab take a look? I'd really appreciate it."

"Sure. I'll check with our lab here in New York. Here's the address. Maybe you can drop it off right away. I'll tell them to put a rush on it."

"Thanks." Zack hung up. *Could it be so simple?*

***

Casey Matheson pulled up the collar on his tan windbreaker, then walked up to the police officer on duty at the door, quickly flashing a badge. Officers never look too closely at another person with a badge. They assume he's a fellow officer in blue.

"Hey, what's up?" the officer asked.

"Not too much." Casey slipped the badge back into his pocket. "I happened to be in the area and Commissioner Tomlinson asked me to come over to check on things."

The mention of the commissioner's name caused the man to straighten. "Is everything okay?" Casey asked. "No one in or out?"

"All quiet."

"You're sure. Nothing going on."

The officer laughed. "Nothing except a cute chick delivering pizzas. What a character."

Casey spotted the danger immediately. A young woman. "How long ago?"

"Maybe fifteen or twenty minutes."

Crap. He ought to ream the guy out for his carelessness, but there wasn't time. "I'd better go up and check things out."

"No need," the cop replied. "She was a cutie. Wouldn't hurt a fly."

But Casey didn't hear the last of his comments as he brushed by the officer and raced for the elevator.

***

When Dog reached the eighth floor, she stepped out of the stairwell and checked each of the numbers for the right door. She stopped for a moment to catch her breath. Uneasy about taking the elevator, she had run up eight floors and was breathing hard. She couldn't look winded when Laura answered the door. Had to look like a real delivery person.

Hoping Kelly would be alone so there would be no collateral damage, she rang the bell. Then she shifted the pizza boxes and pulled out her pistol. Kept it under the boxes, available, so no one could see it and be alerted.

Dog heard a click, then an older woman opened the door. *Shit, collateral damage. Why the hell didn't Kelly answer? Easy in and out. Fucking Kinsey. Her screwup required all of this.*

Dog pulled her hat lower over her face and smiled. "Good evening. I have a pizza order for this address."

"Oh, my, I'm sorry," the woman said. "No one here ordered any pizzas. I was just getting ready to make some tea."

"Well, someone must have ordered pizzas. I got the order at the store." She looked up at the number on the door. "That's right, apartment number 804."

"You must have the wrong number."

Dog had to cut this crap and get out of here. She didn't want to alert the woman and cause more problems. "Let me see. Is there someone here by the name of Laura?"

"Oh yes, she's my granddaughter. But she's sound asleep. Exhausted."

Dog's heart beat like a jackhammer and her pulse pounded. "Look, could you check with her. Kids like pizzas. Please, I've got other pizzas to deliver before they get cold and I lose my job."

"All right," the woman said. "I'll walk back and check with her. But if she's asleep, I don't want to wake her. Both Laura and my friend are sleeping. I'm sure of it, but wait just a minute and I'll go back and double check."

As the woman walked back to look in on her granddaughter, Dog eased her way into the living room and followed a few steps behind the woman. She fought back the urge to run after the woman, shoot her and shoot the damn girl. She needed to get the hell out of here before the fucking cop downstairs got wise.

The woman turned back toward Dog. "You can wait there. I'll check with Laura and be right back."

Dog's heart kept pounding like it would leap out of her chest. *Damn woman taking forever.* Dog debated running down the hallway and getting this over with. She took a few more steps. Then she remembered this Olney was a retired cop himself. She didn't want to get caught too far from the fucking front door.

Okay, just go do it and get the hell out of here.

***

He rode the elevator to the eighth floor and spotted the open door. Peeking around the door frame, he saw the pizza delivery female. He watched as she put down the boxes and started down the hall, pistol in hand.

Hurrying down the hallway behind her, he pulled out his gun and raised his hand to strike the woman over the head. Had to stop her, but he didn't want anyone to see him.

She must have heard his footsteps and started to turn as he brought the gun down on her head. The noise from the shot reverberated throughout the room, but the bullet drilled harmlessly into a wall.

She fell on top of her pizza boxes.

Still trying to shake the noise from the shot, he heard a bedroom door bang open and a woman's scream.

He turned and ran down the hallway toward the door. Another scream.

"Who's there?" a female voice called.

He put his hand over his mouth to muffle the sound of his voice and yelled, "Call 911. Tie her up. The woman is a killer."

Not trusting the elevator, he headed for the stairway, and ran down the eight flights of stairs, completely out of breath by the time he reached the ground floor. He took a minute to catch his breath then pulled the cap lower over his eyes and walked out to the street.

The officer stood with his back to the door.

"Better call 911," Casey said. "Something's going on up there. I've got to take a moment and call the commissioner."

"Wait a minute," the officer said. "What's going on?"

"I'm not sure, but radio 911. I'll wait."

As the officer spoke into his radio, Casey hurried down the street. As he turned right off of Riverside drive, he saw a police car go by, siren blaring. He breathed a sigh of relief.

Hurrying wasn't the way to say alive, but it's what Casey Matheson had to do tonight.

34

Upper Manhattan, Friday, 2:15 a.m.

Zack had been at the FBI lab when he took a call from his mother about the woman who had tried to kill Laura. The officer who had driven him to the lab drove him to Olney's condo building. It took about twenty minutes for them to reach the building, even with the siren.

He leaned forward in the car. "Dammit, hurry."

When Zack arrived at Olney's building, three police cars had closed off the street. As they stopped, Zack jumped out and approached the two officers at the door.

He flashed his ID. "My daughter's upstairs."

"Go ahead, Colonel Kelly." The officer waved him through and Zack ran to the elevator. When he reached the eighth floor, he opened the elevator door and saw a police officer blocking his entrance into the apartment.

He pulled out his ID. "Zack Kelly. You need to let me in."

"Go ahead, Colonel Kelly. I recognize you."

When Zack pushed his way inside, his found his mother and Laura sitting the couch. A heavy-set man in civilian clothes stood in the corner holding a small notebook and talking to Chester Olney. *Damn, Sergeant Dempsey again*, Zack thought. The fucker who gave him a bad time the first day he and Laura arrived.

Zack recognized Sergeant Huna right away. She stood guarding a woman sitting on the floor, handcuffs binding her hands. Huna looked over and nodded to him.

Zack hurried over to Laura and knelt down. He took her hands in his. "Are you all right?"

She stared up at him, tears in her eyes and stuttered as she tried to talk. "The woman on the floor broke in here. She, she ... tried to kill me. She must have been one of the other hijackers on the boat. Oh, Dad, I'm so scared. When will this ever stop?"

Zack rose, ready to beat the hell out of someone. "Right now." He stalked over to that fucking Dempsey. "Your police force was supposed to guard my daughter. You knew someone tried to kill her earlier this afternoon. You were supposed to be guarding her. Now, can you explain to me in plain English how the woman got in here? How the hell did she do it?"

Dempsey stepped back, obviously shaken by the force of Zack's attack. "Now wait a minute, Kelly, you can't do this."

"Oh, yes I can. Now, I repeat, how did the woman get in here? You were guarding my daughter and she walked right in. Now you tell me how it happened."

Chester Olney stepped between Zack and Dempsey. "Hold on a minute, Zack, Martin just arrived. He's trying to sort out what happened, too. Tomlinson placed a guard on the door downstairs. The woman apparently posed as a pizza delivery person and somehow talked her way past the guard. It shouldn't have happened, but it did. Martin is trying to figure out how and why."

"Where were you, Chester?" Zack asked, starting to cool a little. "You were here. How did the woman get past you?"

Olney looked down for a moment, then back up at Zack. "To be honest, I was asleep in the back bedroom. I had no idea someone would get past the guard or I would have been out here."

Zack turned away, calming himself, and spotted Sergeant Huna watching him. She gave him a nod and a small smile. She apparently didn't care much more for Dempsey than Zack did.

Zack turned back to Dempsey. "Okay, what happened? How did she get in here with the gun?"

Dempsey stayed red in the face, but started talking. "As Chester said, the woman hijacked a pizza delivery vehicle and three pizzas. She sweet talked her way past the guard downstairs. He told me she looked to be on the level so he let her by."

Zack took a deep breath. "Did he ever think to call up to the apartment and ask? What are phones for? All he needed to do was call the apartment and say, 'Hey, did anyone order pizza?' That's not so hard. I just did it in five words."

"You're right, Kelly," Dempsey said. "I told him the same thing. Personally, I think she charmed her way past him. His lieutenant will write him up and discipline him."

Zack still wasn't buying it. "What would they have done if the bitch had gotten up here and killed Laura?"

Dempsey whispered, "Nothing."

"You're goddamn right. Nothing. Now, what happened when she got up here? Did the guard on the door stop her?"

"There wasn't a guard on the upstairs door."

His mother stepped forward. "Zack, please calm down. The woman knocked on the door. Half woke me up. When I opened it. She said she had three pizzas for our apartment. I told her we hadn't ordered any pizza. She said they had a phone order from a Laura."

"What?" Laura turned when she heard her name. "I didn't order any pizza."

"Of course, I didn't know," her grandmother said. "I thought maybe you had gotten hungry or maybe Chester had ordered them, so I walked back to the bedroom to ask. As I reached Laura's room and opened the door, I heard a scuffling out here, then a very loud gun shot.

She put a tissue to her eyes.

Zack walked over to take her hands. "I'm sorry you had to go through all this."

A slight smile. "Me too. I turned around and took a step into the hallway to see a tall man hit the woman over the head. He hit her with a pistol. Then he ran out the door yelling, 'Call 911.' "

Zack shook his head in disbelief. "Did he have on a blue jacket and a Yankee cap?"

"No, a tan jacket and a baseball cap from some club. It wasn't the Yankees. The cap covered much of his face and he'd already turned away from me."

"Could it have been the same man from this afternoon?"

"I didn't see him, remember? From what you said he looked like, it could be the same man."

Zack just stared out the window. How did the man know Laura was in trouble? "He saved her life twice today."

"I know," his mother said. "I know. If he hadn't been here..." She gave a sob.

Zack hugged her. "I'm so glad you were here for her."

***

It took about an hour to clean up everything. The staff from the crime scene lab cut the bullet out of the wall, dusted for fingerprints, bagged her gun. Sergeant Huna and two other officers took the woman away. She refused to say anything.

Chief Tomlinson arrived about the same time as they were taking the woman away.

"Zack," Tomlinson said, "I don't know what to tell you, but I've got to apologize for the actions of my men. That woman never should have gotten up here. Never."

"We agree on that, Commissioner," Zack said. "I hope the people you have on duty now do a better job. I'd stay here myself, but I have sent some material to the FBI crime scene lab, and I want to go over and check it out."

"What did you send over there?" Tomlinson asked.

"Just something in the forensics package. The angle the bullet entered. Didn't seem to make sense. Should have been from the front, but it seemed to be from the side."

"Maybe your father turned at the last minute," Tomlinson said.

"Possible, but I think it's something worth checking out."

"Absolutely," Olney said. "You need to follow every detail until you're comfortable with the investigation's conclusion. Your dad was killed by one of those drug bastards. A terrible thing."

Maybe, Zack thought, maybe. But maybe not. He wasn't going to quit until he knew.

"Who do you think this Good Samaritan is?" Tomlinson asked. "I mean, if he's the same guy, he saved Laura twice. Who in the hell is he?"

"I've been racking my brain," Zack said, "but nothing I come up with makes any sense."

"It has to be someone who knows what's going on," Olney said. "He had to know Laura was here and this woman might be coming after her. Maybe he's a retired FBI agent?"

"Well, he probably figured the bitch had missed once and would try again," Zack said. "But how did he know where Laura would be? Has to be someone on the inside."

"It certainly is an option." Tomlinson said. "Anyway, I've got one officer on the front door, one on the elevator, and two up here. I'm placing a sergeant in Chester's apartment to coordinate things and to make damn sure nothing else happens. She'll be safe."

Zack stood. "I sure as hell hope so. Can I get a lift to the crime lab?"

Tomlinson nodded. "I'll take you myself."

"Thanks." Zack continued to believe Tomlinson could be involved. Staying close by to check on me. Who the hell could he trust? Maybe the man in the jacket and no one else.

As Zack stepped out the door and into the hallway, his cell rang. He motioned to Tomlinson and Olney to wait a minute. "Colonel Kelly."

"Colonel Kelly, this is Amanda Frost."

So much had happened, Zack had to think for a minute to place Amanda Frost. "Who?"

"You and your friend stopped by our house a couple of days ago to talk to my husband about what happened to your father."

"Of course, I remember you, Mrs. Frost. How's your husband?"

"It's Amanda, Colonel Kelly. He's doing much better. For the first 24 hours, I wasn't sure if he would ever be okay again. I mean, who in the world would shoot him?"

Zack wished he knew, but waited for her to continue.

"My husband is awake and would like to talk with you. He told me he's been thinking a lot about what happened to your father, and he's concluded the cover up just wasn't right."

Zack lowered his voice and stepped away a few steps. He whispered, "Did you say cover up Mrs. Frost?"

Tomlinson and Dempsey looked at him.

"That's what he told me," Mrs. Frost continued. "Can you come by the hospital room sometime today?"

"I certainly can, Mrs. Frost. And I want you to know I'm so glad he's doing better. I could probably be there in a couple of hours."

"Thank you, Colonel Kelly. He said he had some important things to say."

"Okay. I'll be leaving here in a little while and will come over to the hospital. And by the way, it's Zack."

"Thank you so much, Zack. We'll see you soon."

"Who was that?" Tomlinson asked.

"Just Amanda Frost. She said her husband is doing much better."

He hoped Tomlinson and Dempsey hadn't been alerted by the call. He needed to get to the hospital as soon as he could. Damn, he needed sleep. His brain cells were running low.

He stopped and turned back again to Chester Olney. "Keep a sharp eye out for them, Chester. I don't completely trust the guards after what just happened."

"Don't worry, Zack," Chester said. "You can count on me."

"Thanks." Zack was glad he had someone he could count on.

***

The phone rang on the chief of staff's desk. He picked it up. "Hello."

"I need to talk to the man."

The chief knew the caller and put him right through.

"Yeah, what do you want? I'm really busy."

"You're not too damn busy to hear this," the caller said.

"Okay, what ya got?"

"It's possible old Curly Frost is going to spill something to Kelly."

"What? He knows better than to say anything. What happened to him should have been a sufficient warning."

"Guess not. I heard he wants Kelly to come by the hospital. It might be nothing, but I don't think we can trust him."

"When was this?"

"Maybe about thirty minutes ago. Kelly had a couple of other things to do. I suspect we don't have much more than a couple of hours."

"Shit. Okay, I'll take care of it."

The line went dead.

35

Hospital, San Antonio, Friday, 6:00 a.m.

Garcia must have dozed for a few minutes. She shook herself awake and stretched. All quiet in the surgical recovery ward. Paul moaned in his sleep. Poor guy. The pain still making him thrash around. She wished she could do something to help him. She checked her watch. Six o'clock. She felt like shit but at least she was alive. *The nurse should come by in a few minutes.*

Checking her cell, she spotted a text from Admiral Steele that he wanted an eight o'clock conference call. Getting up, she used the restroom and splashed some water in her face. She'd needed a coffee hit. Oh, man, lots of coffee.

Stepping out into the hallway, she nodded to the guard, then called Ryan. When he answered she said, "It's Garcia. Admiral Steele, would like a conference call at eight o'clock. Can you join us? I'd like him to hear what you know. You're more current than I am."

"You bet. We've rounded up four persons we believe were involved in the takeover of the Alamo. None of them have admitted it, but I think it's just a matter of time. What's Steele's number again?"

She gave it to him. "Talk to you in a little while."

She hurried down to the cafeteria and pulled a cup of coffee. When she returned, she sat in a chair in the hallway and pushed in the Admiral's number.

His receptionist answered on the second ring. "This is Garcia calling from sunny San Antonio. I understand the boss wants to get us together."

"Right. I'll plug you in. Colonel Kelly is on already."

"Agent Ryan, who has been working with me on the case should be calling in a few minutes."

"Great. I'll plug him in when he calls."

"Thanks."

She heard a click then the Admiral's voice "Garcia should be calling in ..."

"Here, sir."

"Hello, Garcia, Zack is on the line."

"Yes, sir. Agent Ryan, my FBI counterpart, should be checking in soon."

In a moment, Ryan's voice came on the line.

"Okay, Zack," Steele said, "why don't you summarize what happened with the Staten Island Ferry and where all of that stands."

"Will do, sir." Zack went through step-by-step the clearing of the ferry and the explosion, then the rescue operation. "Let me bring in Agent Fairchild to give an update on where we are."

"Good morning, sir, Fairchild here. We believe we have two of the hijackers in custody. We're questioning them as we speak. They were smart. When they set the explosion and got everyone off the ferry, it was hard to sort out the good from the bad. They had an inside man, but we haven't caught up with him yet. Laura identified Kinsey Cartwright who was one of the hijackers, but she got away. Zack, why don't you take it from there."

"Right." Zack updated the call about the attack on Laura."

"Who's the hero?" Garcia asked.

"I don't know," Zack answered, "but he saved Laura's life twice."

"Was it the same woman who tried to kill Laura before?" Garcia asked.

"No," Zack replied. "The first attack was by this Kinsey Cartwright. The woman in the apartment hasn't said anything, but it's not Cartwright. Laura had never seen her before."

"Let me add something here," Steele said. "The FBI has identified the pizza shooter. Her name is Macy Blank, a young woman who left the military with a serious case of PTSD. She enrolled at George Washington University, but dropped out.

The FBI is going through the campus and identifying all of Cartwright's and Blank's friends. Shouldn't be long before we start pulling in the other hijackers by putting the pressure on."

"Was the second one alone?" Ryan asked.

"No," Zack replied, "but her accomplice managed to drive off before the cop on the door realized it. The officer believes the driver was a male."

"I received an interesting call from the undersecretary of state," Steele said. "Kinsey Cartwright worked for her as a young Air Force sergeant. She said Cartwright served in an outstanding manner, and she is shocked to hear she's involved in all this. Can't believe it. Okay, Garcia, let's hear your side."

Garcia summarized what had happened to her and her near death experience. "I'm at the hospital now with Paul Cartwright. He told me he has four brothers and four sisters. His brother, Frank, is the one who tried to kill me. He does have a sister named Kinsey."

"There's the link," Steele said. "Fairchild, do we know where this Kinsey Cartwright is?"

"Not right now, sir, Fairchild said. "But we've got check points at all transportation avenues out of Manhattan, and her picture is plastered everywhere. It's a huge task, but I think we'll come up with her."

"I wonder," Garcia asked, "do you suppose she's heard about her brother, and is on her way to San Antonio?"

"Good point," Steele replied. "Let's cover his room just in case. We will get a photo of Cartwright to you."

"That's great," Ryan said. "We do have a guard on his room and a photo will help."

"Now, were there many injuries or deaths from either one of these incidents?" Steele asked.

"No deaths in San Antonio," Ryan replied, "and I don't believe we've had any serious injuries."

"Here in New York, there are a few seniors who've suffered exposure from the cold water, but it looks as if everyone will recover," Fairchild replied.

"The explosion they set in San Antonio was more to cover their escape as opposed to damaging anything," Ryan said. "I think the idea was to make a point, and not to do any real harm to the site or injure anyone."

"Okay," Steele said. "Keep me advised. I'll need position papers on what you've told me. Anything new hits in the meantime, give me a call. The president is very interested. And Zack, take good care of Laura."

"Thanks, sir. We've got her under guard," Zack said. "Say, I heard Governor Harbaugh is likely to be on the ticket in the upcoming election?"

"You've hit on a sore point," Steele replied. "It's likely he'll be running on the ticket as Vice President. And of course, they're blaming the president for the hijacking, so the Governor won't take the hit."

"How can they, for crap sake?" Garcia asked.

The admiral laughed. "Politics. They're saying if the VA had been doing its job, there wouldn't have been a need to blow up anything."

"Oh," Garcia replied. "Politics."

"You got it," Steele said. "Politics is a spectator sport and whoever can get the most hits on their opponent, wins."

Garcia disconnected. She nodded to the guard and pushed the door open, stepping back into Cartwright's room. Saw Paul still asleep. She had planned to get some more coffee, but decided to sit in the chair for a few minutes and close her eyes before she walked downstairs for breakfast.

In a moment, sleep over took her.

***

At the hospital, Zack rode the elevator up to the surgical ward. He hadn't had a chance to evaluate the forensic package the lab had given him yet, but figured he could talk it through with Fairchild later on. Important to meet with Frost. He must have something critical to say.

When Zack stepped off the elevator, something seemed wrong. Hospital personnel hurried back and forth, and a number of police officers were huddling at one end of the hallway.

When he got near the end of the corridor, a police officer held up his hand. "I'm sorry, sir, but you can't go any further. We're investigating an incident."

"Look, my name is Zack Kelly. I've been working with Chief Tomlinson, and he just had one of his officers drive me over here to see a retired detective named Frost. What's going on?"

The officer got a puzzled look on his face. "Just a minute, sir. I'll need to check with my superior. Please wait here."

Zack didn't like the sound of this at all. Did something happen to the Frosts? He tapped his foot, waiting for the officer to return.

In a moment the officer came back down the hallway, followed by a police lieutenant Zack thought he recognized. "Colonel Kelly, Lieutenant Marvel. How may I help you?"

"Look, I received a call from Amanda Frost a couple of hours ago. She told me her husband wanted to see me. Apparently he had some information for me."

Marvel looked at the other officer then said, "You'd better come with me."

Zack followed him down the hall. When they turned a corner, Zack saw more hospital personnel and more police. Crime scene tape spread around the corridor.

Marvel stopped. "You talked to Amanda Frost a couple of hours ago?"

"That's right. What's going on?"

"I'm afraid Curly and his wife were killed a short time ago. A grizzly murder."

"Oh no." Zack slumped against the wall and put his head down for a moment. Not again. These two wonderful people brutally killed. Why in the world? Who would want to kill them? How did the killers get into the hospital?

"Are you all right?" Marvel asked.

Zack straightened. "Do I look like I'm all right?"

"Pretty dumb question," Marvel replied. "Let's go over to the nurse's station and get a cup of coffee. You can tell me what you know."

Marvel poured Zack a cup, then one for himself. He looked around. "Let's go in that room over there."

When he sat down, Zack took a sip of coffee, feeling the buzz of the caffeine, then shared with Marvel everything from his first visit to Frost to the phone call from Amanda Frost.

Marvel's eyes widened. "You think these murders are tied to the call?"

"It's certainly possible. Otherwise, why would it have happened within two hours of the call."

"How would anyone know about the call?" Marvel asked.

Zack thought about that for a moment. No way could he blame it on Tomlinson. Marvel would assume he had to be a nut case. What the hell to do? "That's the million dollar question. Is there a chance the phone line is tapped here at the hospital?"

Marvel got a puzzled look on his face. "Doesn't seem likely. Where were you?"

"Chester Olney's apartment. Do you know Chester? He's a retired police officer. My dad's partner on the force many years ago."

"Who else was there?"

"Only my mother, my daughter Laura, Chief Tomlinson and a couple of police officers who were assigned to guard the place after someone tried to kill my daughter earlier."

"Let me call the commissioner. He probably doesn't realize this has happened."

"Do you mind if I go back to Frost's room?"

"I don't think you want to go in there. A mess and the crime scene team is working it over. They'll be at it for a while."

"Please let me know if you're able to identify the killer. They were nice people, and I feel badly someone murdered them.

Marvel put his cell up to his ear. "If you've been working with the commissioner, I'll let him decide what to share with you."

Zack had to call Fairchild immediately before things got any worse. Try and sort out their next step. Things were moving fast now.

***

He kept his police scanner on low to try and stay involved in all the police activity. It sounded like a murder. He turned the radio up to see if he could determine who. He also kept the TV on mute. When he spotted the breaking news about Curly and Amanda Frost, it hit him in the gut. Not Curly. Not Amanda. Things were building, and he assumed the murders were somehow tied to Zack's review. Yet he didn't seem to be able to get ahead of events.

Should he go over to the hospital? No. Nothing he could do there. What now?

Casey thought for a few minutes, then knew what he had to do.

36

Hospital, San Antonio, Friday, 9:00 a.m.

Garcia shook herself awake and checked on Paul. Still asleep. Poor guy must be in a lot of pain because he kept moaning in his sleep. Time to get more coffee and something to eat. She checked on Paul once more, then opened the door.

She greeted the guard again. "Be sure and stay alert. It's possible his sister may be headed this way. She was one of the hijackers on the Staten Island Ferry. My boss is sending her photo to you."

"Just got it," the guard said. "I'll be watching."

She took the elevator to the hospital food court and poured herself a welcome coffee. Ordering a couple of breakfast tacos, she carried her food into the lunchroom. Picking up a San Antonio paper, she walked to a table and spread it out.

The newspaper was chocked full of information about the takeover at the Alamo plus information about the shooting at Paul's office. After reading the articles and checking for any other information, she decided to take the paper, a second cup of coffee, and head back up to Paul's room.

When she arrived, a new guard stood by the door. Garcia showed her ID, then the guard checked the roster and opened the door. "I got the photo of this Kinsey Cartwright."

"Thanks." She stepped into the room and had to smile. "My goodness, welcome back to the land of the living."

A groan.

"Hey, how are you feeling?" Garcia asked.

"Like shit. Everything hurts."

"Getting shot isn't as much fun as people say, but I do thank you for stepping in front of me and saving my life. You're probably aware your brother is going to spend time in jail for his actions."

Cartwright nodded. "Frank always was a hothead. Does things before he thinks about the consequences. In any event, I couldn't let him shoot you." He chuckled. "We haven't finished our talks."

Garcia broke out in laughter. "I'm glad you feel that way. I wouldn't have been much company with a bullet in my chest."

"I will have to say I enjoyed meeting and spending time with you, Garcia, even if it was under pretty unusual circumstances."

"I did too. Finding you took some fancy footwork. I remembered your special motorcycle and that gave me the clue I needed. It surprised me to meet Frank when I arrived. He seems like a pretty nice guy."

"He is," Paul said. "He has always been the good guy in the family, but since he's been in the wheelchair, he's changed. Moody, generally unhappy."

"I can certainly understand," Garcia said. "Losing your ability to walk is damn tough."

"He also has a pretty severe case of PSTD to battle through. Forgetful, mood swings, all of the above."

"What about your sister?"

"Which one?"

"I think you probably know which one. Kinsey."

"Oh, that one."

"How many brothers and sisters do you have?" Garcia asked.

"Four and four," Cartwright responded. "All of us have served in the military. Kinda knocked into us as kids. Our dad was a sergeant major in the Marines."

"Bet he was a tough guy."

"Oh, yeah. Really hard on the boys, not so much on the girls. He liked it when we all went into the military. My older brother died in Afghanistan. I often think to myself, for what? What have we gained? It seems we're right back where we started from. And what pisses me and a lot of guys off is no one cares. That's what we were trying to get across. Soldiers are being killed and maimed and no one cares. That has to change."

"Volunteer army gives us really good troops, but narrowed the groups who serve. Many families have never had anyone in the military. No idea what it's like."

"So true."

The door opened. Cartwright looked up and his mouth dropped open.

When Garcia turned, she saw a young woman standing there, dressed in a white nurse's uniform with a blood pressure cup in one hand. She pulled a Glock out of a pocket in her dress with the other, then kicked the door shut with her foot.

Realization fell on her like a brick. Oh, crap. How could the guard miss her? Damn nurse's uniform. "You must be Kinsey."

"How did you know?"

"Well I guess the Glock in your right hand is a clue. Your brother told me about your family. I figured you would be here to visit him."

Kinsey walked over to Paul's bed and took his hand. She kept the gun on Garcia. "Just stay in the fucking chair and don't move."

"Don't worry," Garcia said. "I won't."

She bent down and gave her brother a kiss. "How are you?"

"Feel like shit, but starting to mend."

"How long will you be in here?"

"I'm told probably a week. You shouldn't be here."

"I wanted to come and get you out of here. We can go someplace together."

Garcia watched the exchange, wondering where it was headed.

Paul glanced over at Garcia. "I can't get up and motor out of here. You should go. You were lucky to get by the guard. It won't be long before the cops will come after you."

"I understand Frank is in jail for shooting at some colonel." She scowled at Garcia. "Is she the bitch who caused it all?"

Oh, oh, Garcia thought, *doesn't sound good.*

"You know Frank has always been a hothead. Colonel Garcia has been a friend to me." He nodded at Garcia. "A smarter friend than I thought as she found my office through my motorcycle."

Kinsey kept her gun trained on Garcia, "Yeah, but if she hadn't found you, you and Frank would have been gone."

"I don't want to spend the rest of my life on the run. What kind of a life would it be. I plan to stay here to be with Frank. Help us both through our trials."

"I can help you," Garcia said. "Let me help."

Kinsey pointed the gun at Garcia. "Shut up, bitch. You've done enough."

Paul tried to sit up and groaned for the effort. "Let her help you. She has connections. She's been straight with me."

"Are you aware I tried to kill Laura Kelly. She is the only one who could point the finger at me. Some hunk in a blue jacket stopped me."

Garcia leaned forward. "Don't make it any worse than it is. Together we can mitigate what's going to happen to you. You're young, have a lot of living ahead of you. Let me help."

Kinsey grimaced. "Shut up. I told you to shut up."

Paul reached up and took Kinsey's hand. "This whole thing started because we wanted to help veterans and their families. It's gotten completely out of control. If you turn yourself in, I know Garcia will help you."

Kinsey glared at Garcia. "Fuck."

"No, it will mean a lot if you turn yourself in. If you run, they'll kill you. I know it." Tears formed in his eyes. "I couldn't stand to know you were spending your life running and probably getting killed. This has to stop and stop now."

Kinsey slumped down and started to cry. "Eagle will find me and kill me."

"Look," Garcia said, "I'll get you into protective custody until we round up everyone who was involved. No one else needs to die. You all were trying to do something good and, like sometimes happens, it spiraled out of control. Kinsey, please listen to your brother."

Kinsey sat on the bed and leaned down for her brother to hold her. "Oh, Paul, this is so fucked up. All I wanted to do was help our friends."

He hugged her close. "I know, sweetheart. I know. Now, give Garcia the gun. You have to do it willingly. Garcia can testify you surrendered voluntarily."

Kinsey got up from the bed and handed the gun to Garcia.

"Thank you, Kinsey. I'll help you. I promise."

Kinsey laid back down next to her brother and the two cried together.

Garcia pulled out her cell and dialed Admiral Steele. *What a relief.*

***

Zack and Fairchild sat in an empty office at the New York City FBI office, each with a cup of coffee. Zack had dozed for a few minutes and struggled to focus.

"We need to report in to Admiral Steele. This is getting way too complicated." Fairchild took a sip of coffee. "I sent a message to the boss and he's in his office. He wants us to call him right away."

They got Admiral Steele on the line, Zack updated him on everything that had happened in the last few hours.

"That's crazy."

"I know, sir. The only two who knew where I was going were Chief Tomlinson and Detective Dempsey. Then a couple of hours later the Frosts end up dead. How else can we play it? Got to be one of those two."

"Did both of them know your dad?" Steele asked.

"Tomlinson led the team the night the dealers killed my dad. I don't know if Dempsey was on the task force that night, but he knows who I am and why I'm here. Then, he mysteriously shows up at Chester Olney's condo right after Laura and I arrived. He held a gun on us until I could prove Laura and I had nothing to do with the attack on Olney."

"I checked," Fairchild said. "Dempsey was on the force when your dad died, but on leave the night it happened."

"Anything else?" Steele asked.

"Zack picked up the forensics material from the New York police file on his dad's shooting and took it over to the FBI lab here in New York," Fairchild said. "They checked and everything seemed fine except the angle of entry of the bullets don't make sense. There were two bullets and both entered his chest from the side."

"Wait a minute," Steele said, "the bullets should have entered from the front. Weren't they in a shootout with these dealers in a building? How could the entry have been from the side?"

"You'd think the drug dealers would be firing from the front." Fairchild turned to Zack. "Was there any evidence in the file someone kept shooting from the side?"

"I checked," Zack said. "From what's in the file, all of the dealers were in the building in front of the task force."

"Does that mean one of the police officers took the shot?" Steele said.

"Certainly is one possibility," Fairchild replied. "There is one other thing I found in researching our files. There were many charges of corruption in the New York City Police Department at the time. FBI files revealed we opened an investigation into the corruption and several agents were dispatched to check out the claims."

"Were they ever substantiated?" Steele asked.

"No proof of any wrong doing, but many of the agents testified there were indications of problems. There may have been police officers involved in the investigation to work with the agents."

Zack jumped on that. "Was my dad asked to help the FBI?"

"I don't know yet." Fairchild said. "I'm trying to find out, but I need the okay from the director to reopen the file."

"Let me know if you have any trouble getting the information," Steele said. "If you do, I'll call him. We need the information."

"One other thing," Fairchild said. "I checked and it turns out Governor Harbaugh was the police commissioner at the time."

"Holy crap," Zack exclaimed, "he's the current governor now. I've gotten to know him through this mess with the ferry. Come to think of it he mentioned my father."

"Get on it," Steele said, "and let me know as soon as you find out anymore."

"Will do," Fairchild said.

"Just a minute," Steele said, "I just got a note from Garcia. Okay, great news. She captured Kinsey Cartwright."

"Must have been at the hospital," Fairchild said. "That's wonderful."

"Apparently Garcia and Kinsey's brother talked Kinsey into giving up her gun," Steele said. "So at least Laura is safe from her now."

"Thank heavens," Zack said, "but who else is out there?"

"I don't know who," Fairchild said, "but I'm sure someone."

37

Whitehall Ferry Terminal, Friday, 11:30 a.m.

Zack and Fairchild waited outside the room where Governor Harbaugh had set up an office to monitor the hostage rescue operation. Most of the families had been reunited and sent home after their harrowing experience on the ferry. The press continued to wander around searching for more stories, but without much success.

"How should we play this, Zack?" Fairchild asked.

"I think we tell him about the Frosts, then ask him about charges of corruption during his tenure as police commissioner. See what he says."

The governor's chief of staff came over to where they were sitting. "He will see you now."

Zack and Fairchild followed the chief of staff into an office where Harbaugh sat talking on the phone. He motioned them to sit in the two chairs in front of his desk. "Coffee?"

"Great," Zack said. "Two please."

The chief of staff brought coffee to them, then withdrew and shut the door.

When the governor finished on the phone he turned to them. "Now, how may I help you?"

"Sir, you may remember we talked about my father who was shot and killed in a drug raid some thirty years ago."

"Yes, I remember. Roger Kelly was a good man."

"My understanding is whoever shot him was never arrested and prosecuted."

"We know he was shot by one of the drug dealers, but we were never able to prove which one did it."

"Well sir, the forensics report from the FBI lab determined the angle of the bullets entered from the side, indicating the shots could have been fired by one of the other police officers."

The governor's eyes widened. "Now, wait a minute, that's a pretty serious accusation."

Zack nodded. "Yes, sir, I know it is. But the evidence points in that direction."

The governor watched him for a moment. "All right, let me think a moment. Seems to me the conclusion from the testimony was he might have turned right to look back before some of the shots rang out."

"I don't remember seeing any testimony to that effect," Zack said.

The governor took a sip of coffee. "It's been a long time. We may not be able to resurrect all the evidence again."

"I agree it could be difficult," Zack said, "but another disturbing thing has happened. Someone shot Detective Curly Frost."

"Detective Frost," the governor exclaimed, "I knew him. Seemed to be a good man."

"Sadly, he was seriously hurt two days ago in front of his house," Zack replied. "He's been in the hospital recovering from his wounds."

The governor reached to his desk for a pencil and started to write. "I'll have some flowers sent to the hospital. Hopefully, he'll recover soon."

"You will be too late, sir. Both he and his wife were murdered a few hours ago."

"Good God," Harbaugh said, "I haven't heard any of this. Course this hostage situation has consumed my time."

"All this gets murkier, sir. Two hours before someone shot him, his wife called me and told me Frost wanted to talk with me. By the time I got there, both of them had been murdered."

Harbaugh stared at Zack for a moment. "I don't understand what's going on."

"I think I do," Zack replied. "Someone is trying to cover up what happened to my father years ago. They shot Frost to shut him up."

"How do you think this is all tied together?"

"When Mrs. Frost called me, there were two other police officers who heard the call and knew where I was going. I don't think they knew why."

Harbaugh leaned forward. "Who were they?"

"Commissioner Tomlinson and Detective Dempsey."

"You can't possibly think the Commissioner is involved in all this?"

"It's too early to make any accusations. Frankly I don't know what to think. I'm here because you were police commissioner at the time, and I wonder what your take is on all this." Zack decided to not mention the issues of corruption in the force.

Harbaugh leaned back for a moment and took a sip of coffee. "My people told me Internal Affairs thoroughly investigated the case and one of the dealers shot your father in a gun battle. Later, two of the dealers testified your father was on their payroll. They wanted to make sure he died so it would never turn up."

"I plan to continue investigating," Zack said, "until I find the truth. I never believed my dad was a dirty cop and I still don't."

"I certainly understand what you're saying," Harbaugh said, "and I'll do whatever I can to help you. Please keep me informed of what you find."

Zack leaned forward. "Yes, sir, I will."

The two stood, walked back to the door, opened it and walked out, closing it behind them.

***

Harbaugh sat at his desk, staring at the closed door. Any hint of a scandal of this magnitude would quench his chances to be vice president. He'd been working too long and too hard to let it happen.

He pressed a button on his phone and his chief of staff hurried into his office.

"Yes, sir, I figured you'd want to talk about Kelly."

"Kelly is asking all kinds of questions, questions which could bring out more than we want. He knows about the angle of the bullet and is aware the death of Frost is somehow tied to his father's death. I'm afraid we can't let this sit any longer."

"Does he have any information about the scandal in the department?"

"If he does, he didn't mention it. But it probably won't be long before it comes up. What bothers me is both he and Fairchild work for the president's national security advisor who can open any door anywhere in the government."

"Perhaps he should meet with an accident?" the chief said.

"Too obvious. Not after all the other things that have happened. I think we need to be direct and wipe out him and his family. It's going to cause a lot of publicity, but then it's over. Kelly won't ever stop, but someone else probably won't be so thorough."

"I don't see how we can work it out now, not with so much else going on. Maybe a bomb? Or a fire in Chester Olney's apartment. That's where his family is staying."

Harbaugh smiled. "Now you're thinking. I pay you to take care of these things. Get on it and get it done."

The Chief stood. "Yes sir."

"See that you do."

"Don't worry, sir, I have the action." His chief of staff turned and walked out of the office.

Harbaugh leaned back in his chair. He decided to not call the presidential candidate. No need to bother him. Kelly would soon be out of the equation.

***

Garcia rolled Cartwright's wheelchair out of his room and down the hall to a small porch with a view of downtown San Antonio. She pulled a chair up next to him and sat quietly, waiting for him to talk.

Tears filled Cartwright's eyes. "Damn hard to see Kinsey taken away by the police."

Garcia shook her head. "I can't imagine."

"Our whole effort has gone up in smoke. I've watched Frank day after day in his wheelchair. Always such an active guy, and now he's stuck in the chair for the rest of his life. The damn politicians, they're not stuck in any damn chair like Frank. Out playing golf. Fuck."

Garcia put her hand on Cartwright's arm. "The politicians all applaud the military, then sit down and eat their big dinners and drink wine while the wounded warriors hobble around." She glanced up to see Agent Ryan walking down the hall and waved. "Hey, Ryan, over here."

When he reached the porch, Garcia said, "Agent Frank Ryan, meet Paul Cartwright."

Cartwright straightened. "Hope you don't want me to jump to attention."

Ryan laughed as they shook hands. "We've met, but at the time you said you were with the Texas Highway Patrol. Garcia hasn't rubbed it in. At least not yet."

Garcia chuckled. "We'll see."

Cartwright rubbed a hand across his eyes. "The cops came a little while ago and took my little sister away. Broke my heart."

"Fortunately she didn't kill anyone," Ryan said. "If she had killed Laura Kelly, I suspect she might have gotten the chair. Whoever the guy in the jacket was, he probably saved both of their lives."

"What do you think will happen to her?" Cartwright asked.

"Oh, man," Ryan replied. "Really hard to say. Hijacking a ship and putting those passengers through all that crap is pretty serious stuff. To say nothing about their plan to kill Laura."

Cartwright flinched. "I know, I know. Believe me, I know."

"From what I understand," Ryan replied, "no one on the ship died. Some of the passengers suffered from exposure, but I don't think anyone is critical. A lot could be determined by what Laura has to say. If she doesn't want a pound of flesh, maybe a few years."

"Have you rounded up our crew?" Cartwright asked.

Ryan nodded. "We went right down your list and picked most of them up. Some of the folks couldn't believe you had ratted them out."

"You would have gotten them anyway," Cartwright said. "We didn't want to hurt anyone. Just get people's attention."

"You did it," Ryan replied. "Fortunately for you there wasn't much damage at the Alamo from the explosion."

"That's the way we planned it. One of our guys is a bomb expert. We needed an explosion to cover our escape. Once Garcia tagged me, the jig was up. If I had gotten away, I'm not sure you would have ever caught us."

"I suspect we would have," Ryan replied. "You had fifteen people in the mix. Something always gives. Someone talking out of school after a few drinks, a finger print on a fountain, always something to trip people up. Particularly in a high visibility escapade like this."

Garcia put her hand on Cartwright's arm. "I will have to say saving my life certainly put you on the top of my hit parade."

Ryan nodded. "Those actions will speak well in your defense. I'm afraid your brother won't fare so well. Attempted murder is a bad rap."

"I couldn't believe it when I saw him planning to shoot Garcia. Couldn't believe it."

"Well, I'd better get moving. Tons of paperwork." Ryan looked over at Garcia. "What about you? Do you need a lift anywhere? Place to stay? Anything at all. You did a bunch of stuff to stop this thing before it got any worse."

"No, I've got my motorcycle and will probably head back to Austin this evening. To be honest, I'm enjoying hanging out with the guy who saved my life."

"I can see you two are doing okay. I'll be leaving the guard on duty here. When you're released from the hospital, we'll move you downtown to a holding cell. Then, who knows."

Ryan turned and headed down the hall. He looked back. "I'll have to say you're a pretty good egg, Garcia. I enjoyed working with you."

"Same here," she called. "Take care and have fun with all the reams of paperwork."

As he headed down the hallway, she turned to Cartwright. "Now what should we talk about?"

"How about a little about you," Cartwright said. "I don't know a thing about you, and I'd really like to know more. First of all, are you married or have a boyfriend?"

Garcia laughed. "No, I'm a free agent."

He took her hand. "Good. Would you come and visit a guy in jail?"

"Depends who it is. I think you'd be a good candidate."

38

On Board the Staten Island Ferry, Friday, 2:00 p.m.

Zack stood at the railing of the Staten Island Ferry, watching as they passed Liberty Island and the Statue of Liberty. The sun cast a shadow from the statue across the bay and Zack was happy Laura and his mother were now safe in Olney's apartment.

The ferry that had been hijacked was in dry dock where teams were working to repair the damage from the fire. Fortunately the damage wasn't extensive. Zack heard it would be back in service within a couple of weeks.

He tried to process what had happened since he had last ridden the ferry. First of all, was meeting Shelia again, then the shooting of the Frosts during his visit to their house.

The phone call from Amanda Frost still bothered him. Must have been a professional hit. Tied to his father's murder. Only thing that could possibly make any sense.

Finally the attempt to silence Laura at Olney's apartment. The attacks on Laura were one thing, probably tied to what happened with the ferry, but the attacks and murder of the Frosts had to be a separate item and tied to what happened to his father.

Either Tomlinson or Dempsey had to be involved with the Frosts' murder. They both witnessed the phone call. But why? A plan to silence Frost.

Now, where to start? This was giving him a headache.

Okay, just start with one step at a time. Once he claimed his truck from the terminal parking lot, he could drive over to the Navy Lodge and pack up all of their luggage. Then he'd drive into Manhattan and drop Laura's and his mother's stuff off at Olney's. Step one. Check.

Step two. Shelia had invited him to stay with her. He could drop all of his stuff off at her hotel, have a good dinner, stay the night, and get to where he could think straight. After all this mess was over, he had to figure out what sort of a future the two of them had.

Next, he needed to check in with Fairchild. See what she had found out about his father's FBI files. Key item.

Zack decided to take a minute to enjoy the sights. He'd learned in Afghanistan to be watchful. With all that had been going on, he needed to double down on watchfulness. Something nibbled at the back of his neck, making him look around. He felt eyes on him. Hard to explain, but he felt sure someone watched him.

When he turned to check, he spotted two guys standing at the other end of the ferry. Had they been on the same subway he'd ridden? They looked familiar. Might just be a coincidence. They could be taking the ferry to Staten Island just like him.

Both were large, muscular looking men wearing trench coats. Both had hats pulled down over their eyes. No question they could be trouble. When he looked their way, the two men quickly shifted their gaze to the water.

He turned back, glanced out at the water, and pulled out his cell. He pushed in Fairchild's number. Too much had been going on. This mess wasn't over yet.

She picked up on the first ring. "Agent Fairchild."

"It's Zack. I'm on the ferry headed to Staten Island."

"Take care, Zack. With all that's been going on you've got to be careful."

"That's why I'm calling. There are two grungy looking blocks of muscle who I think were on the same subway line to the White Hall terminal with me. Now I just spotted them at the other end of the ferry. I have the uneasy feeling they could be planning something once we make it to Staten Island."

"Well, I've been checking with the FBI to gather all the information I can on the investigation of the NYPD at the time someone shot your dad. It's considered classified and the files honchos won't release it without all kinds of authorizations. I'm working with Admiral Steele's office to get approval to have it released. I should have the files soon, then I'll be able to review them. Once I can go through them, I will give you a call."

"Sounds good. Let me know as soon as you have any concrete data."

"What I'm saying is there is more here than we know. Someone is trying to keep what happened years ago from seeing the light of day. If you're being followed, those guys could mean business."

"I'll be careful. I have a weapon locked up in the gun safe in my truck. Once I get there, I should be fine."

"Do you want me to alert the Port Authority? Maybe see if they can place a couple of their guys with you."

"I don't think it will be necessary. I'll feel pretty silly if it's all my imagination."

"I know you better than that, Zack. If you think something's up, you're probably right."

"They're not going to pull anything in broad daylight. Not in the middle of town. Besides, I want to find out what these guys want. They just might want to talk. If we arrest them now, we can't charge them with anything other than riding the ferry. We may miss an opportunity to find out who they are and what they know."

"Zack, be careful."

"I always am."

"Good."

***

As Zack's ferry neared Staten Island, Casey Matheson sat in his room scanning the New York Times, trying to determine the status of the investigation into the ferry hijacking. It appeared from what he'd heard on television, the majority of the hijackers had been captured and put in jail. What a relief. Should help ensure Laura's safety.

Taking a sip of coffee, he turned the page and saw the story on the murder of Curly Frost and his wife, Amanda. Sadness rained in on him and he felt himself tearing up. He couldn't believe these two were dead. Zack Kelly's investigation must be heating things up again. After all this time, people were getting hurt. Exactly what he didn't want to happen.

He tried to prioritize possible courses of action. Doing nothing didn't seem feasible. Besides it wasn't in his personality. He hated to sit still.

The thing which seemed to make the most sense was to catch a subway out to Olney's building. He could set up in the park across the street from the Olney's apartment where he wouldn't be seen, but where he could keep an eye on things. There was nothing currently on his police scanner. Worry trailed him like a dark cloud. He had to do something.

Okay. Get out to Olney's. Stay abreast of the news. Be ready for whatever might hit. And something undoubtedly would. Always did.

Damn right. He'd be ready.

***

Zack made his way to the back of the ferry, watching the two men over his shoulder. They hadn't moved from their original spot, still talking to one another. Maybe they were just innocent passengers who were headed to Staten Island. With all that had happened in the past three days, he could be overreacting.

He continued to weave through the crowd until he reached the rear steps. The ferry scraped the dock with a bump. Zack looked forward to picking up his truck, getting all of his family's luggage, then clearing out of the Navy Lodge. They had been very helpful when Zack told them all that had happened. Same as the Port Authority. They emailed him a pass so he wouldn't be charged for the number of days his truck had been sitting in the lot.

As soon as the gate opened, people poured off the ferry like a stream of fish. A little pushing and shoving, but not too bad now. It would probably pick up later in the afternoon which would have made it easier to lose these clowns in the crowd.

He walked through the glass doors and down the hallway. Glancing over his shoulder, he didn't see either of the men. Surprised him to see the crowd at midday. Could be tied to the hijacking of the other ferry still out of commission. People hadn't been able to use it for two days.

He passed a police officer and nodded to him. Security had picked up since the hijacking of the ferry. Even more so compared with when he had arrived three days ago. Was it really only three days? Seemed like three years.

Stepping into the bathroom, Zack made his way into one of the stalls where he could watch the entry way without being seen. He waited, hoping neither of the men would appear. Hoping he was only being too careful.

Then he spotted one of the men from the ferry. He had added a green baseball cap, but it was definitely him. *Got ya,* Zack thought.

Zack watched the man's gaze sweep the bathroom obviously looking for someone. He turned and hurried back out without using the bathroom. Definitely something going on and he was damn sure he had to figure out what it was.

Zack waited a few minutes, then stepped out of the stall and took off his coat. He turned it inside out, then stepped out into the hallway. Green cap was facing the other way, talking to his partner, a slightly taller man in a trench coat. Little warm for a trench coat, but probably necessary to hide a sidearm. No doubt these guys were following him. *Now what the hell was he going to do about it?*

Stop a cop? Safest course of action, but not a problem solver. *The cops would stop the two, but on what charge? Riding the ferry. Going into the bathroom?* Wouldn't accomplish anything.

Zack ducked down a little, making himself shorter, and slipped over to follow a bulkier man hurrying down the hall. He fell in step with the man on the far side of where his two followers were standing and hurried down the hall.

He'd almost made it when green hat pointed at him and looked like he was almost ready to yell. The other guy glanced over at Zack and glared. They obviously weren't worrying about hiding their identity any longer.

Zack hurried down the hallway, staying close by the man blocking for him. He sped past the waiting room, the restaurant, and the paper store. He burst out of the glass doors toward the parking lot and took the stairs two at a time. When he reached the base of the stairs, the shuttle bus stood waiting to take passengers to their cars. What a break. It was just pulling away, but Zack jumped on board, the door closing behind him.

"Almost didn't make it," he said to the driver.

"I saw you running down the stairs and figured you were really in a hurry."

"Thanks." Zack decided to level with the guy. He needed a little help to get to his truck and have time to get his pistol "I know it sounds a little weird, but two men are following me. I'm not sure why, but they don't look like very nice folks."

The driver glanced in his mirror. "If it's the guy in the green hat who followed you down the stairs, he and his partner just jumped into a black car and they're following the shuttle."

Oh, shit, Zack thought, he didn't want to be trapped. Not before he got to his truck and retrieved his Glock.

Zack leaned over and whispered to the driver. "Look, I've been helping the NYPD investigate the hijacking of the ferry, and I think those two might be involved. Could you drop me at my truck? I don't want anyone else to get hurt."

"You got it," the driver said. "Show me where you parked."

Zack gave him directions. The driver pulled into the lot, then up to his aisle. The driver dropped him right behind his truck.

"I'll stay here for a minute to shield you until you're inside the cab of your truck. Then I need to get moving before my passengers riot."

"Thanks, man, you're a lifesaver."

As Zack got in his truck, he called, "Thanks again." And he meant it.

Twirling the dial for his gun safe, he pulled out the Glock. He looked in the mirror to see a black car, he thought an Olds, pulling close to him. He pulled out two magazines and jammed one into the handgun, slipping the other into his pocket.

Zack started the engine. He backed up the truck and drove

over the lawn to the gate. Fortunately there weren't any cars in line so he showed the attendant his pass, then pulled out onto the street and drove past the bus platforms to the first stop sign.

Glancing in the mirror, he watched the black Olds pull out behind him. At the stop sign, he turned right and followed the road up to the stop light at Bay Street.

Zack debated running the light and pulling onto Bay Street, but decided to wait. He needed to be sure who these men were before he risked involving the police.

When the light changed, he turned left onto Bay Street, the Olds close behind him. Zack blended into the flow of traffic, maintaining a moderate rate of speed. He checked his mirror again and, yes, there was the Olds two cars back. Obviously they were trying to maintain a little distance.

He continued on Bay Street, passing the National Lighthouse Museum on the left. In two more blocks he passed Tappen Park on the right. Need to make something happen.

When he reached Broad Street, he turned right, spotting the Richmond University Medical Center on his left. He reached Tompkins and turned left. Slowing down he waited, then sure enough in his mirror, he saw the Olds follow his lead onto Tompkins.

Should he contact Fairchild and ask her to notify the cops? But first he wanted to find out who these guys were. Doing anything now wouldn't solve anything.

He reached Vanderbilt, turned left and drove to Bay Street, where he took a right. The Olds stayed a respectable distance behind him.

In a few more blocks, he reached the Fort Wadsworth Light House and ahead he saw the Verrazano Narrows Bridge. He'd almost reached the Navy Lodge. *What should he do without endangering anyone else?*

Just take it one step at a time.

39

Navy Lodge, Staten Island, Friday, 3:00 p.m.

Zack drove under the bridge and pulled into the Coast Guard station, checking to see if the Oldsmobile stayed behind him. Two blocks back, but definitely still there.

He passed the Coast Guard Exchange, then pulled up to the front door of the Navy Lodge. Shutting off the motor and getting out of his truck, he spotted the Oldsmobile about a block away, creeping his way.

Checking back, he felt the reassuring lump of the Glock tucked in his belt. Zack walked inside the front door and stood at the desk.

The clerk came out from the tiny office. "May I help you?"

"Yes, I'd like to pick up my luggage. You have it saved for me in a back room. Name is Colonel Zack Kelly."

"Yes sir. I'll go back and get it. Probably take me a few minutes."

"I suggest you not hurry. There's a guy I don't really know who's been following me. I plan to go back outside and see what the deal is."

The clerk's eyes widened. "What?"

"I don't think you're in any danger. But just wait a few minutes before you come back out to the desk. If there's a problem, call 911."

The clerk turned to walk back to the storage area. Zack slipped down the hall and out a side door. He walked around the back of the Navy Lodge and peeked out in the front.

One of the three men got out of the car and walked over to Zack's truck. He leaned in, then pushed the door shut, walked to the front door of the building and stepped inside.

Zack took that opportunity to duck down and run over to the car, staying behind a hedge for cover. He took his Glock out and pulled the back door of the Olds open, slipping inside. Pushing the Glock up against the neck of the man in the passenger seat, he said. "All right, asshole, don't move or I'll blow your fucking head off. You at the wheel, start the car and drive slowly away from the curb.

The driver looked over his shoulder. "What the hell?"

"Just drive and don't say anything," Zack said.

The Olds pulled away from the curb. Zack waited until he saw Tappen Park on his left, then took his Glock and hit the man in the passenger seat over the head. With a low moan, he slipped down in his seat. "All right, you driving, turn right at the next corner and pull over to the curb."

"What?" the driver said.

"Pull over. Are you not only stupid, but deaf?"

"Just don't shoot."

"Do what I say and you have about a 50/50 chance of staying alive."

"Okay, okay. Just take it easy."

The driver turned the corner and stopped. Zack pulled the gun from the holster of the unconscious man and reached over to open the door. He pushed him out of the car. The man fell out and lay spread eagle in the grass next to the curb.

He pulled the door shut and said, "Okay, let's go. Drive slowly and don't pull any shit. You dorks have been following the wrong guy, and I'm about to show you why. You have no idea how many jerks like you I've shot in the military so don't tempt me."

"Goddamn, don't kill me."

"That's completely up to you."

***

After they had driven along Bay Street for a few more minutes, Zack picked a quiet street away from the main part of town. "Okay, turn here, pull up and stop."

The man did as he was told. "Look man, I'm just the driver. I don't know nothing about why they was following you."

Zack held his Glock to the man's head. "Just stay quiet while I check you for weapons." He found a pistol, pulled it out of the holster, and slipped it in his belt. "Now reach in your back pocket slowly and give me your billfold."

The man passed his billfold back to Zack. "Look, I don't know nothing."

"We'll find out in a moment. Cause whatever you know, you're going to tell me." He checked through the man's billfold, then pulled out his cell and dialed Fairchild.

In a minute he heard, "Fairchild."

"It's Zack. I'm in the back seat of the Olds that was following me. The driver's name is Domenico Salvestro. Let me spell it for you."

"Thanks."

"Maybe you can check him out for me."

"Will do."

"Two of the guys decided to leave the car. One is back wandering around the Navy Lodge looking for me, and the other is next to the sidewalk just across Bay Street from Tappen Park. He's sleeping soundly from a blow on the head."

Fairchild laughed. "My goodness, you've been a busy boy."

Zack chuckled. "Yeah, I guess so. Would you call the locals and ask them to pick up both of those guys? I don't know how the man at the Navy Lodge will respond. They need to be careful with him. I believe he's the chief of their little tribe."

"Okay, I'll get the police on it," Fairchild said. "Probably best if I send a couple of agents from our office to meet them. Hopefully the little tribe will have interesting things to tell us."

She returned on the phone line in a moment. "Okay, I've got the pickup working."

"I'm with the driver. I believe he has a few things to tell us so will you pull out a tape recorder?"

"Sure. Just a minute." There was a pause. "Okay, you're on."

Zack checked the man's billfold. "Your driver's license reads that you are Domenico Salvestro. Is that correct?"

"Yes."

"Yes, what?"

"Ah, I don't know."

Zack pushed his weapon up against the man's head again. "Some respect."

"Ah, yes, sir."

"Much better. You keep it up and we'll get along fine. Now who do you work for?"

"I work for the guy you left at the Navy Lodge."

"What is the name of the man who fell out of our car?"

"Shit, you pushed him."

"A detail." Zack kept his pistol against the man's head. "What is the name of the man who fell out of the car?"

"Stefano Lodovico."

"You know, my friend is checking all of this while we're talking. If I find out you're lying to me, it's going to go very badly for you. And I don't think you want that."

"It's the truth, man."

"Okay. Now, what is the name of the man who decided to stay back at the Navy Lodge?"

"Shit man, you tricked him."

"When I want your opinion, I'll ask for it. Now what the hell is his name? I'm getting kinda pissed at your bullshit."

"His name is Niccolo Frosino."

"Okay, Fairchild, see if you can find Frosino. He should be wandering around the Navy Lodge, probably pretty pissed off by now. He may call someone to pick him up so you'd better put a rush on it. While you're doing that, I'm going through this clown's billfold." Zack held the pistol to Salvestro's head again. "And if you're lying, it will go very badly for you."

"Yes sir, I understand."

"Much better."

"Hey, Zack, this is interesting. It says this Salvestro is a security consultant for the governor."

"What? The governor? Harbaugh?"

"That's exactly right. He is a security consultant for our very own governor."

"How about the other guy?"

"He is too."

Zack thought about that for a moment. "We may have hit on the critical link. Harbaugh was the police commissioner when my dad was shot and killed. If he's trying to hush things up, then things are finally starting to make sense."

"Okay," Fairchild said. "The police are on the way. Should be at the Navy Lodge in a few minutes. They'll pick up the guy near Tappen Park."

"I'll wait for the police at the Navy Lodge and hand over my driver friend. Then, I can pick up my truck and head back toward Manhattan. While I'm waiting, I'll update Admiral Steele. The problem is we still don't have any proof."

"But, we're getting close," Fairchild said. "We're finally getting close. Maybe we can break one of these guys."

***

Fairchild closed off the call from Zack and called in three of her fellow FBI agents. She explained to them what was going on with Zack and what she had done to date. "In addition to the locals, I'd like to get three agents over to Staten Island. We can't afford to let this go wrong."

"I agree," Agent Schultz a short, blond-haired agent said. "We've got to move fast, but carefully. I'll get a warrant to go through their stuff. I think what they have done to Zack will hold up with our judge."

"Okay, get moving," Fairchild said. "I've got a chopper waiting for you."

As soon as they left, she picked up the phone. She needed to check and see if she could get her hands on the complete case file from the corruption investigation of the New York Police Department.

"Records," the voice said.

"This is Agent Fairchild calling again. I'm still trying to obtain the remainder of the corruption file on the NYPD."

"You're in luck. I just got the word it has been released. You've got friends in high places. This is the first time I've seen something this sensitive released after over thirty years. Apparently there are a number of hot shots who have been protecting this."

She said a quiet thanks for Admiral Steele. Without him, she doubted she could have gotten it. "Could you messenger it over to me?"

"Will do. Should be there in thirty minutes."

As soon as she got off the phone, she called the FBI witness protection office. This was going to be a battle, but one she needed to win. The last two times she'd called, she was told they couldn't release the file because of national security. Now why the hell was that?

When the clerk answered, she said, "Agent Fairchild again. I've got to obtain the witness protection folder that tracked with the corruption investigation into the NYPD thirty years ago. I've been trying for three days."

"You're in luck. We just received a release signed by the president himself."

Fairchild gave herself a thumbs up. "Can you messenger it to me?"

"Give me your address."

40

Navy Lodge, Staten Island, Friday, 4:30 p.m.

Zack beat the police back to the Navy Lodge by a few minutes and had the driver pull over and stop off to the side. He stayed in the car because he didn't know where Frosino was. Couldn't risk him sneaking up behind him.

When the police arrived, Zack got out and pushed Salvestro toward one of the officers. "Will you cuff and keep an eye on this clown until we can find his partner. I believe he's inside."

Another police car arrived and a slender, athletic looking man stepped out with the name tag Captain Walt.

"Are you Kelly?" Walt asked.

Zack nodded.

"Okay, what's going on?"

Zack provided Walt with a statement about what had happened and why he had taken the actions he did. "I'm convinced that if I hadn't done what I did, they would have kidnapped me and who knows what they would have done."

"I don't think we have enough evidence to hold them very long. I suspect they'll be lawyered up as soon as we hit the station."

"I understand," Zack said. "I'll leave those problems to my friends in the FBI. Let them sort it out."

"We found the guy across from Tappen Park, still out cold. You did a job on him. He's being moved to the station as we speak. We'll get a doc to check him over. We can probably hold the three of them for twenty-four hours, but without any more evidence, I suspect we'll have to release them."

"Can you take the car into your garage and get the lab guys to check it out?"

"Will do. What else can we do for you?"

"I need to get inside and pick up all of our luggage. I suspect my daughter and mother will be delighted to get their clothes. They've been making due and without a resupply, they'll be on the town buying everything in sight."

"For sure you don't want a buying spree." Walt motioned to one of his officers. "You two stay here and keep an eye on things in case the other man returns."

Zack thanked the captain and walked into the front door of the lodge. He spotted the manager behind the counter. "I'm sorry to have dumped the clown on you. I wasn't sure who he was and what would happen, but I needed to get the other two to the police before they got away."

"Actually, it wasn't too bad. The man came in and told me he was looking for a Colonel Kelly. I told him you had gone back to check on the luggage you had left here and showed him where the room was. He came back in a little while complaining you weren't there. Then he hit the roof when he noticed the car was gone."

Zack had to laugh. "I bet he did."

The manager chuckled. "He pulled out his phone and called someone. In a little while a car came and picked him up. I got the license number."

"Outstanding." Zack pointed toward the officer standing outside. "Please give the number to the officer over there"

Zack loaded the luggage from the storage room. Thanking the Navy Lodge manager for all his help, Zack pulled out of the parking lot and drove across the Verrazano Narrows Bridge into Brooklyn. It took him a little over an hour to fight his way through Brooklyn and into Manhattan. Then another twenty minutes to work his way over to Chester Olney's apartment. On the way, he called Shelia and told her what had happened.

"Be careful, Zack," she said. "I've been so worried about you and am looking forward to seeing you. I think I'll take a shower and not bother to get dressed. Just let myself air dry."

***

Agent Fairchild waited impatiently for the corruption file the staff in the FBI office of records had promised to forward to her. It always seemed when you were in a hurry, things took longer.

While she waited, she decided to call the local police who had picked up the two on Staten Island. "This is FBI Agent Tara Fairchild. Can I speak to whoever picked up the men at the Navy Lodge?"

"That would be Captain Walt. I'll get him for you."

In a moment she heard, "Walt speaking."

"This is Special Agent Tara Fairchild. I wanted to thank you for your quick response to my request. I understand you have two of the characters in custody."

"Correct. A guy named Salvestro and a stiff named Lodovico. Lodovico is still out cold. Kelly must have really whacked him."

"Well, I think it was a case of whack or be whacked."

Walt laughed. "You're right."

"Did you find Frosino yet? He's the third guy and I suspect the one in charge."

"Holy, crap," Walt said, "did you say Frosino?"

"Yes I did. Do you know him?"

"You bet. He's one of the local Mafia hoods. I don't think very high in the system, but reputed to be a member of the Angelo family. We'll find him. I know where he hangs out."

Fairchild took a deep breath. They now had another link they could use. A tie to the governor and a tie to Angelo. "Would you call me as soon as you find him and bring him in. It's imperative I speak to him. And would you carefully check the Oldsmobile. I have reason to believe it may have been used in a shooting, and I'm hoping those dumb shits left the rifle in the car."

"Okay," Walt replied. "I'll get a team of officers going over the car. Let you know as soon as we find Frosino."

"Thanks so much."

Fairchild hung up. Things were coming together. If we can track those clowns to the shooting and then to the governor and Angelo, we'll have a case.

A messenger brought in the corruption file. She signed her name for what seemed to be the hundredth time and set the file on the table. Spreading it out in front of her, she began to read, making notes as she went.

Holy crap, she thought, the police commissioner was one of the suspects in the corruption case, but nothing could be proved. A number of statements read that Roger Kelly could have been shot by one of the police officers, but there was not sufficient proof to press any charges. They must have done a lousy job with the forensics.

She had to contact Zack and warn him about what she'd found. She dialed his cell, but it went to voice mail. She tried again, but still voice mail. Come on, pick up, Zack. You always answer your phone.

"Pick up," she thought. "For God's sake, pick up."

41

Chester Olney's Apartment, Manhattan, Friday, 6:30 p.m.

When he arrived at Olney's building, it was almost six thirty. Damn rush hour traffic always a challenge. He could spend some time with Laura and his Mother, then head over to Shelia's place. She brought a smile to his face. It would be nice to spend some time with her after three very long days.

He dialed Olney's number to ask Laura to come downstairs and help him with the luggage. The phone rang but went to voice mail. *That's funny*, he thought, *they should be there. Maybe they decided to go out for a walk.*

Figuring he might as well get started, he picked up two suitcases and headed toward the front door. Apparently, with the arrest of Kinsey, the police had removed the guard from their front door.

He rang the buzzer but no one answered. This was starting to piss him off. Fortunately one of the ladies he had met earlier happened to be leaving.

She smiled when she saw Zack. "My goodness, you're got a load of luggage there."

Zack set one of the suitcases down. "That's not all of it. Got a stack more in the truck. But I'm sure my mother and daughter will be glad to get it. I'm having trouble raising them."

"That's funny," she said. "I thought I saw them come in a little while ago. They should be upstairs."

"Well, they must have gone out for a walk or could be taking a nap. My mother loves her naps."

"How are you doing?" she asked. "I've been following all you've been through. My goodness, it must have been awful."

"A bunch of events I never want to repeat. Thanks for opening the door for me."

His cell rang. He checked the number and realized it was Fairchild. He figured he could call her back once he got upstairs. Not have to balance suitcases.

He took the elevator to the eighth floor, opened the door, and stepped into the hallway. All quiet. What had happened to everybody?

He knocked on the door to Olney's apartment. No answer. *Oh, shit,* he thought, *this is getting to be a real pain.* He set the bags down and started back toward the elevator. As he waited for it to arrive, the door to Olney's apartment opened and Chester stood in the doorway.

"So there you are," Zack said. "I tried to call a number of times, but got no answer."

"Sorry about that," Chester replied. "I guess we had the TV too loud."

Something sounded wrong in his tone, but Zack felt exhausted, and he wanted to get inside to see Laura. "Let me bring some of these bags inside, then Laura can come down and help me with the rest."

"That's fine. Come on in."

Something strange about the way he talked. No emotion. "Are you all right?"

"We're fine. Come on in."

Zack picked up the two suitcases and hauled them into the apartment. When he got inside, he saw Laura and his mother sitting on the couch. "What's going on? Why didn't you answer my call? I've got all of our luggage, and I'd sure like some help bringing them up."

He set the bags down and turned to go back out the door.

Chester stood looking at him, a Glock in his right hand.

"Sorry, Zack. I wish it hadn't gone this way."

***

Zack stood there dumbfounded. Then it dawned on him. *Olney, fucking Olney. He needed to stall for time. Figure a way out of all this mess.* "Chester, what are you doing?"

"I'm really sorry, Zack. Why couldn't you have dropped all the poking around and moved on? You have no idea what you're getting into."

Zack began to understand what he was getting into. The dirty rotten bastard. "You were the link to the Mafia. You were the guy who shot my dad. That's why the bullets entered from the side rather than the front."

"That's right, Zack. If you had dropped it, we all could have gone on with our lives. But no, you had to keep pushing. Kept blindly pushing. Even when all the signs were there to stop."

Zack paused for a moment. "When we found you after the assault and in all the pain, it was the Mafia hoods telling you to keep your mouth shut. They didn't need a key. You let them in."

"Well, you're right. They were very insistent. They didn't have to worry. I would have stayed quiet. What would I have gained by talking to anyone? I would have gained nothing."

Zack was so goddamn mad, but he needed to stay cool. Whatever Olney had in mind, Zack couldn't let him shoot Laura or his mother. "I want you to know I met all three of those clowns this afternoon. All three are in the custody of the Staten Island police. I can't remember their names, but they're in jail and probably singing their hearts out by now."

"Again, Zack, you have no idea who you're dealing with. Those three will be out of jail by now and probably headed this way. They need to get rid of evidence and you are evidence."

Zack sucked in his breath. He had to keep Olney talking until he could think of a way out of this.

"You can't hurt Laura or my mother. They didn't do anything to you. Mom flew out here to help you. Laura did everything she could to help you. How can you hurt them?"

"Again, you don't understand, Zack. It's not me. If I don't do it, someone else will. And they would be a whole lot worse than me. Those Mafia guys are monsters. I plan to do it quickly, then we will destroy the evidence. Never to be heard from again."

"No way. I work for the president's national security advisor. My partner is an FBI agent and she knows exactly where I am. She just tried to call me. It won't work. Right now you can help us and your actions will go well for you. I don't know what you've done, but murdering three harmless people isn't going to help your case."

Olney laughed. A sad laugh. "You may be right about Laura and Ethel, but you are certainly far from harmless."

Zack thought he heard a click sounding from behind him. Maybe Fairchild? He needed to keep Olney talking. Keep him facing away from the door. "I'm not sure why you're still involved after all these years. Isn't it time to drop it all?"

"You never get out from under the thumb of those bastards. Once they have you, they have you forever. If I don't kill you, they will kill me."

Olney turned slowly. When he got half way around, he noticed a shadow moving in the doorway.

The man in the doorway held a Glock in his hand. "Don't even think about it, Chester. I will blow your head off if you try anything. And it will be my pleasure."

Olney's face turned white, as if he had seen a ghost and he had. "Roger, my god, Roger ..., you're dead. I shot ..."

42

Upper Manhattan, Friday, 7:00 p.m.

Fairchild sat in the backseat of the police cruiser next to Commissioner Tomlinson and kept trying to reach Zack as their convoy raced, sirens screaming, through the rush hour streets of Manhattan. Following their car was a van with members of the FBI SWAT team and behind the SWAT team two other police cars.

When they reached Riverside Drive and 110th street, she directed the officer in the front seat to kill the sirens. Once the caravan pulled up in front of Olney's building, she jumped out of the car, Commissioner Tomlinson right behind her.

The SWAT team commander hurried up to her. "How do you want to do this?"

She pulled out her cell. "Let me try once more to reach the people inside. In the meantime, place some of your team in back. I'll take the rest upstairs with me." She glanced up and spotted the helicopter hovering overhead. She wasn't taking any chances.

Police officers began setting up barriers, and detouring traffic off Riverside Drive.

Fairchild spotted Zack's truck, still loaded with luggage. She pushed in his cell again and was forwarded into voice mail. "Zack, where the hell are you? Why aren't you picking up?"

Glancing at Tomlinson, she said, "We can't wait any longer. We need to get inside. See if you can raise anyone to open the door. If not, we'll have to break it down. Four of the team go up the stairs and three go with me on the elevator. Once we get to the eighth floor, it's a small corridor. No one goes in until I say so. I don't want anyone killed who just happens to be standing there."

"Got it," Tomlinson said. "I''ll coordinate things here on the street and call for backup in case we need it. Who the hell knows what we're going to find."

She thought of Zack's family and shuddered. "Okay, let's do it."

Tomlinson nodded and the chief of the SWAT team sent one of him men back to the van to pull out the battering ram in case they needed it. He hurried back to where Fairchild stood.

"Okay, one more try and we go."

***

Zack stood in the center of the living room, frozen in place. His dad? His father alive? How the hell could that be? He'd attended his father's funeral. Mourned him for the past thirty years. He glanced over at his mother whose eyes bulged out, hand over her mouth.

Olney stared, eyes wide as did everyone else. Finally squeaking out, "Roger. Roger, you're dead. The funeral, the memorial service, everything ..."

"Well, I'm back from the grave and ready to take care of what I should have thirty years ago. Now Chester, put the gun down on the floor or so help me I will shoot. I've been wanting to kill you for the past thirty years so don't tempt me. Not for one minute."

Olney bent over and placed the gun on the floor.

"Now kick it over toward Zack."

He did. Zack bent over and picked it up. Looked at his father. "Where the hell have you been?"

Roger Kelly kept his eyes on and gun pointed at Olney. "I'm not really sure where to start. First of all, my current name is Casey Matheson, only one of many. I was approached by one of the senior FBI agents about six months before the shooting. I had worked with him on a couple of cases. A really good guy.

We hit it off. He told me about evidence of corruption in the NYPD."

Zack's rage hit the boiling point. All they had been through and his goddamn father was alive. "Why the hell didn't you tell us? Why? All the pain. All our misery. All the mourning. And all the time you were alive and hiding away."

"Zack, I know you're upset," his mother said, "but let your father talk. I buried my husband thirty years ago and I'm willing to let him talk." Then she smiled, a small sad smile. "But by God, this had better be damn good."

Roger smiled back at his wife. "Thank you. You always made the most sense of anyone I've ever known. When I woke up after surgery, I found myself in a hospital room with three federal agents standing around my bed. They told me what had happened and that everyone thought I had died from the gunshot wounds. I asked to see you right away."

Ethel put her hands on her hips. "Why didn't they tell me?"

"The agents were convinced if Angelo knew I had survived, he would kill me and if need be, my entire family. Anything to keep me from talking. I couldn't risk anything happening to you or the kids. The agents told me the only way my family would be safe would be for me to enter witness protection. No one would know I was still alive and a potential danger to them.

"But…" Zack started.

His father held up his hand. "With a normal case it probably would have been possible to get word to your mother. But the FBI suspected the involvement of the police commissioner himself. Their concern centered on the fact that when they told the commissioner, it would get back to Angelo." He looked at Ethel. "Please understand, I couldn't bear to have anything happen to you because I had acted as an informant for the FBI. He'd think nothing of killing you."

Ethel teared up. "Oh, Roger, what a burden."

He turned to Olney. "Chester, I can't understand how you could have shot me, then lied about it. We were partners for Pete's sakes."

"Roger, I got in over my head. A classic story. First a little help with my rent. Then a little extra money if I turned my head. Once I was into them, I couldn't get out. They would have killed my wife and me if I had tried."

"We were friends."

"I know and I'm sorry. I've never been able to forgive myself."

Zack exploded. "That's a bunch of crap. You've been doing great as far as I can tell. Living the good life while all the time knowing the suffering you've caused."

Chester shook his head. "I'll never be able to explain and I'll never forgive myself." With that he turned and ran toward the window, shattering the glass as he jumped. A scream and he was gone.

***

Fairchild tried one last time on the phone and turned to give the order to knock down the door when one of the officers cried, "Watch out."

She looked up in time to see the body falling, hitting the roof of one of the police cars with a sickening thud. "Who the hell is that?"

She rushed over, but didn't recognize the body.

Tomlinson came over. "Holy, hell, it's Chester Olney."

About then, her cell rang. "Fairchild, it's Zack. We're inside Olney's apartment. Everyone in here is all right. Olney just jumped out of the window."

"I know. Jeez. I know. I'm outside the building in the street with Tomlinson. Olney just arrived via air mail. Ruined the hell out of the roof of one of Commissioner Tomlinson's best police cars. You all are okay?"

"Yes. My dad is here. He's been in witness protection all these years."

"I know," Fairchild said. "I finally had a chance to review all the folders. Tried to call you."

"Sorry, but I've been kinda busy."

"I guess you have. Now if you'll let us in, I want to get you the hell out of there and into an FBI safe house before anything else happens to you. And I've got an army of cops to keep you and your family safe."

"Okay, come and get us."

"On the way up, my friend."

43

FBI Safe House, Lower Manhattan, Friday, 9:45 p.m.

It took a little over an hour to move Zack and his family, including his dad, to an FBI safe house in lower Manhattan. They were escorted by the SWAT team and a bevy of NYPD police cars, sirens blaring until they closed in on the safe house.

When they pulled up to the back door so they could safely enter, Zack smiled to see Shelia standing next to the door.

Fairchild bumped his arm. "I thought Shelia would improve your morale. You deserve a bonus after all you've been though."

He reached over and gave Fairchild a hug. "Thanks. And thanks for all you've done."

"You're welcome, Zack. What a time."

Sergeant Huna stood next to Shelia. She smiled and waved when she saw Zack. "Hey, Zack, welcome to safety. You deserve it."

"Thanks so much." He hurried up to Shelia, gave her a hug and a big kiss.

She hugged him back. "I've been so worried."

Zack leaned back. "I think it's finally over."

They settled in each of their rooms, then an hour later gathered in the living room. They were all shaken by the death of Chester Olney and the miraculous return of Roger Kelly from the dead.

Fairchild took charge of the group. "Welcome to all of you and a special welcome back to Roger Kelly."

He stood "Thank you. You have no idea how great it is to be with my family again." He smiled at Ethel. "I know it will be a long time before we've settled everything between us."

Ethel smiled back. "Who knows? Maybe not too long."

Fairchild opened two bottles of champagne. "It's time we celebrate." When everyone had a glass she said, "I propose a toast to all of us for a job well done."

"Will we have to spend the rest of our days in a safe house?" Zack asked.

Fairchild shook her head. "Probably only three or four days. Captain Walt caught up with Froscino. He searched the black Oldsmobile and found the rifle they used to shoot Detective Frost."

"Can we tie him to the shooting?" Zack asked.

Fairchild nodded. "We have Froscino's prints on the rifle, and the bullet that injured Frost was fired from the rifle. We're negotiating with him now, and I suspect he'll turn states evidence when he finds out he could be facing life in prison. If he gives up the governor's chief of staff, we should be able to get the governor."

"What you have just said is the news I've been waiting thirty years to hear," Roger Kelly said. "What about Angelo?"

"I believe we have enough to put him away for twenty years," Fairchild said. "But we'll have to wait and see. He'll be lawyered up, and we'll need to keep Frosino alive long enough to testify against him in court. Not an easy task"

Roger Kelly took his wife's hand "I'd like to say again how sorry I am for what happened to you and for what happened to us. I'd like to spend the rest of my life making it up to you."

She turned toward him. "Well, I don't know, but we need to take it one step at a time."

"The agents told me based on what they knew, they believed the fact I worked undercover for them had leaked and why Angelo ordered me shot."

"Oh, Roger," Ethel said, "all you went through must have been awful."

"You have no idea, Ethel. I loved my family more than anything and the thought I might be responsible for their deaths was intolerable."

Ethel smiled at him. "Go on."

"They told me no one outside of a few FBI agents knew I had survived the attack. As soon as Angelo found out I was alive, he would come after me. The bastard was a killer and the agents were convinced he would not only kill me but also my family. They knew if Angelo didn't get me, threatening my family would ensure my silence."

Laura started to cry. "Oh, grandpa, what an awful position to be in."

"Sweetie it was. What made it so impossible was the fact the police commissioner himself could be involved. If anyone in the NYPD found out I was alive, the commissioner would know. They figured he would tell Angelo."

Fairchild checked her watch, then walked over and turned on the teleconference monitor. "Gather round. We have someone who wants to talk to us."

In a moment, Admiral Steele's face came on the monitor. "Good evening, all. I'm so glad everything worked out and you are all safe. Garcia is on the video teleconference with us from San Antonio."

Garcia's face popped up on the screen. "Hi, everyone. What a week. I'm so happy it's finally over."

Admiral Steele looked to the left of the picture. "Here he comes."

The president's face appeared on the monitor. "Admiral Steele, I just wanted to say how much I appreciate all you and your team have done over the past week. In New York, you helped bring the hijacking of the Staten Island Ferry to a successful conclusion. And in San Antonio you stopped a bigger problem at the Alamo. And most of all, I'm glad to see Roger Kelly is back with us. Zack, you solved the corruption problem in the NYPD and brought those responsible to justice."

He smiled. "And I'm delighted the governor of New York will not be running for vice president. This should help me in my campaign, and it will help me keep this marvelous team together."

Admiral Steele came back on. "Thanks to everyone. Now take a week and enjoy yourselves. You've earned it."

The picture went black.

Roger Kelly moved over to sit by Ethel. "Did you hear the admiral? We should relax and enjoy ourselves. I'm looking forward to getting to know my beautiful granddaughter."

Laura giggled. "I love you, Grandpa."

He looked at Zack. "I don't know how I can ever thank you for what you did."

Zack smiled. "What say we take in another Yankees game? It's been over thirty years since my last one, and I'd like to show Laura and Shelia the ins and outs of baseball."

Roger put his arm around Zack. "Sounds great to me."

Ethel stood up. "You know, I might even enjoy attending my first baseball game. But you all have to promise to teach me the rules."

Roger Kelly laughed. "That's a deal."